ONLY WOUNDED

BY PATRICK TAYLOR

Only Wounded
Pray for Us Sinners
Now and in the Hour of Our Death

An Irish Country Doctor
An Irish Country Village
An Irish Country Christmas
An Irish Country Girl
An Irish Country Courtship
A Dublin Student Doctor
An Irish Country Wedding
Fingal O'Reilly, Irish Doctor
An Irish Doctor in Peace and at War

The Wily O'Reilly: Irish Country Stories

"Home Is the Sailor" (e-original)

ONLY WOUNDED

STORIES OF THE IRISH TROUBLES

PATRICK TAYLOR

A TOM DOHERTY ASSOCIATES BOOK NEW YORK

ONLY WOUNDED

Copyright © 1997 by Ballybucklebo Stories Corp.

Maps by Jon Lansberg

A Forge Book
Published by Tom Doherty Associates, LLC
175 Fifth Avenue
New York, NY 10010

www.tor-forge.com

Forge® is a registered trademark of Tom Doherty Associates, LLC.

The Library of Congress Cataloging-in-Publication Data is available upon request.

ISBN 978-0-7653-3520-3 (hardcover)
ISBN 978-1-4668-2144-6 (e-book)

Forge books may be purchased for educational, business, or promotional use. For information on bulk purchases, please contact the Macmillan Corporate and Premium Sales Department at 1-800-221-7945, extension 5442, or write to specialmarkets@macmillan.com.

First published in Canada by Key Porter Books Limited

First Forge Edition: June 2015

Printed in the United States of America

0 9 8 7 6 5 4 3 2 1

ACKNOWLEDGMENTS

This book would not have been written without the faith and guidance of:

Jack Whyte, a Dreamer of Eagles, who showed me how to dream and keep the dream alive.

George Payerle, author of *Unknown Soldier*, and Carolyn Bateman, who edited the manuscript with consummate skill and patience. Bless you, both.

Jim Scott, who read the drafts and from his own depths gave me new insight into my own work.

Adrian and Olga Stein, without whose support the book would not have seen the light of day.

Todd McEwen, author of *Fisher's Hornpipe* and *MacX*, mercy-killer of superfluous modifiers.

To them I offer my deepest gratitude for their professionalism and, more important, their friendship.

The book is theirs as much as mine.

CONTENTS

IRELAND

— Provincial boundary
••• County boundary
▓ Northern Ireland

0 ——————— 30 miles
0 ——————— 30 kilometres

DONEGAL

Londonderry
LONDONDERRY

ANTRIM

U L S T E R

TYRONE

NORTHERN IRELAND

Bangor

Belfast

Sligo

FERMANAGH

MONAGHAN

Armagh
ARMAGH

DOWN

Strangford
Lough

CAVAN

C O N N A C H T

Dundalk

Drogheda

Athlone

Galway

L E I N S T E R

Dublin

Kilkenny

Limerick

M U N S T E R

Waterford

Cork

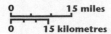

ONLY WOUNDED

INTRODUCTION

Flames devouring Isaac Agnew's Volkswagen dealership on the Falls Road in Belfast were the first television images I ever saw in colour. Much of the city of Belfast was burning. The pictures rocked me like none before or after. At the time, in the summer of 1969, I had just arrived in Alliston, Ontario, as a locum general practitioner. Canada had colour television. Back home in Northern Ireland we still had black and white, and a citizenry that was equally polarized.

The horrifying pictures were not my first experience of sectarian warfare. Two men and the car in which they were riding were totally destroyed by an explosion outside the wall of Campbell College, Belfast. On that mid-fifties day, I was a schoolboy playing cricket on the other side of the wall.

On October 1, 1964, riots broke out on Divis Street, a Catholic neighbourhood of Belfast, when the police tried to remove a flag of the Republic of Ireland being flown in defiance of Northern Ireland laws. I was a casualty officer at the Royal Victoria Hospital and worked round the clock with my colleagues treating the large number of people injured in the fracas.

These and other episodes of caring for the human wreckage of internecine warfare, while living in Belfast until late 1970 were the extent of my personal involvement with the Troubles.

But I grew up in Bangor, County Down, eleven miles away from the city and have always loved my part of the island of Ireland. I have loved her loughs and mountains, lakes and little fields, small towns, and ugly, careworn, raggedy old Belfast.

The demands of a career led me to Canada in 1970, shortly after the beginning of the Troubles that form the background to the stories in *Only Wounded*. It would be presumptuous of me now, at such distance, to attempt to disentangle the rights and wrongs of the civil war that raged with such ferocity from 1969 until 1994. I simply note with deep sadness that during those years there were more than 35,000 shooting incidents, more than 14,500 explosions, and 3,268 people killed.

In this book you will see events of those years through the eyes of committed Loyalists and Republicans—Protestant and Catholic— and those without strong political views who, like the majority of the citizens of the six counties, were simply trapped in the middle of the war.

The counties, cities, towns, streets, and places like Strangford Lough, Ballysallagh, the *Club Bar*, and the *Crown Liquor Saloon* are real, and although the characters in the stories are mine and the events portrayed are fictional, they reflect the reality of men and women caught up in circumstances over which they had little or no control.

The short sections between stories are only too horribly real and are matters of record. They are by no means an exhaustive history of the Troubles and were selected in an arbitrary fashion to give context to the fiction from an endless catalogue of similar episodes. No attempt has been made to explain the political background to these matters in detail, nor, I hope, to take sides.

What is so chilling is that all these violent acts did happen. The atrocities were committed by a relatively small number of people from both sides of the sectarian divide. The rest suffered the grinding civil war with dignity and courage. It was with them in mind, the ordinary folk, that these stories were written.

Some readers who are unfamiliar with Irish history may wish to know a little more about the background to the events in Northern Ireland. To you I offer a few short paragraphs of explanation.

Until 1922 Ireland was one country of four provinces, Ulster, Munster, Leinster, and Connaught, and thirty-two counties. The old Ireland was ruled from Westminster. Today, twenty-six counties belong to a sovereign state, the Republic of Ireland, which was recognized in the Ireland Act of June 1949. Six of the original nine counties of Ulster remain a part of the United Kingdom of Great Britain and Northern Ireland.

There are those who wish for reunion of the six counties with the Republic of Ireland. They insist the province be known as "Northern Ireland." Those who wish to remain an integral part of the United Kingdom are proud to call their home "Ulster." When men can disagree so vehemently over even the name of such a small piece of land, it is little wonder that passions run high.

King Henry II took possession of Ireland in 1155. Since then the fates of Ireland and England have been inextricably entwined. The native Irish race has always wanted the English to leave.

In the early seventeenth century, Scottish artisans and farmers were deliberately settled in the northeast corner of the island, in the province of Ulster. The native Irish were Catholic, the settlers Protestant. While the Protestants were the dominant culture in the one province, Ulster, they were in a minority in the whole of Ireland.

So were sown the seeds of the troubles of Ireland. Two threads run through a history reaching back eight hundred years: the desire of the Irish for independence from England and the fear of the Protestant minority in the north that they might be overwhelmed by the Catholic majority in the rest of the country if such independence were to come to pass.

Modern Irish history can be traced from 1914 with the enactment of a home rule bill granting Ireland dominion status patterned along the lines of that already possessed by Canada and Australia. The act was not to become law until the cessation of the First World War.

While welcomed by many, the bill was bitterly opposed by the Protestants of the north. They raised 90,000 armed men to resist home rule.

The legislation did not satisfy those Republicans who would settle for nothing but total independence. Two thousand Irish Nationalists rose at Easter 1916 believing they could secure Irish independence by force. They were crushed. Four hundred and fifty lives were lost and 2,614 people were wounded.

In 1918, as the details of the political settlement that would result in the partition of Ireland were being hammered out in London and Dublin, hard-line Republicans who would accept nothing short of a thirty-two-county Ireland, independent entirely from Great Britain, began military action. The rebel military force of the south was the Irish Republican Army. A truce was signed on July 11, 1921. The treaty establishing the twenty-six-county Irish Free State and a six-county British Northern Ireland was ratified on January 7, 1922.

The treaty was anathema to those who wanted complete independence. Civil war broke out pitting the new government of the Irish Free State against the IRA. Irishman against Irishman. The new dominion was born in bloodshed until a cease-fire was declared on May 24, 1923.

The IRA, while defeated politically and militarily, did not vanish. It formed an Army Council, with no ties to the Irish government, to direct army activities aimed always at reunion of the thirty-two counties and complete independence from Great Britain.

An abortive IRA bombing campaign was mounted on the British mainland in 1939 but failed to produce any political results. Military activity was suspended until 1951, when a series of arms raids was carried out on British military establishments.

"Operation Harvest," IRA attacks on targets in the north, began at midnight December 11, 1956, and ended on February 26, 1962. It was during this campaign that I had my first encounter with the bombers.

It must not be thought that all Catholics were Republicans nor all Protestants Loyalists. There were moderates on both sides. Many moderates. In the late sixties, a growing, non-denominational civil rights movement began to demand equal treatment for the Catholics of Northern Ireland. The civil rights activities provoked a Protestant backlash. By August 1969, the situation had deteriorated so badly that the Royal Ulster Constabulary could no longer cope. On August 14, a company of the First Battalion of the Prince of Wales Regiment was inserted to quell a demonstration in the Catholic Bogside area of Londonderry.

The sectarian rioting in Belfast and Derry worsened, and the population of the Catholic areas turned to the IRA for the protection it was unable to provide. A schism developed and grew among the leadership of the IRA. A few days before Christmas 1969, a Provisional Executive and Provisional Army Council were established. This group divorced itself from the traditional or "Official" IRA, and became the Provisional IRA, The Provos. Their initial priority was to establish effective defence of the Catholic neighbourhoods. Their ultimate goal was to go on the offensive, using force of arms to remove finally what they perceived as the British forces of occupation and at last realize the dream of a united Ireland.

Loyalists in Ulster were not prepared to let this happen and such paramilitary groups as the Ulster Defence Force and the Ulster Freedom Fighters were formed.

So was the scene set for the events of the last thirty years, events that with the explosion of an IRA bomb in the Canary Wharf district of London on February 9, 1996, again filled the headlines. In that explosion, two people were killed and more than 100 wounded.

It is in those thirty years that the stories in *Only Wounded* are set.

Again, for those who may find some nuances of Northern Irish idiom and some historical figures unfamiliar, and all aspects of Ulster politics confusing, a short glossary has been provided at the end of the book. Paramilitary and political organizations and the Security Forces are described, and some general information is provided. Readers may find a preliminary consultation of this information to be of value.

For anyone who wishes to learn more, a short list of suggested reading is supplied.

STRANGFORD LOUGH 1964

"Keep your head down," Neill whispered urgently from where he huddled in the angle between two rough stone walls. He glanced away from the target to make sure Pat's balaclava no longer broke the skyline. In the near-dark, the white of the skin around his eyes peering through the slit in the woollen helmet would be enough to betray his position. Not much point taking cover if you let your head stick out like a sore thumb. Still keeping his voice low, Neill said, "I'll watch them. I'll tell you when." He stared back into the half-light of the false dawn. For a moment he could see nothing. Had they turned away? His eyes caught a flicker of movement. They were closer now. Still coming. He tightened his grip on the frigid barrels of his shotgun. God, it was cold out here, the wind howling in from the south like a stepmother's breath. "Come on. Come on." He crouched lower and lifted the twelve-bore, tucking the butt into his shoulder. "Come on." Almost in range. Six of them. He held his breath. Ten more yards. Five.

"Now."

Neill uncoiled, aimed, and fired. He heard Pat's shot, then almost as one the crashes as both guns fired again.

Four ducks flared wildly, wings beating frantically as the birds turned, climbed, and hurtled downwind. The lead mallard and a bird to his left folded in mid-flight and plummeted earthward, one falling on the land, the other into the sea, thirty yards out.

He heard Pat whoop. The silly bugger always cheered when he had a bird down. "Good shot, Pat."

"Good shot, yourself." Pat propped his now empty shotgun against the wall of the old ruined sheep pen. "Let's get the birds."

"Come on, then." Neill tucked his gun into the crook of his left arm, barrels pointing down, and led the way. Grouse, his big, black Labrador at his heels, sniffing the wind, tail going twenty to the dozen.

"God," said Pat, "there's no happier animal than a retriever in the shooting season."

Neill smiled and thought, Except you and me, Pat, back here again on the Long Island.

Neill watched Pat walk over the tussocks, striding easily, head turning from side to side as he sought the place where his bird had crashed.

The gravel of the foreshore crunched underfoot as Neill took Grouse to the water's edge. "Hi lost, Grouse." The dog needed no second bidding. He charged into the water. Head high, he swam strongly through the dark sea, only visible because of the white wake of his passage.

Neill hunched his shoulders into the collar of his heavy coat and tried to ignore the biting rawness of the wind that tugged at him. He shivered. It was probably true, he thought, leaning into a gust, that all wildfowlers are mad. But the cold was a small price to pay for the sheer pleasure of being on Strangford Lough, away from work, in his own universe, shared only with Pat, a day's fowling ahead.

Neill looked out across the stretch of water between the island and the shore. The light was better now. He could see that Grouse had taken the duck in his mouth and had turned back. Behind the dog the distant shoreline was becoming visible. A small flock of ducks flew low over the water, lifting to clear Gransha Point, bent like a dog's hind leg and stretching for more than a mile into the choppy waters.

Gransha. Neill remembered the day there last season when Pat had shot a goose. Why had Grouse not been with them? Was that the time he had a torn pad? The bird had fallen in the water and Pat had stripped down to the buff and swum out to make the retrieve. The image of Pat, clutching the greylag, his white skin pimply like a freshly plucked bird, brought a smile to Neill's cold lips. Daft bugger.

He ran his gaze along the familiar coastline from Gransha, round a deep bay to the bulk of the Castle Hill, dark and brooding against the lightening sky. The sycamores at the hill's crest had always been a good spot for wood-pigeons. Perhaps, he thought, we should give it a try next weekend.

Grouse was closer now. He was swimming in on a line from John Dunlop's farmhouse. Its red roof stood out against the paleness of the surrounding fields. The house itself was set in a sheltered hollow. Neill stuffed his hands into his coat pockets. It would be warm over there, someone putting on the kettle, stoking up the range. Still, he'd rather be here.

The big Labrador waded through the shallows, his tail thrashing the water in joy. He landed, politely gave the duck to Neill, and shook himself, sending a spray of water droplets into the just-risen sun. Grouse in his element, proud and wet.

"Good boy." Neill thumped the dog's flank and headed back to the hide where Pat waited, leaning against the wall. In his left hand he held a drake, its chestnut throat, metal-green head, and yellow beak bright against the speckled breast feathers. Only two dark spots in the grey showed where the pellets had smashed through.

"Right," said Pat, "one each."

"And no more if we don't get out of sight. Go on in, Grouse."

Grouse slipped through the entrance and curled up in a corner out of the wind. Neill followed Pat inside, frowned, and wished that his friend wouldn't be so careless, leaving his gun propped up unattended like that. Neill reloaded and made sure the safety catch was on. Pat had done the same. Good.

Neill went back into his niche between the walls. "Right. You keep an eye out towards Gransha. I'll watch the other side."

He listened to the wind battering like a wild thing against the stones, howling through the cracks. No wonder folks round here still believed in the banshee. He blew on his hands, tucked himself behind the shelter of the wall, and peered over the top. He watched with pleasure as the sun turned the waters of the lough to grey-green flecked with small whitecaps. The undersides of the clouds were painted with pinks and posies of red and maroon. Far in the distance the indigo line of the Mourne Mountains stood against the morning sky, with Slieve Donard, the highest, solid as a boxer's fist, punching the clouds away.

He hummed a snatch of an old Percy French Ballad: ". . . but for all of their jewels I'd far rather be, where the Mountains of Mourne sweep down to the sea." By God, he would. He'd been born and had grown up in Ulster. Born Catholic, true enough, but in Bangor, a town where sectarian matters played little part in his life. This rough, cold, windy corner of Ireland was home.

"My side. Teal."

Neill dropped lower and turned to look where Pat pointed. Fleeing down the wind a ball of teal rushed on like little rockets. Neill fired twice, and missed. He stole a surreptitious glance to see how Pat had fared. He'd missed, too. Grouse had risen and was looking up, head cocked, ears pricked.

"Lie down, pup," said Neill and was rewarded with the kind of disdainful sneer an English lord might have used while chastising a peasant. Neill bent and patted the dog's head.

"Bugger," he heard Pat say, "the meteors must have been wrong."

"You and your shooting stars." Neill snorted.

"I saw six on the way here in the punt." Pat's voice was serious. "That should mean we'll get at least six birds."

Neill laughed. "We'll get bugger all if we don't shoot a bit better."

"Aye," said Pat as he moved back into position, "and if we don't reload." He broke his gun and pulled out the spent cartridges. "Keep a good eye out on your side."

Neill resumed his watch. Sometimes, he knew from experience, wildfowling could be a slow business. Twice in the next three hours, pairs of mallards flew in, coming head-on at him, looking like airborne beer bottles. Twice he had whispered to Pat, and crouched, pulse quickening, willing the birds to hold course. Twice the ducks had veered away out of shot. The sight of the wing beats, the light reflecting from the drakes' heads, green like molten emeralds, gladdened him. He didn't really regret not firing.

The sun was higher now, and taking some of the chill off the air. It had been bitter on the row out this morning, in the dark. The moon had set and the sky had been as black and clean as a wet blackboard, only smudged here and there by wisps of high clouds, chalked by the myriad stars. The glare of the lights of Newtownards at the head of the lough was too far away to dim their brightness.

As Neill rowed, Pat had scanned the skies and Neill had known that his friend was looking for meteors. Three years ago he had solemnly announced his theory that the number of fire flashes would predict the day's bag.

In spite of himself, Neill had looked up from time to time. He'd counted four, trailing their deaths across the icy heavens.

"Pintail. Three of them."

No mistakes this time. Pat's "whoop" echoed down the wind. Four birds in the hide now. Maybe he was right about the shooting stars, Neill thought, as he turned back to his corner.

Pat and his daft notions. Like making a cannon from an old tin can when they'd both been twelve. The bang had nearly scared the pants off Pat's mother. Neither of their fathers had been amused, and both he and Pat had had to eat standing up for a couple of days.

They'd had a lot of fun together since the day Pat had introduced himself. They'd both been ten at the time. Pat had jumped into Neill's little canvas skiff uninvited, and promptly capsized it. He'd soon learned Pat was never backward in coming forward and Neill was glad he wasn't. How much time had they spent together, pottering around the Bangor seashore, kayaking, fishing, sailing, shooting here on Strangford Lough since they were old enough to carry firearm certificates? Not even Pat being sent off to that posh boarding school in Belfast had made a damn bit of difference. Neill had missed his friend when he was away and looked forward eagerly to holidays. Pat said he always had two priorities when they let him out. Get a decent meal and get round to Neill's house.

And now, with Pat at law school and Neill selling advertising for the *County Down Spectator*, the long summers of childhood were gone but they still teamed up every weekend. Just like today.

For a moment the sun disappeared behind a cloud, throwing a

shadow over the grass of the island. Neill looked up. By the height of the sun he judged it to be past midmorning. He rubbed his right hand rapidly up and down along his left arm. Still bloody cold, but soon the wind would push the cloud away.

Sunbeams spilled and spotlit the crests of the Mourne Mountains. Mountains was perhaps a bit of an exaggeration if you compared the Mournes to the Rockies or the Himalayas, but they suited Ulster. Small as mountains went, but well proportioned to the size of the province. Bracken, soft as the Ulster summer, and heather, its flowers as bright as tiny jewels, grew on the slopes. When the mist was on the hillsides, which it was more often than not, the valleys could be sombre and silent as catacombs.

What did people say? "If you can see the Mournes, it's going to rain. If you can't—it's raining." But see them or not, they were always there. Granite mounds, immovable as an Ulsterman when his mind's made up. The Mournes suited Ulster. And Ulster suited Neill. The day the mountains left the six counties, so would he. Until then, he thought smiling, as the cloud passed and the air brightened, he'd just stay and keep them company.

"Wake up."

Neill started as he heard pinions whicker overhead, the blast of Pat's shot, his yell, and moments later the "whump" as a bird hit the grass.

"Could I trouble you to send Grouse?"

Neill laughed. "Hi lost, pup."

"I thought you'd done a quick Captain Scott." Pat rubbed his hands together.

"What?"

"Frozen to death. It's not like you to miss seeing a bird." Pat blew on his hands. "I'm foundered. This would freeze the balls off a brass monkey."

"Right enough. That south wind gets into your bones." Neill stooped and took the duck from Grouse's mouth. "Into the corner." The dog obeyed.

Neill pointed across to the mainland. "I'd not mind being in the Dunlop's kitchen."

"With a big mug of hot tea." Pat motioned towards Neill's game bag. "Any tea in there?"

"No." Neill unloaded his shotgun and propped it against the wall.

"No? No tea?"

Neill waited just a moment longer, letting Pat believe that there was nothing hot to drink, then said, "Do you fancy a cup of coffee and a sandwich? See if that'll warm us up a bit. Must be damn near lunchtime anyway." He rummaged in his game bag and produced a Thermos, pouring two steaming cups of coffee.

"You'd me going for a minute there." Pat parked his weapon and accepted the filled lid of the flask. "Ta, mate." He cradled the cup in both hands. "That's better." He drank and turning his back to the wind, said, "Do you think we'll get another shot?"

Neill shook his head. "Not for a while. Not until the tide turns. It's on the way out now." He pointed at the punt, which was now fifty yards from the water's edge, a hump above the grey shingle, standing out like a small, beached whale. "That beach is a pretty sight."

The tiny pebbles of the strand were dotted with rocks and clumps of seawrack. Small flocks of oyster-catchers, black and white and scarlet-billed, trotted from seaweed clump to seaweed clump probing for crabs. A knot of greenshanks whirled like tossed smoke along the water's edge.

Neill looked out to a sandbar halfway between the Long Island and the shore, the sea between, rushing, driven by the south wind.

"We'll have to wait until that bar's covered again. The widgeon'll be browsing on the mudflats." He finished his coffee, tossing the dregs to the grass floor of the hide. "There's enough shelter under the lees of the islands for the mallard and teal. They'll not budge until the tide pushes them out."

"I suppose you're right." Pat sat and pulled his balaclava up over his face, showing Neill a downy fair stubble and a pair of blue eyes. "We might as well take the weight off our feet. Here." He handed the lid back to Neill. "What about those sandwiches?"

Neill sat. "All right. And no complaints about cold sausages."

Pat rolled his eyes. "Not again. Jesus, Neill. Could you not think of something different? Just once."

"Why? I like things that don't change."

Pat accepted a bridge roll. A ketchup-smeared sausage stuck out from each end. He looked at it, sniffed, and took a healthy bite. "It's my turn next week. I'll bring curry in a Thermos."

"Fair enough." Neill bit into his roll. Curry indeed. There was nothing wrong with good Ulster bangers—from Cookstown. Best sausages in the world. "What's so great about change, anyway?"

"Come on. The whole world's changing. The Beatles. The Rolling Stones."

"That music's just a fad."

"Right. You haven't got over Buddy Holly's plane crash yet have you?"

Neill laughed. "I liked Buddy Holly. And the Big Bopper."

"I suppose all those Sputniks are just a fad too?"

"Do you see one up there with the Red Hand of Ulster on it?"

Pat frowned. "What are you talking about?"

"As far as I know the shipyards are still building ships, not satellites. Things don't change as fast here and that suits me fine."

"Well, they're on the move everywhere else."

"Where?"

"Do you not read your own newspaper?"

"Aye."

"There was a story a week or two back about Canada. They've changed their flag."

"I didn't see that."

"Funny looking thing. Red and white with a maple leaf."

"They threw out the Union Jack?"

"Aye." Pat held out his hand. "Give us another roll. Ta."

Neill rubbed his chin, feeling the roughness of the unshaven skin. "Hard to believe. Flags can mean a lot."

Pat almost choked on his sausage. "Bloody right. How many nights did they riot on Divis Street up in Belfast in October when the police tried to haul down the tricolour?"

Neill snorted. "What do you expect? Sinn Fein runs up the flag of the Republic over their constituency office. Paisley yells bloody murder that it's against the law, and our brilliant prime minister sends in the riot squad."

Pat shook his head. "The orange and the green. I suppose you don't want that to change either."

Neill thought for a minute. "Of course I do. But it is changing. Do you think a Catholic like me and a Protestant like you could have been mates forty years ago?"

"No."

"See what I mean? It is changing." Neill pointed his half-eaten roll at Pat. "That nonsense on Divis Street? Just a bunch of hooligans. That's over now. One of these days Ireland will get back together again, peacefully, but it won't be the end of the world for me if it doesn't."

"Jesus," said Pat, "Ireland reunited? If Paisley could hear you, he'd have a canary." Pat shook his head in short jerks and said in a deep voice, "Gawd is a Pratestant."

Neill laughed at his friend's imitation of The Reverend Dr. Paisley and started repacking his game bag. "I don't care what God is. I'm an Ulsterman. I'll stay an Ulsterman."

Pat stood and looked all around. "Me too." He waved his arm in a great arc. "Just look at this place. Could you imagine living anywhere else?"

"What?" Neill's head jerked back. He thought for a moment that the question was rhetorical and yet, there was an edge in Pat's voice that seemed to want an answer. "Somewhere else? Not at all. Could you?"

Pat did not reply immediately. "Some of my friends from school have gone to Canada. They say it's great."

"Aye. With a bloody great red and white maple leaf for a flag. Not for me. I'd miss Strangford too much. And the ducks."

"Ducks. Now there's a thought." Pat lifted his shotgun. "I think I'll just take a wee dander down to the low hide. The odd bird might fly in. Come on down in a while."

"Fair enough." Neill watched his friend leave.

It was comfortable in the sheep-cot. The sun was at its height over-head and the coffee and food had warmed him. Neill reckoned he'd just sit and enjoy the day, just like old Grouse, curled up with his tail over his nose. Pat was welcome to the low hide. It was a lot more ex-posed and the wind had not abated. There'd be no ducks for at least an hour. Pat and his optimism that the ducks would come, and his blethering on about change. And leaving Ulster? What a load of rub-bish. Neill chuckled at the thought of Pat and his daft ideas.

Through the gap in the wall, Neill watched the grass of the island, green and wind-tossed, rippling like the waters of the lough between the island and the shore. Strangford Lough, he thought. It never changes. The Vikings had named it *Strangfjard*, "the shallow inlet with the swift current," because the tides at the narrow mouth between Por-taferry and Strangford Town could run up to ten knots. His dad had explained the difference between the Norse "Fjord," deep inlet, and "Fjard," shallow inlet. That was also the day his father had told Neill how a long-ago shipwrecked sailor of the great Armada and some soft Irishwoman had started their family. The Spaniard had given the men dark hair, dark eyes, and a solid build. Men who had shot here on the lough for generations.

"You'd not want the place to change, would you, Grouse?"

The black dog looked up questioningly for a moment, stood, turned round and round, flattening the grass, then settled with a sigh, and curled up, square head on his forepaws.

What a great day. You couldn't beat it with a big stick. Wildfowl-ing had more to recommend it than merely shooting ducks. It was the excuse. The excuse to escape from the grime and the mundane reality of adult life.

Neill stood and looked out over the Lough. He must have been imagining things when, for an instant, he had thought Pat was seri-ous, asking about living somewhere else. Neill couldn't imagine leav-ing Ulster. He would miss Strangford too much. And the sailing at Ballyholme, the trout in Ballysallagh Reservoir, the way cloud shad-ows ran over the hills and little fields, the dew of a summer morning heavy with the scent of a badger, sleeping in his sett under the roots of the oak near Portavogie. He'd miss the people. Solid, down to earth, funny as all get out when the mood was on them. And where else could a man get a decent pint?

Neill loved the history of the place. The old sheep-cot was more than a hundred years old, and the Castle Hill over on the shore—that was a hill fort. It had been battled over by bonnaught, Irish mercenaries of the Normans, and gallowglass, fierce Scottish soldiers brought to Ulster by the Lords of the O'Neill to defend the O'Neill lands from the Norman invaders hundreds of years ago.

The locals still believed that the sycamores at the summit were a fairy ring. He remembered one evening in the gloaming. He and Pat had waited among those trees for wood-pigeons. As the night fell, Neill had been sure he could hear the clash of broadsword on battle axe.

He idly pulled at a tuft of grass growing between the stones of the wall. It would not budge from the earth. The roots must run very deep.

Two shots cracked from the far end of the island. Neill swung to see if Pat was up making a retrieve. No sign of him. Probably missed. This was about the time the ducks would start to move.

Grouse was on his feet. "Come on, you lazy lump. We should take a wander on down to the low hide and see if we can't get another bird or two. We're still one short of the six meteors."

Grouse waited, tail waving, until Neill had slung his game bag and picked up his gun. "Do you think Pat's going to get a few more?"

The big dog cocked his head to one side.

"Go on. Get out."

Neill set off along the east side of the island, Grouse quartering the ground ahead through the swaying grass and tufts of rusty benweed. A snipe sprang from beneath Grouse's feet and flew low, kraking hoarsely and jinking.

He walked out along one of the long, low arms of the island and stopped where many years before fowlers had thrown up a rough circle of boulders to make a hide. Pat had heaped piles of seaweed on the rocks. He was tucked in behind the improvised breastwork trying to remain concealed from any unsuspecting birds.

Neill saw the balaclava and called, "Any luck?"

Pat half-rose, shaking his head. "Come on, on, on, on, in."

Neill laughed at his friend's use of the Belfast vernacular, told Grouse to lie down on the grass, and stepped over the wall of the hide. He crouched beside Pat and waited. The tide rose slowly, washing round the rocks in the bay, hiding the kelp-beds.

The eagerly anticipated wildfowl did not come. Neill turned and sat with his back to the wall of boulders and weed, smelling the salt of the kelp. The tide rose higher. The sun moved round the heavens. The wind eased and whispered to the grass. In the distance the Mournes turned from blue to deep purple. It would soon be time to go home to Bangor.

Pat grunted, "Down."

Neill turned, hiding the white of his face against the wall of the hide, peering in the direction where Pat was staring so intently. A single teal had turned into the bay and was flying straight for them.

"Your bird, Pat."

Pat stayed hunched. He was going to fire from a kneeling position. The teal must have seen the two men below and rocketed straight upwards. As it reached the zenith of its flight and momentarily stalled, motionless against the blue sky, Pat swung the shotgun. Neill flinched as he saw the barrels rush past his face. The shot was deafening, the muzzle was so close to his ear.

The bird fell, but there was no yell from Pat. "Shit, Neill. I'm sorry." His blue eyes were wide, and he held one hand over his mouth as he stared down.

Neill shrugged. It hadn't been that close. Just that old Pat could be careless sometimes. He shook his head. "Never worry. You missed me."

Pat still looked horrified.

"Hi lost, Grouse." Grouse took off running.

Neill put one hand on Pat's arm. His friend was trembling. "Come on, Pat. I told you. It wasn't even close."

Neill moved his hand to the barrels of Pat's twelve-bore. The metal was warm. "Just remember." He laughed to show he held no grudge. "That thing's for shooting ducks. Not people."

1969

On New Year's Day, 1969, members of an organization called The People's Democracy began a march from Belfast City Hall. They intended to cover the seventy-five miles between Belfast and Derry, in the spirit of the Selma to Montgomery march that had been led by Dr. Martin Luther King in 1965. Their goal was to demand increased civil rights for the Catholic community of Northern Ireland. They were harassed by Protestant Loyalists, the most violent confrontation occurring at Burntollet Bridge, near the village of Claudy, where one young woman was beaten unconscious and left lying face down in a stream. She survived. The fallout of the march was the inflammation of sectarian passions as severe as those of the Troubles of the 1920s.

From August 12 to 14, rioting in the Bogside, a Catholic enclave in Derry, led to the first involvement of British troops, a detachment of eighty men of the Prince of Wales Own Regiment.

On August 12, rioting spread to other cities and towns, and in Belfast, by August 15, six people had died or had been fatally wounded. John Gallagher was the first fatality of the new Troubles. On October 11, Constable Victor Arbuthnot was the first member of the Royal Ulster Constabulary to be killed.

1969 Dead 13   **Total Dead 13**

GERRY

Much of Belfast owes its being to the Victorian linen mill masters, who, with true Christian charity and a shrewd eye for productivity, built row upon row of workers' houses marching with the symmetry of the Brigade of Guards, terrace following terrace in anonymous uniformity. In the very heart of the city, narrow streets run between the Protestant Shankill Road and the Catholic Falls Road.

Many Shankill Protestants are staunchly Loyalist. They salute the Union Jack, believe God to be an Orangeman, and Ian Paisley his anointed. In the Falls district, committed Republicans fly the tricolour of Eire in defiance of the laws of Northern Ireland and belong to such outlawed organizations as the IRA and Sinn Fein. The factions are barely separated yet for years they managed to co-exist despite their deep differences—until the Troubles.

Gerry Connolly was born before the Troubles, on the seventeenth of January, 1950. He came into the world in a corridor of the Royal Maternity Hospital. Too many patients were labouring and being confined for his mother to be afforded a room to herself. His birth occasioned no great stir. He was neatly fielded, eyes swabbed, cord clamped, bottom slapped, wrapped in a towel, shown briefly to his semicomprehending mother, and taken off to an aseptic nursery, where he spent the next six days in the company of fourteen identical infants. At least he had a cot to himself.

Mrs. Connolly took him home to Cupar Street to a small house where a crucifix hung in the bedroom and a plaster image of Saint Bernadette of Lourdes stood on an old dresser in the front parlour. For the first five months of his life he slept alone in a drawer at the foot of his parents' bed, but when his early morning noises became too much for old man Connolly, he was transferred to the room next door, where three elder brothers shared a double bed, and Brendan, only thirteen months his senior, had, until Gerry's arrival, the monopoly of a crib. Brendan did not take kindly to having to double up. From the moment of his birth Gerry was rarely to be entirely alone.

His mother died, quietly, unobtrusively, and with a sigh of relief, bearing the eighth Connolly baby, leaving Gerry a sturdy child of six, already able to hold his own with the other boys in the street. His father, a welder in the shipyard, was too preoccupied with feeding eight mouths to take a very active part in his children's upbringing, but there was a rough affection, a sense of family.

Gerry lived in a crowd. He played on the streets, and on the bomb sites, reminders of the nights the Luftwaffe had visited Belfast, the arse of his trousers torn, his upper lip shiny with a snot track, periodically rubbed away with a grubby sleeve. People, noise, congestion were all part of the normal pattern.

Saint Gall's, where Gerry went to school, was run by priests. The building, of ageing red brick, softened by drizzle and pitted by corrosives from the factory chimneys, squatted in a tarmac yard facing Cupar Way. The fathers, well-meaning men, struggled with their primitive surroundings, the gloomy passages, the high-ceilinged barns that did service as classrooms, and the feeling, prevalent among the children, that book learning was a waste of time. Gerry's lessons were confined to the three Rs and Irish history, taught by a bitter, stunted Nationalist whose idea of the torments of purgatory was to live forever in an Ireland "crushed beneath the Saxon's heel." Gerry did not grasp the imagery of the little priest's diatribes but was made to see clearly the fate of any Catholic foolish enough to become involved with the Protestants.

His early indoctrination was tempered by Father James. The tubby cleric taught by example and illustration, leading rather than driving, rarely having to resort to the cane. Father James, as well as teaching maths, had a special responsibility for religious instruction. He discharged this duty with an eccentric disregard for dogma and preferred to instill a code of behaviour based on the work of Kipling rather than the Holy Writ. Above his lectern a framed copy of "If" took the place of the more customary biblical scene and was religiously recited at the beginning of each lesson. Gerry soon learned the poem by heart and sometimes wondered if Mr. Kipling had written any others.

Gerry was a poor student, but he liked Father James and paid attention in his classes, trying to please. He felt shame beyond endurance when, aged twelve, he was caught copying his homework, and in an effort to save his own skin, told. The priest made Gerry wait behind after class and gave the boy the thrashing of his life, punctuating each stroke with the same words. "Don't you ever tell tales again." Gerry, sobbing, had sworn not to and was dimissed with a curt reminder that a promise was a promise.

Father James had one other talent. For such a rotund man he was remarkably nimble and as a boy he had been a keen boxer. He taught Gerry how to box.

Gerry left school at sixteen. He was a stocky youth, black haired, dark eyed, with a bent nose he'd picked up in the ring. He could read and write and number well enough to know if he had been shortchanged on a packet of cigarettes. He was a Catholic, more by conditioning than from any deep conviction. Unemployment was high in Belfast, and the shipyard where Gerry was to have joined his father as an apprentice plater was not taking on. He joined the queues at the Labour Exchange, "the burroo," instead and drew his unemployment benefit from a myopic blonde clerk who, secure in her job, dispensed the money with the condescension of royalty on Maundy Thursday. From time to time he sought work on building sites, travelling on corporation buses packed with men in Dexter coats and smelling of damp undervests. He met with prejudice and was usually turned away disappointed. No one ever asked his religion. The simple question "What school did you go to?" was sufficient to identify him. An inborn acceptance of his inferior status, rather than any generosity of spirit, kept bitterness from marking him.

His days were long. There wasn't much to do but stand on street corners with other men, smoking, talking, wasting his time. Wasting his life. Sometimes to amuse his friends he would recite "If." They would always have a good laugh at the bit about filling the "unforgiving minute with sixty seconds' worth of distance run." All their days were full of unforgiving minutes and nowhere to run to.

Often the conversation would turn to what might happen if the six counties could be reunited with The Republic. Gerry found the visions of Celtic Twilight romantic but unrealistic. He could see that if it happened, his chances of getting a job would be no better and the British dole was higher than the handouts from the Irish government.

And he needed the cash. He had to chip most of it in at home for board and lodge. Da didn't let Gerry keep more than a few bob for pocket money. Enough for fags and beer and the occasional trip to the Palace Ballroom. When he met Bridget there, his life brightened for a while. She was pretty decent about paying her whack, she could afford to, Gallagher's cigarette factory gave its women workers a fair wage, but she drew the line at buying his pints or cinema tickets. Good thing she got lots of free samples of smokes.

Sometimes Gerry would spend a few bob on science fiction magazines that he bought in a second-hand bookstore in Smithfield Market. There he came across an old copy of *Rudyard Kipling. Selected Verse.* He thumbed through the pages looking for "If." He felt as though he had found an old friend, gave a moment's thought to Father James, and bought the book.

It took him several months to read it all. He did not understand a lot of the poems, but some of the ones about soldiers, the ones that told stories, were as exciting as any of the Buck Rogers stuff. Kipling's far-away places were closer than Altair or Beetlegeuse, though Gerry realized that he was as likely to go to Afghanistan or India as to the Spiral Nebula. "Fuzzy-Wuzzy" was his favourite poem. He found something heroic about the soldiers of the broken British square, even though he knew he should be pleased about anything that gave the Brits a poke in the eye.

He'd tried to read some Kipling to Bridget but she'd thought it was silly. She didn't like poetry much. In fact, she didn't really like Gerry much anymore. Any man good enough for her had to have a steady job.

For several months he missed their heated fumblings in the back rows of cinemas or the dark alleys of the Falls. She'd never let him go all the way, but then he hadn't expected to. Girls brought up at convent schools were like that. He hadn't bothered much with girls since. He'd put away the Kipling, too.

He settled for loitering with his mates and his rarely successful attempts to find short-term labouring jobs. Sunday was the bright spot of most of his weeks. Da and Gerry and the rest of the boys would go to Casement Park and watch Gaelic football or hurling matches. They'd done that for as long as Gerry could remember. Da was funny about Sundays. He insisted that after the game the whole family would sit down for the supper Gerry's sisters had prepared. Da said it kept the family together.

Fridays, dole day, Gerry spent the afternoons in betting shops and the evenings in the pub. Over a pint of stout, he was as happy as the next man to blame all his troubles on "Them" at Stormont but in reality understood little of events in the political world, events over which he had no control.

Robert Atkinson, Her Majesty's Minister of Industry and Commerce, sat in an oak-panelled office in London. He had a hangover, which put him in remarkably bad humour. The occasion responsible for his pounding head had not been pleasant. Last night he had been taken to dinner by some very strong-willed men from Ulster who had come to persuade him to give more money to the already shaky shipyards. They kept him in conversation for much longer than he had anticipated, the while plying him with a very excellent brandy.

His temples throbbed and his mouth felt gritty. No doubt the shipbuilders had made convincing arguments, but so had the people who wanted his ministry to fund a hydroelectric scheme in Scotland. The Highlands were as economically depressed as Northern Ireland. He was supposed to have dinner with the Scots delegation again tonight, and, perish the thought, they were probably hoping to sway him with single malt whisky.

He saw little to choose between the two proposals. In the end it all boiled down to politics. The Scots if disappointed would not vote Labour in the next general election, and the Scottish seat was marginal at best. Ulstermen? They had no choice. No matter what he did they'd vote Conservative and Unionist if they wanted to keep their gloomy six counties part of Great Britain. The Tories had played that card since the days of Lord Edward Carson and Winston Churchill. Besides, he would have to visit the recipients of his industrial grant and the salmon fishing was a damn sight better up north.

The insistent ringing of his telephone intruded, and he was less than pleased to hear the nasal voice of the head of the Ulster delegation.

"Well, minister, have you decided yet?"

He sighed. "Terribly sorry, old man. There's simply not enough to go round. I only wish there—"

"Bugger you." The line went dead.

Robert Atkinson sat back in his chair, closed his eyes, and hoped that the repercussions of his decision would not be too catastrophic.

On the day that this conversation was taking place, Gerry was trying—and failing—to find work. It had been several months since his last job, and the boredom of enforced idleness made the hours hard to fill. He placed a few hopeful bets at the bookie's, killing time between races in a pub across the street. He took his pint with spiritless men, long unemployed, who sat on rough benches, drank from straight pint glasses of watery porter, reminisced, swore, spat in the sawdust, resignedly tore up losing tickets, and selected more runners from dog-eared copies of the local paper.

Gerry rose from his seat. He'd had enough of the cramped room. The cigarette fug made his eyes water. He might as well go home. None of his horses had come in.

He stepped out onto the street and pulled a few coins from his pocket. Shit. Not even enough for bus fare. Ach well, he was in no rush. The walk would fill a bit of time. Those other fellows in the pub were enough to make anyone miserable. He felt cleaner just being in the open air, such as it was in the city. He walked on. An unimaginative display in the window of an army recruiting office briefly caught his eye. He smiled. He didn't need to break his stride to know that it promised "A Man's Life." Had they used posters like that when Mr. Kipling was writing?

Gerry felt the unspoken, subdued feeling of apprehension the moment he arrived home. His father, naturally inarticulate, was even less communicative.

"What's up, Da?"

"Yard's going to lay off more men."

No wonder the old man was tight-lipped. Liam, one of his younger brothers, had been given his cards last week.

"What about them bosses that went to London?"

"There's a rumour out they done no good."

"Have you not seniority, Da?"

A derisive snort. "Served my time before you were born. Fat lot of good it'll do me if they close the graving dock."

"Maybe the rumours is wrong?"

"Aye. Maybe." Da's eyes held little hope.

The blow fell three days later.

"Twenty-seven fucking years at the Big Yard." Da stood looking out the kitchen window, his back to Gerry. "D'you know that song, 'Belfast Mill'? '. . . I'm too old to work but I'm too young to die.' That's me, Gerry." Da turned. "I'm not saying it's because I'm a Catholic but a brave few of the Protestants got kept on. I just don't know how we're going to get by."

Gerry soon saw how strapped the family was. He tried desperately to find work.

He and Da went down together on Friday to collect their dole. Da counted the few notes.

"Ach, to hell with it, Gerry. Come on. I'll buy you a jar. Just the one."

On the way to the pub they passed the army office. The recruiting poster still hung in the window. Gerry stopped and stared. "Come here a minute, Da."

His father turned back. "What?"

"I could join up."

"Not at all. England's always fought her wars on the backs of the Irish. Come on." Da strode off.

Ach, well. It had only been a notion anyway.

They stood together at the bar. The pub was packed.

Da took a deep swallow of his pint. "Were you serious?"

"About what?"

"The army."

Just like Da. Say "no" then think a thing over.

"Well, it would be one less mouth to feed at our house, and the pay's not bad. I could maybe send a few quid home." I could get out of Belfast, too. Even see Mr. Kipling's India, he thought. That idea was suddenly appealing.

"We'd miss you, son."

"Aye, but I'd get home on leaves. I might even get sent to Palace Barracks at Holywood."

Da finished his drink. "Get that down you. We'll go and have a word with the sergeant. You're under age at seventeen. I'd need to sign some papers."

Gerry wished the sergeant wasn't in such a hurry, rattling through the routine. The little ceremony was important to Gerry. The papers were quickly completed, Da signed, and Gerry found himself holding a Bible and taking the oath of allegiance. The phrases were solemn, and their sounds pleasing. The soldier sitting at the desk opposite might not care, but as Gerry returned the book he suddenly remembered Father James and heard his words, "A promise is a promise."

"Right, then," said the sergeant. "Come back here next Monday. Bring your suitcase. I'll have your orders and a travel warrant."

"Yes, sergeant." The man didn't look a bit like Gerry's image of the colour-sergeant in Kipling's "Danny Deever."

Da grunted. "That's that then." He took Gerry's arm. "Come on. We'll have one more wee wet. Going away present."

And Gerry saw that Da's eyes were misted.

It would be two years before Gerry returned to Belfast. A very different Belfast. Much was to happen to him in those two years. At Catterick Camp in Yorkshire he was surprised by the impersonality of induction, but was no stranger to the indignities of communal living. The jostling, like cattle, in a mass of bodies through the showers, hair cuts, inoculations, free-from-infection-inspections, and kit issues did not bother him. Nor did the idea of sleeping twenty to a barracks, messing in echoing halls with crowds of other bewildered recruits.

He soon settled into the life of a peace-time soldier. "Boots—boots—boots—boots, movin' up and down again." He didn't mind. The discipline was tolerable, and Sergeant Edwards, in charge of Gerry's hut, may have been a living caricature, but he was no worse than many of the priests at Gerry's old school. The course of Gerry's basic training, where he learnt the intricacies of the about-turn on the march, the workings of the FN rifle, and the traditions of his regiment, passed uneventfully.

He liked the traditions and was sure Mr. Kipling would have approved, and among the men of his platoon he found a new family. Most of the men were Cockneys. At first he ignored their teasing about his being Irish, but when a big lad from Bermondsey called Gerry a "thick bloody Paddy" once too often and the other men laughed, Gerry snapped, "Fuck off."

The ensuing brawl might have been just another barracks scrap if Sergeant Edwards hadn't arrived, dressed both men down, and ordered them to the gymnasium. Gerry had learned Father James's lessons well. He demolished the big private in the first round, and Sergeant Edwards promptly put Gerry on the boxing team where he managed to win a lot of bouts and quite a bit of money for his platoonmates. The English squaddies soon became his friends.

Anne didn't approve of his boxing, and Gerry, not wanting to do anything that might displease her, packed it up after the Regimental finals.

He'd met her one Sunday. He had gone by himself to Richmond, a town a few miles north of the camp. Usually he went out with his mates but sometimes he just wanted to be on his own. He would take long walks over the Yorkshire Dales, never ceasing to marvel at their peacefulness. The first time he had stared out over all that empty space he had felt a little frightened. All his life he had lived in crowds, comfortable with people and narrow places. Once he had recovered from his initial unease, he found that up there in the hills there was a tranquillity he had never known existed. And there was something wonderful about being alone, feeling like the only human being on Earth. It was good to be solitary but The Dales were even better when Anne came along.

Before he met her that day he'd been sitting on a dry stone wall reading Da's last letter. It contained the usual, "Thanks for the money. Nobody can get work. When are you coming home, son?" Da had asked that in his last letter, and the one before. Gerry sighed. The army had opened a new world to him. He didn't want to leave it. Ever. He'd stuffed the letter back into his pocket and headed back to the small town. He knew he should go to Belfast. Maybe on his next long leave. It would be good to see Da again.

He'd fancied a cup of tea and had gone into a small café. He was struck by the hazel of the waitress's eyes, a dimple that appeared on her left cheek when she smiled, and how freshly she smelled. Not like that Bridget back in Belfast.

He often wondered why she had said "yes" when he'd plucked up enough courage to ask her out.

They walked the Yorkshire moors together as often as he could get free. He fell in love.

One Saturday afternoon they sat together in the lee of a wall, high on a ridge. Gerry looked down over the brown and purple heather, studded with white sheep, to a granite cottage snug in its farmyard in the valley.

He'd proposed to her that day, in a roundabout kind of a way. She'd asked why he never went back home and he'd tried to explain that he sent his da money and never had enough left for the fare. Then he'd blushed and said he should go because he wanted his folks to meet her. She'd pretended not to know what he meant but had happily accepted his stumbling, "Because I want to marry you." When he had tried to explain that because she was a Protestant and he was a Catholic there might be some difficulties, she had indignantly demanded to know what that had to do with anything?

Gerry, so enraptured with her, had forgotten for a while what he had said that afternoon, but he soon had cause to remember his reply. "Where I come from, it matters a whole hell of a lot."

Indeed it did. Soon after Gerry proposed, the situation started to deteriorate in Northern Ireland. In their letters Da and the married sister Eileen mentioned that things were getting worse. Gerry felt vaguely concerned for his family yet delighted to be well away from the place. Sure Da and the others would be all right.

Gerry couldn't afford to marry until he was promoted to lance corporal, and he had every reason to believe his advancement was imminent. They kept their engagement secret. Until things settled down a bit in Ulster he was even more concerned about how Da would react to the news that his son wanted to marry a Protestant.

In August 1969 all hell broke loose. The Royal Ulster Constabulary, no longer able to contain the riots in Belfast and Londonderry, asked for help from the British regiment garrisoned in Ulster. The General Officer Commanding Forces (NI) sent a terse request to the War Office for more men.

The Honourable Ronald Atkinson, moved in a recent cabinet shuffle from Commerce to the Ministry of Defence, made the case to cabinet. They approved. He phoned the Joint Chiefs of Staff, and the decision was made. The first battalion was already stationed in Ulster. It would make sense to dispatch the second battalion from Catterick, a battalion where private Connolly of B

Company Rifle Platoon was ordered to pack his kit and prepare for embarkation.

The mess hall was packed. Gerry, sitting in the middle of the crowd, watched a young captain mount the podium.

The buzz of conversation stilled.

"Good evening. I am Captain Bristow. I want to tell you a little about what's going on across the water."

It seemed that in early 1967 a civil rights movement had been founded in Belfast. The students of Queen's University had felt it to be their sacred trust to protest. Copying the Americans, the captain suggested. It was unimportant what they protested about as long as they made themselves heard. One or two attempts to publicize the plight of the Biafran refugees and the war in Vietnam had failed in the face of public apathy.

No one, said Captain Bristow, was exactly sure who had the inspiration to demand fair treatment of the Catholic minority, and although this was something the populace could be expected to understand, it was probable that even this bit of agitation would have fizzled out had it not been for the inevitable backlash from right-wing Protestants. There had been ugly scenes in January when protesters had tried to march from Belfast to Londonderry. In the next six months, name-calling had turned to scuffles, scuffles to riots, and riots to a state close to open civil war. The guns were out on the Falls and the Shankill, and men were dead. That was why the army units already involved in peacekeeping were being reinforced. Their job would be to keep the two sides apart and protect the Catholic population.

He went on about not upsetting civilians, cooperating with the police, details of troop movements, but Gerry was more concerned for his family and worried because he was not going to see Anne. The convoys to the troopship waiting in Liverpool were leaving tomorrow. All passes were cancelled.

He was able to phone her, tell her how much he loved her, ask her to wait, but Gerry was still worrying as the ship docked at Queen's Quay. He stood at the rail. The docks looked the same. He had left from this very berth only two years before.

He forgot about Anne as he sat near the tailgate of a one-tonner while the convoy made its way slowly through the city. He caught glimpses of broken glass, boarded-up windows, dirty black scars where petrol bombs had melted the tarmac. The shells of burnt houses, black like rotten teeth, interrupted the regular terraces. Over all hung a mist of smoke, acrid in his nostrils.

He shrank from the jeers as the lorry went past sullen knots of men and women. The people, he realized, had been scorched too.

Once in the barracks, unpacked and properly fed, Gerry's platoon was ordered to report to Captain Bristow for a further briefing.

The captain used a wooden pointer to demonstrate on a large scale map of Belfast.

"There are gangs of hooligans here, here, and here."

Gerry strained to make out the street names and flinched when he saw that the stick rested one street north of Cupar Street.

"We are not yet prepared to patrol at night in the alleys between the Shankill and the Falls. Headquarters thinks the IRA may be on the streets there. Those boyos are almost certainly armed."

There wasn't even a phone in Da's house. Gerry could only hope the old man was all right.

"Ardoyne and Turf Lodge are the responsibility of first battalion. It's coming under control up there. When the rest of your unit arrives, second battalion will move into the Falls. Now. Any questions?"

Gerry had one, but before he could ask a Cockney voice shouted, " 'Ow can we tell the difference between Catholics and Protestants, sir?"

"You've heard that Orange song, "The Sash My Father Wore"? Whistle it. If you get to the second verse and still have your teeth— you're whistling at a Protestant."

He waited for the laughter to subside.

"Very well. Last thing. If there are any men here who come from Belfast, report to my office. Dismiss the men, sergeant."

Gerry reported to the company office.

"You must be very worried, Private Connolly."

"Yes, sir."

Gerry remained at attention.

"At ease."

Gerry obeyed.

"You've family here?"

"Up the Falls, sir. Cupar Street."

"Mmm." Gerry watched as Captain Bristow consulted a sheaf of documents. He looked up. "There was a Connolly family on Cupar Street."

Was? Christ.

"They've been rehoused in a block of flats on Divis Street. Here."

"Are they all right?"

"Sorry. Can't tell you that." Gerry could see concern in the captain's eyes. "That's their new address and I've given you a pass until ten tonight." He handed Gerry the papers. "Do not try to go there in uniform. Good luck, Private Connolly. Dismiss."

Gerry slammed to attention, saluted, made a smart about-turn and marched out. Jesus. It had been all very well over there in Yorkshire, pretending to himself that he had left Belfast behind, but Da and the lads could be in all kinds of shit. Gerry's hands trembled.

He changed into civvies and took a taxi to the address Captain Bristow had given him. It should have been a twenty-minute journey but it seemed to be taking forever. Detours past the worst-hit areas accounted for some of the lost time, but the continual checking of credentials, both by the military and by self-appointed civilian groups, caused the most delay. Jesus, this was bad.

The taxi stopped again. A soldier stuck his head through the driver's window. "Driver's licence, please."

Enough. Gerry looked at the meter and thrust the notes at the cabby. "I'll walk from here." He climbed out.

"Just a minute, sir." The soldier, menacing in full riot gear, grabbed Gerry's arm. "I'll have to see some identification."

Gerry pulled out his army paybook. "Here."

The soldier scanned it. "I'd not go up there if I was you, mate. They've all gone fucking mad."

Gerry grabbed his paybook and ran. The evidence of the rioting was everywhere. Some of the terrace houses were gutted, stark, pitiful in their nakedness. Smoke and tear gas fumes stung his eyes and made them water. Broken glass crunched underfoot. He stopped to catch his breath and bent over, hands on knees. As he straightened up, he came face to face with a group of men. Men carrying pick handles. One spoke.

"Who're you?" His voice was flat.

Gerry let his natural Belfast accent thicken as he said, "Gerry Connolly."

"Where are you going?"

"Home. Cupar Street."

"You're a fucking liar." The big man hefted the pick handle. "Cupar Street was burned out two nights ago."

"I know that, for Christ's sake, but my da and my brothers is here." He dug in his pocket and handed the address to his interrogator.

"Say your name was Connolly?" another man asked. "Have you a brother, Brendan?"

"Aye."

"Brendan Connolly?" The man handed Gerry back his paper. "He's with us."

Gerry did not like the way the men were looking at him.

"Hang about. You the Connolly that joined the army?"

Gerry heard the suspicious tone of the man's voice, but if they knew Brendan he must have told them about his brother in England. There was no point lying. "Aye. What about it?"

The big man took a step forward. "We hate fucking soldiers."

For a moment Gerry thought he was done for until another of the group intervened. "Hold on, Huey. The Connollys is decent folk. Leave the lad alone. He's a Catholic."

"I just want to see my folks. See they're all right, like."

"Leave him be, Huey."

Huey lowered his club. "Aye. All right. Come on. Me and the lads'll take you down there."

Gerry had not realized he was holding his breath. He exhaled. "Thanks very much."

Ten minutes later he stood in the shabby hall of a six-storey block of flats. His escorts had left. Huey had said, before turning away, "Don't you come back round here again. I told you, we don't like fucking soldiers."

Gerry wiped his sweaty palms along the sides of his trousers. He took the lift to the sixth floor and hunted along the narrow corridor for number 605. There. Plastic numerals hung lopsidedly from a door that had long ago been brown but now bore deep gouges and scrawled graffiti. He rang the bell.

Da answered the door. Gerry flinched when he saw how much his father had aged—once thick black hair now thinning and greying, a paunch that had not been there before.

Da growled, "Where'd you come from?"

"Palace Barracks. My unit's been sent here." Gerry pushed past his father into a cramped room, furnished with a cheap table and chair set and two large armchairs. The stuffing was leaking from one of the armchairs. "Are you not pleased to see me?"

Da closed the door. "Decent of you to let us know you were coming."

Jesus, but Da could be sarky. "Come on, Da. I'd no chance to."

"All right. Sit down."

Gerry sat. No wonder Da was upset. It must have been bloody awful, being burnt out. "Look, I'm sorry. Fair enough? How're you doing, anyway?"

Da took the seat opposite. "I suppose I'm all right." His voice was listless. "Me and Brendan and Liam and Turloch's living here now. Home away from fucking home."

The bitterness in his father's words hurt. Eileen had said in one of her notes that their da was turning sour. No wonder.

"It's been bad, like?"

"You never seen anything like it. Two nights ago . . ." He sat hunched forward, forearms on his knees, staring into Gerry's eyes. "There was hundreds of the buggers. Hundreds. They chucked bricks, chunks of iron manhole covers." He shook his head. "Some Protestant fucker threw a Molotov cocktail through our front window." He sat back and pointed at Gerry. "The young lads weren't in. Me and Brendan was bloody lucky to get out alive."

"I heard about the riots, Da. I've seen some of the wreckage. It must've been bloody awful."

"You don't know the half of it. It's a damn good thing Liam and Turloch was out."

"The boys is all right then?"

Da relaxed a bit, crossing his legs, scratching his head. "Your big brothers is well out of this. You mind they left home after you joined up?"

Gerry wanted to ask about them, but Da ploughed on. "Eileen and her man popped in last night, just to see how we're doing here, me and Brendan and the two youngest ones." He waved his arm round the little room dismissively. "How the hell would we be getting on, four of us in this pokey wee place?"

"Right enough. It's not Buckingham Palace. I suppose it could have been worse."

"Worse? How could it have been worse, for Christ's sake?"

"You could all've been killed."

"Fuck." Da rose from the chair and stood, arms hanging limply. Gerry noticed the stoop in his father's stance, saw his lower lip begin to protrude. "We bloody nearly were. Jesus, Gerry, it's desperate the way things are going. Minding your own business. Some Prod git throws a petrol bomb into your parlour—" Da raised his voice and shook a fist under Gerry's nose. "I worked bloody hard to buy that house an' rear you youngsters right."

Gerry pulled his head back and took a deep breath. "I know, Da. I know." He stood and hugged his father. "I'm just glad to see you in one piece. I've been away near two years, you know."

His hug was slowly returned. "Ach, Jesus, Gerry. I'm just mad, that's all. You're right. Sit down. Tell us what you've been up to." He lowered himself into the chair, but Gerry remained standing.

"My platoon only just got here. My officer's a decent man. He give me a pass so I could come over. See how you were, like."

"Aye. Well. You've seen."

"I know. It's not great."

"Gerry, you feel so fucking helpless."

"Maybe now there's more of us soldiers we can help."

"Fat lot of good the soldiers have done so far. They're meant to protect the likes of us." Da laughed derisively.

Gerry sat and put one hand on his father's arm. "Da, they're doing their best."

"Aye. Well, it's not good enough. The Lord helps those that help themselves. Brendan and the boys are out tonight." He grimaced. "They're for getting together a bunch of the rest of the folks and tomorrow night the lot of them are going down the Shankill. Show those Protestant fuckers." He looked at Gerry for a long moment. "Would you go with them?"

Gerry pulled his hand from his father's arm. "Ach, come on, Da. You know I can't get into anything like that." He tried to make a joke of it. "My sergeant wouldn't like it."

"Look, Gerry, you're a Connolly, an' a Catholic. I want you here."

That was an order. The old man was asking for the ranks of the family to close. Gerry found he was at a complete loss for words. He needed time to think.

"D'you hear, Gerry?"

"I'm a Connolly right enough, Da. And I go to mass on Sundays. But I'm a soldier too, so I am. You were there the day I took the oath." Gerry looked for some sign, any sign that Da had understood. "I can't get into civvy fights, sure you know that."

Da's nostrils flared. He clenched his teeth and growled, deep in his throat. "You mean you won't. Away on back to your English friends." He pointed, his finger quivering. "You needn't come round here till you're with us."

"Da, don't be like that."

"Get out." Gerry felt himself seized by one shoulder. "Get out, you turncoat. You're no son of mine!"

Gerry rose slowly. "I'm sorry, Da." He had to make one more attempt. "Look, I can't go back on my word."

"Get out. Get out. I'll hear no more."

Gerry was close to tears by the time he found a cabby who was willing to drive out to Holywood. He sat in the backseat, wishing he had brought a warmer coat. It was cold in the taxi, as cold as Da's, "You're no son of mine," which refused to stop repeating in Gerry's mind. Maybe if he had come for a few visits in the last couple of years, Da would have understood. Still, he couldn't desert, could he? He owed loyalty to his own flesh and blood, but he owed allegiance to his mates in the company and the traditions of the regiment. And then there was Anne. God, but he missed her.

"Two pound fifty."

"What?"

"You're home, mate."

Gerry stared through the window at the high barbed-wire fence. The posts and coils of razor wire were stark against the dusk sky.

"Right." He paid the driver and identified himself to the sentry. As the gates swung shut, Gerry paused and looked at the tarmac parade ground, the rows of wooden huts, the red brick headquarters building, the flagpoles with the Union Jack and the regimental colours. The whole place seemed pretty bleak, but the driver was right. It was home now.

Some home, he thought, as he tossed restlessly in his cot. Lights out had been hours ago, but sleep would not come. All around him men snored or muttered. The place stank of farts and dirty socks. He closed his eyes and tried to picture the peace of the Yorkshire Dales but all he could see were burnt houses, shattered glass, charred timbers—and the look on Da's face, "You're no son of mine."

What the hell was he going to do? Da had reared them all after Ma died. God only knew how hard that must have been. He owed Da. But he owed the army too. Blood's thicker than water. A promise is a promise.

He drifted into an uneasy doze and woke before reveille. As the weak light of a watery dawn crept through gaps in the curtains he decided. He'd have to go back and see Da. Try to explain. Hope that the old man had been so mad with worry and his desire for revenge that he hadn't been thinking straight.

Other men stirred. Usually most of his mates liked to stay in their sacks until the very last minute but today was going to be different. No wonder the rest of the lads were rising early. As soon as the rest of 2nd battalion had been briefed, his platoon would be going on the streets. And after what he had seen last night he knew that it would be no Sunday School picnic.

Gerry just had time for a quick wash and a hasty breakfast before the Motor Transport lorries started to arrive.

The one-tonner stopped on the Grosvenor Road. Gerry smelled the fear of the men around him, yet sensed that his mates, like him, were taking comfort from the nearness of well-known faces.

Sergeant Edwards formed them up on the pavement.

"Right, you lot. Next street up's the Falls Road. The bobbies are in a bit of bother there. Our job's to dig 'em out. And, remember what our officer said. 'Be nice to the civilian population'."

Gerry had never seen such a sneer on the company sergeant's face.

He soon understood why.

The platoon advanced and turned the corner. Gerry could only stare, open-mouthed. A group of green-uniformed RUC men was hemmed in by a mob of rioters. The policemen had been backed up against the wall of Isaac Agnew's burnt-out car dealership and were trying to take cover behind their long perspex shields. Their attackers pelted the hapless men with a constant barrage of rocks and bottles. A Molotov cocktail arched through the air, smashed on the ground, and flared into stinking petrol flame.

The noise deafened him. Shrieks, curses, yells of pain, and a savage metallic clamour like a demented Jamaican steel band. Women standing in doorways, beating on dustbin lids with wooden spoons.

And the sergeant expected them to go into this? Jesus. It wasn't "Gunga Din" anymore. More like "Fuzzy Wuzzy," and the people in that mob were the savages.

Gerry glanced at the private in the rank beside him. The Bermondsey man. He saw stark terror in his eyes.

"Platooon. Shun." The sergeant's orders could hardly be heard above the earsplitting row.

Crash of boots on tarmac.

"Sloooope arms. Poooort arms."

Gerry held his FN aslant across his chest.

"Forwaaard march."

Gerry took a very deep breath and stepped out.

He heard someone yell, "Here come the fucking soldiers!"

His world dissolved into a blur of missiles, swinging rifle butts, egg stains on a child's torn sweater disappearing under a flood of blood from the boy's split head. The lad going down shrilly screaming, "Baastaards!"

A jagged piece of concrete thumped Gerry on the shoulder. He would have fallen if another soldier hadn't grabbed his arm.

Gerry had tried to avoid hitting anyone. These were his own people after all. The piece of concrete changed that. He waded in swinging the riflebutt not caring if teeth were lost or bones shattered. The platoon slowly gained ground. The mob was losing. That was all that mattered.

How long the battle lasted he had no idea. All he knew was that he was desperately relieved to be sitting back in the one-tonner. His shoulder throbbed, but by the looks of some of his friends, he had escaped lightly. All of the men were filthy, many had jagged tears in their uniforms. One sat forward, holding his head as blood dripped on the lorry's floor and a medical orderly tried to staunch the flow.

Gerry's old boxing opponent sat on the bench opposite, wiggling a tooth between his finger and thumb. "Fuck it. I'll lose this one." He raised his eyes to heaven. "You're all right, Gerry, but the rest of that lot are nothing but a bunch of thick bloody bogtrotters."

Gerry was in no mood to be offended. This was the bloke who had hauled him to his feet when the concrete struck. "How do you mean, thick?"

"Christ, mate. We took a bit of a pasting, but did you see what we did to them? Paddies, two. Army, two hundred."

Gerry knew his platoonmate was exaggerating, but he also recognized the truth. It was fucking madness to pit civilians against armed troops who were trained in riot control.

"They are bloody stupid. You're right."

Gerry lapsed into silence. Now that the action was over he could not help thinking about Da and what he'd said. Brendan and the rest were going to start a street fight tonight. They'd be massacred if the troops were sent in. He'd have to warn them. He'd have to.

Captain Bristow had given Gerry another pass and he stood in the flat's foyer willing the ancient lift to return to the ground floor. He was wet and out of breath. He'd had to run all the way from the City Hall. Through the pissing downpour. The taxi driver had laughed. Drive onto Divis Street? Not bloody likely.

Gerry had not liked the look of what he had seen on his way. There was an awful lot of sullen people on the streets, and curfew time wasn't far off. Those folks shouldn't be there, he thought, as he stabbed at the call button again. At least he hadn't run into Huey and his crowd.

Come on. Come on. He hit the call button. At last the doors opened. Gerry jostled a fat woman as he ran in and pushed the button for the sixth floor. He had to be in time to stop Brendan and the rest.

He left the lift, tore down the hall, and pounded on the door of 605.

Da answered. His face lit up in a huge grin. "Gerry, I knew you'd come. I knew it." He grabbed Gerry's hand and shook it. "Go on now, boy, away on down. If you take the back alley, you'll catch the rest of the boys. They've only gone about five minutes." He clasped his son's upper arm. "They wouldn't take me with them, said I'd to stay on here and mind the place, but they'll be as pleased as me to see you."

Gerry heard the pride in his father's voice and for a moment wanted to obey.

"Come on, boy, what's keeping you? Have I to say I'm sorry for roasting you last night? You know I am."

"That's not why I came, Da."

"What?"

"I'm having no part in it. I came to get you to see sense. There's no good fighting. You'll only get hurt worse." He sank into one of the armchairs, head bowed. "Ach, but it's no use, there's nothing I can do now." Gerry waited. Then he looked up.

Da was shaking his head slowly, like a dazed prizefighter. Did he still not understand? "You're not going? You mean that? You're not going?"

After last night Gerry had expected Da to rage, but instead he sounded sad. Defeated. "I don't understand. I just don't understand. Why?" There was a catch in his father's voice as he took the chair opposite. "Do we mean nothing to you anymore? Haven't you seen what's been going on?" He reached over, lifted Gerry's face, looked deeply into his eyes. "Are you scared, is that it, are you scared? I know I was wild. I said you were no son of mine—am I right, Gerry?"

Gerry had never heard his father plead. He usually demanded. It was unsettling. Gerry spoke slowly, his voice tired. "Yes, I'm scared, but not the way you think, Da. I was in one of those riots today, I seen what happens to people down there. Da, the soldiers'll murder the boys. They've no mission." Gerry saw the hurt on his father's face. "Don't you see, Da? There's nothing to gain from getting your head split. It won't get you back to Cupar Street. It won't make the Prods love you."

All the time they had been talking Gerry had been aware of noises coming from the street below. Suddenly the clamour became louder.

He stood and stepped to the window. Below him a crowd was retreating towards the flats. They were being pushed back by a squad of soldiers, helmeted, rifles at the high port.

"Da, come here and look at this."

Gerry felt the presence of his father by his shoulder, heard the old man say, "Ah, fuck."

Gerry didn't turn to Da. He could not tear his eyes away from the scene below. Behind the soldiers a police water wagon, armoured, repulsive as some of the bug-eyed monsters he'd read about in his science fiction stories, poured high-pressure jets at the demonstrators. He watched as a woman was caught and hurled aside. Her forearm, stark white against the black of the tarmac, was bent at an impossible angle. The bone must have snapped. Paddies, two. Army, two hundred.

Behind him the door slammed open.

Gerry spun and saw his brother Liam standing there soaked, dishevelled, panting. "For God's sakes, Da. It's a fucking shambles down there."

Gerry went to hug his brother but was stopped dead when Liam snarled, "What the hell are you doing here?"

"Jesus, Liam."

"Da told us you were here last night. You wouldn't come with us."

Da put up one hand. "Easy, son. Sit down for a minute and gather yourself."

"Sit down? Sit down?" Liam dragged in another great breath. "There's no fucking time for sitting. Brendan's in deep shit."

"Is he hurt?"

"Worse. He shot a policeman."

Da crossed himself.

Gerry looked from Liam to his father and back again. No one spoke. Finally Da begged, "Are you sure?"

"Of course I'm fucking well sure. Wasn't I with him?"

"Oh, God, Liam. Where is he now?"

"Dunno. Him and me got split up. The last I seen he was charging up a back alley. I think he got away all right."

"God, I hope so. If the soldiers catch him, they'll murder him."

Gerry moved to the centre of the room, away from Da and Liam, away from the hellish racket below. He flinched as shots punctuated the eldritch howling. There was no mistaking the sounds of gunfire, clear and staccato above the rumbling of the armoured car. He slammed his hands over his ears, but they did not stop him hearing Da say, "Right, we'll need to get Brendan and Liam over The Border. Brendan will likely make for here and between the four of us we'll manage it."

"How, for fuck's sake?" Liam asked.

Da spoke rapidly. "We'll hide him till, you, Gerry—Take your hands off your head and listen."

Gerry bit his lip as he obeyed. He couldn't get involved in this.

"Go an' get your uniform."

What was Da asking him to do? Gerry shook his head.

"Gerry. Go and get your fucking uniform. When Brendan comes, you can escort him and Liam past the patrols. Tell the Brits the lads are your prisoners. If they can get out of the Falls, they can steal a car and head south."

Gerry straightened his shoulders. He wasn't a youngster anymore to do as he was bid. What Da wanted him to do was wrong. He clenched his teeth. "No."

"What?" Da's voice rose to a high-pitched shout. "I'm talking about the family."

"No."

"So Da was right about you?" Liam hawked and made as if to spit. "Blood's not thicker than water?"

Gerry looked at his brother's face and saw contempt, anger and hatred.

"Keep you out of this, Liam." Da pointed a finger at his younger son. He turned to Gerry and pleaded. "Gerry, Gerry, you told me why you wouldn't fight, but—this is your brother we're talking about. For the love of God, you must help. You must." He seized Gerry by the shoulders.

"I can't, Da." Gerry felt like he had as a wee lad when Da had wanted him to catch a hurling ball in his bare hands. He'd known it would hurt and had begged his father not to throw. The old man had kept on and on until Gerry had caved in. The hard ball had stung his hands and he'd cried. He looked Da in the eyes and said, as distinctly as he could above the din, "No. Now let me be."

"Ah, Jesus. Why not?"

It was the hurling ball all over again. Da simply did not know when to quit. Gerry began to tremble, but fought back. "Because—I told you this before—do you remember the day you signed me in? Do you remember me with a Bible in my hands swearing an oath? Remember?"

"Is that all it is?" For God's sake, Da was smiling. "What's your word to the English anyway? How often have they kept their word? If you've any love for us, any love at all, you must help." He spoke softly, gently.

More shots rang out from the street. Da's grip on Gerry's shoulders tightened, and he pulled away. Keep your bloody hurling ball, Da. "Let me be." Gerry's eyes pricked. He broke from his father's grasp. "Leave me alone!" The door of the flat was still open. He ignored Liam's yell of, "Come back here, you," and rushed through, up the stairs and out onto the flat roof. He stood, oblivious to the downpour. His ears were filled with the clamour from the street below.

Fuck them. Fuck the rioters. Fuck Liam, who wouldn't understand. Fuck Da and his going on and on. The Connolly family or the army? Gerry saw the knot of khaki uniforms below and ached for his platoon. He wanted to go back to them. He wanted to go back to the wild solitude of the Yorkshire Dales. He wanted Anne.

Below him he could see that the worst of the fighting had moved away from the flats. He stepped back from the edge, took a deep breath, and swallowed. He'd go back to his unit. The road was clear. He'd go back home.

As he passed the mouth of a narrow alley, strong arms encircled his throat. He flailed helplessly as he was dragged into the darkness. He dimly recognized the voice of big Huey saying, "You, you shite. You fucking British shite. I told you not to come back," seconds before a pick handle beat Gerry's head to a bloody pulp.

The Honourable Robert Atkinson was on the telephone.

"I see, General. So your boys over in Ulster are taking a beating are they? One killed last night? Pity."

He toyed with a marble-based Parker pen set as he listened.

"Why do you think he was a deserter?"

That was a very elegant piece of marble.

"Just because he was found in a Republican area and didn't come back from a pass doesn't mean he ran, surely? Oh, I see. So you think your chappie might have been trying to help his brothers go South?"

Robert Atkinson frowned. There could be a lot of bad publicity over this.

"Tell you what. See if you can put a good face on this one. Claim he was abducted trying to return to his unit."

Atkinson sighed, the miserable little province seemed to dog his career, and said, "Why? For the sake of his family."

1970

On March 31, the Junior Orangemen paraded. They were attacked by groups of Catholic youths. Seventy soldiers of the Royal Scots who were sent in to control the riot were pelted with stones, bottles and petrol bombs.

On July 3, rioting was so intense that the Falls Road, a predominantly Catholic part of the city of Belfast, was placed under curfew for thirty-four hours. Three people were killed and 1,600 cannisters of CS gas were fired.

1970 Dead 25   **Total Dead 38**

1971

On February 6, Gunner Robert Curtis became the first British soldier to die while on duty. He was killed during a riot in Belfast.

On August 9, internment without trial of suspected IRA sympathizers was instituted as a security measure. More than 300 people were incarcerated.

On December 4, fifteen people were killed by a Loyalist bomb in Mc-Gurk's Bar in Belfast.

1971 Dead 174   **Total Dead 212**

SHE MOVED THROUGH THE FAIR

"... Another martyr for old Ireland, another murder for the Crown...."

Mary sat on the sofa beside her friend Carol and sipped the remnants of a vodka and orange. Bridget was singing another of her rebel songs. A girl from Kerry, in a Belfast flat, bawling about Irish Republican heroes. The words seemed to mean little to her and the three other party-goers, who stood, arms round each other, belting out the words of 'Kevin Barry.' Mary turned to Carol, who was keeping time with one high-heeled shoe held loosely in her right hand.

"Do you think we should be having songs like that?"

Carol looked over her spectacles. "Why not?"

"Well, with all the riots and shootings."

"There's no riots in here." Carol giggled. "Yet." She finished her drink. "It's your party. You can tell them to shut up if you want, but everyone's friends here and tonight no one gives a bugger about the Troubles. They're miles away."

"I suppose so." Yet hadn't a bomb killed five people in a bar on the Shankill Road yesterday, only five miles from this house?

"You 'suppose so'? Jesus, Mary. You're getting married in two days. Relax a bit."

That was Carol all over. Live for the minute. She was right. Forget about the Troubles. "Come on, then. Let's have another drink."

"Now you're talking." Carol managed to slip her shoe on at the second attempt. She rose a bit wobbly and took Mary's glass. "Vodka?"

"Please." She smiled as she watched Carol head for a long table, pushing her way past the rest of the twenty or so revellers. They were all listening to Bridget's quartet, which was now in full flight. Bless Carol. She'd made all the arrangements for tonight. The buffet had looked so inviting four hours ago when the guests started to arrive. Amazing what a bunch of hungry student nurses could do to food. All that was left was a few dried-up sandwiches, the bone of a ham looking like something a hyena had chewed, and a few scattered nuts hanging on forlornly.

"Kevin Barry gave his young life, for the cause of liberteeee . . ."

That was hard on the ear. Bridget would have had a brassy voice if there hadn't been so much tin in the alloy.

"Here." Carol handed Mary another drink. "Get that down you. It'll do you good." She waved her own glass at the choir. "Maybe if they stopped standing on its tail, it would stop howling."

Mary laughed at the old joke.

"Tell you what. When they've done you give us 'She Moved Through the Fair'."

"Ach, no, Carol."

"Ach, yes. I love that song, and you do it so well. You've a lovely voice."

"No. I don't want to sing a song about a bride who drowns herself on her wedding eve."

Carol laughed. "The only one likely to drown herself here is me if I've much more rum. Anyway, you're not getting married tomorrow. It's the day after." Before Mary could stop her, Carol yelled, "Wheest now, you lot. Mary's going to sing 'She Moved Through the Fair'."

Realizing that further protest was useless, Mary stood. Everyone was looking at her. "Go on, Mary. Give it buckets of nyah." The Kerry girl, Bridget, was still swaying as if in time with her own song.

"All right." Why, she thought, do I always have to be persuaded to sing? I love to and, damn it, I have a good voice. Mary took a deep breath and closed her eyes.

"My young love said to me my mother won't mind,
Nor my father slight you for your lack of kine . . ."

The laughter and general conversation stilled. Bridget wants nyah? Mary put vocal grace notes on the words. She gave herself to her music until the song ended,

... "My drowned love came in,

so softly she moved that her feet made no din.

She laid her head by me and this she did say,

"It will not be long love, till our wedding day."

She opened her eyes to smiling faces and a round of applause. Bridget was in tears. "Jesus, Mary, and Joseph, that was grand. Would you look at me," she sniffed, "that bloody song always makes me cry, and this to be a grand happy night for the bride. Sorry about that." She waved her half-empty glass. "It must be the drink." She giggled. "Come on! We'll have a chorus of 'We All Whipped the Knickers off the Queen'."

"Another murder for the Crown." This was no pub song about the Republican medical student Kevin Barry, hanged by the English. This was a flat statement of fact spat out by a hunched, scowling man, a man with the pockmarks of old acne on his face. Kieran McKenna put down the *Belfast Telegraph*, sat back, and folded his arms.

So, he thought, the Brits had killed Ronnie Hogan last night. "A known terrorist." Ronnie was no terrorist, for fuck's sake. He was a freedom fighter of the Provisional IRA. Had been a freedom fighter. Well, we'll find a way to mark your passing, Ron.

Kieran picked up the phone. "Hello, Seamus, did you see the paper? Aye. He was a good man. I know. It's too bad. I think you and me and the others should have a chat. Can you get ahold of them and tell them to be roun' here about ten? Fair enough. I'll see you then." Kieran narrowed his eyes. By the time he had finished, even if the original plan had to be changed, there would be a fresh headline for the *Telegraph*. Of course, according to the Brits, it wouldn't be "terrorists" dead. It would be "innocent victims." But there were no innocents. This was a war, for Christ's sake. Whatever it took, however long it took, Kieran McKenna knew he was in for the duration. The more dead, the more disruption, the sooner the British fuckers would go home. For good. He rose and went to a cupboard. He must get the device ready.

Of course, Siobhan would have to agree to go along.

Mary woke late with a heaviness behind her eyes. What did the Sister Tutor call it? "Self-inflicted injuries." Too many vodkas the night before, but it had been a great party, the last she'd go to as a single woman. Tomorrow at two o'clock, in Fisherwick Presbyterian Church, she would become Mrs. Brian Robinson. "To love, honour and cherish." None of this "obey" rubbish. This was the '70s.

Get up you idle hussy. The day after tomorrow you can lie in bed, with him, for as long as you like. She hugged herself, rubbing her hands along her upper arms, feeling little goose pimples.

The eyes that looked back at her from the bathroom mirror were bloodshot. But they'd be bright and green tomorrow.

Brian, when he'd finally got round to telling her he loved her, had said he'd fallen for her eyes. She peered more closely. They were probably her best feature. The nose was a bit narrow. Lips? They'd do.

She combed the tangles out of her hair, dishevelled after sleep. As usual it was like a black haystack, but it would be all right once the hairdresser had cut it to swing forward to frame her face.

As she brushed her teeth, Mary wondered if Brian would be able to do anything with his hair. She thought of his turned-up nose, slight double chin, and the fair tuft that always stuck up on his crown, no matter how carefully he tried to smooth it down. He was certainly no Adonis. Persistent man. He wouldn't take no for an answer. The first time he'd asked her out, she'd turned him down. And the second.

Her father's razor lying on the glass shelf caught her eye. She picked it up, remembering how a razor had made her relent and accept Brian's third invitation. She'd been sent to prepare a man for surgery, had to give him a pubic shave before his hernia operation. He'd promptly had the most enormous erection and was clearly delighted by her embarrassment—until Dr. Robinson walked behind the screens and pricked the man's balloon. Brian had taken the straight razor from her and announced, "Right, nurse. Let's get this circumcision over with. We'll not need an anaesthetic." She could have kissed him.

Mary went back to her bedroom and let her night-dress slip to the floor.

She did kiss him that night, outside the nurses' home and had been surprised by his gentleness. He wasn't the first man she'd gone out with, but he was the only one who hadn't tried to grope her on a first date. Randy lot, medical students and housemen. Brian was different. That's when she'd started to fall in love.

Mary cupped her breasts, feeling the warmth. Feeling Brian's hands. The first time he'd undressed her he'd got her bra strap caught in a ridiculous string vest she was wearing.

She opened a drawer and removed her shapeless white cotton knickers—what her friends in nursing school called "passion killers." She saw the cream satin bikini panties and half-bra, took them out and tried them on. She examined herself in a long mirror, turning this way and that. The tiny panties were cut high and made her slim legs seem longer. The bra lifted her breasts and let her nipples peep over its lacy cups. You'll like this set a lot better than a string vest, Brian Robinson. Mary closed her eyes.

Someone was knocking on her door.

"Are you up, Mary?"

"Yes, Mum."

"Better get a move on. Carol's coming at ten."

"Right." Mary quickly slipped out of her ready-for-tomorrow underwear, slipped them back into the drawer, dressed, and sat at her dressing table to put on her makeup. She had forgotten about the time, and she and Carol had a lot to do today.

Kieran McKenna stubbed out his cigarette and went to answer the knock at his door. He hurried two men and a slight, dark-haired woman into the hall. One of the men carried a suitcase.

The soulless tenement where McKenna lived was on a narrow street off the Falls Road and was part of a no-go area for the Army, the Royal Ulster Constabulary, and the council workmen who, at least officially, were responsible for its upkeep.

He looked rapidly along the bare concrete balcony, cluttered with broken-down perambulators, rusty bicycles, empty beer bottles and rubbish. Washing hung dispiritedly from lines strung from beneath the overhang above. An all-pervading smell of frying fat mingled with the odour of cat piss rising from the stairwells. The whole was shrouded in the smoke-laden drizzle of a Belfast morning. Satisfied that his guests had not been followed, Kieran closed the door.

The woman preceded the serious, tight-lipped, frowning men to one of the chairs at the kitchen table. The others joined her. The man with the suitcase laid it on the floor beside him. Kieran sat like a farmer, feet flat on the floor, knees apart, forearms draped across his thighs, his callused hands hanging limply, the back of one just brushing the other.

"Tonight's off," he said calmly.

"What?" The question was querulous and came from the smaller of the two men. His thin face was disfigured by the scar of a poorly repaired harelip. "What do you mean it's off? I thought we were going to do Palace Barracks." He dropped his hand to the case beside him.

"I know, Paddy," Kieran spoke slowly, "but I had a call early this morning, from one of the boys in Holywood. The Brits have moved the sentry boxes inside the wire." His smile was sardonic. "That place is closer guarded now than Buckingham Palace."

The woman spoke, leaning forward, striking the table with one finger to give emphasis to her words. "So, if it's off, why did you drag us round here?"

Kieran looked straight into her deep-set eyes, wondering why Siobhan always reminded him of a feral cat. "Because, love"—he saw her bristle at the endearment—"because I think there's a better way."

The other man, heavy-set, balding, thrust out his chin and scratched the unshaven underside of his jaw. "It's pretty bloody sudden. What have you in mind?"

"Seamus, I want to get a parcel into a bar in the city centre," Kieran said. "And I want it done today." His eyes narrowed. "I'm not about to let the Brits think they can get away with killing our people."

Seamus drew in his breath. "How the hell can we do that? All them places have security. Everyone's searched."

Kieran laid a hand on the arm of Siobhan's denim jacket, noting how she flinched at his touch. "In the Ladies." He looked at her with one eyebrow raised.

She bit her lower lip, small white teeth stark against the pale pink. "You want me to make the delivery?"

Kieran nodded, smiling. "Aye—and you picked the right word. Delivery."

"What do you mean?"

Kieran stood and walked to a corner of the kitchen. He opened the cupboard and produced a strange-looking contraption, swollen in the front, straps behind. "Try this on."

She stood and took it in one hand, holding it at arm's length.

"Here," said Kieran, "put the bulge in front, the straps over your shoulders and round your waist."

She shrugged and did as she was told. The foam-rubber shell hung in front of her belly.

"Jesus," said Seamus, "hang a dress over that and you'd—" his eyes widened, "you'd swear she was pregnant."

"Aye," said Kieran, more wistfully than he had intended, "but it's quicker than the natural way."

"Don't you wish, Kieran McKenna." Her eyes flashed. There was no humour in them.

Kieran found himself indeed wishing that it could have been so, but he had known Siobhan for four years. She was as wedded to the cause as any nun to the Church of Christ. He'd tried, only once, to ask her out and had been solidly rebuffed. Yet he ached for this tough young woman and even now wondered if it was worth putting her in harm's way. He turned to the man with the suitcase, hiding his feelings behind a façade of business. "Have you the little present in there, Paddy?"

"I have," said Paddy. "It just needs the last wire connected and the timer set."

"Show me." Kieran held out his hand.

Paddy pulled the case onto the tabletop, opened the lid, and took out a slab of slate-grey plastic explosive. The copper top of a detonator was buried in the putty-like material and connected to two small batteries by a red wire. Another wire ran from the batteries to a small alarm clock and was attached to a plate where the alarm hammer would strike. A piece of blue flex hung free from the detonator, its loose end wrapped in insulating tape. "Here."

Kieran took the bomb and turned to Siobhan. "I need to see if it'll fit," he said apologetically, lifting the lower edge of her bulge with one hand, and pushing the device into the hollow with the other. He inadvertently lifted the hem of her T-shirt with the back of his wrist and felt the soft warmth of her belly. "Sorry." He dropped the foam padding. "How does that feel?"

"Cold," she said and her words were icy, "but it fits."

"Right," said Kieran. "Take the thing off."

She did so, laying it on the table and tucking the end of her shirt into her jeans. Seamus, who had been watching the proceedings, pursed his lips. "That's all very well, but even if Siobhan can get into a pub, where's she going to put the bloody thing?"

Kieran ignored him. "Can it be waterproofed, Paddy?"

"No sweat. Just lap it in a couple of plastic bags."

"Good." Kieran lifted the bomb from its nest and handed it to Paddy. "Set the thing to go off at nine. The pub will be full then." He spoke to Siobhan. "If you can get it into the Ladies, all you have to do is set it, wrap it in the bags, and lay it in one of the lavatory cisterns."

She inclined her head. "No problem."

Paddy showed Siobhan what he had done. "See that there?" He pointed to the wire he had just connected to the hammer. "The clock's set for nine." He showed her the red hand on its face. "When the hammer hits the plate, it'll complete the circuit." He put a strip of insulating tape on the plate, smiling. "It's safe as houses until you strip that piece of tape off." He turned to the pock-faced man. "Have you a couple of plastic bags, Kieran?"

Kieran found the rubbish-bin bags in a drawer. He set them ready on the table. "Leave the bomb and the carrier." He turned to the young woman. "Siobhan, you get away on home and put on a big dress." He looked at her short cropped tresses. "And for God's sake put on a bit of lipstick and do something with your hair."

Her lips curled in a sneer.

"Seamus? You drive Siobhan to her place and get her back here for twelve."

"Right."

"I'll look after things from there. Paddy, skedaddle."

"Right," said Paddy, turning to leave. "Don't forget to do up the bags tight after you take off the tape." He smiled at her. "Good luck, Siobhan."

Kieran wondered if she had even heard the good wishes. He watched her leave with Seamus, seeing the proud walk of her, the curve of her small buttocks in her tight jeans, the wisps of black hair at the nape of her neck.

He sat at the table, looking at the bomb. Very ecumenical stuff, plastic explosive. It doesn't care if you are Protestant or Catholic, Hindu or Jew. Given a nudge by its detonator, it will destroy all around it in a completely nondiscriminatory fashion. All he had to do now was wait.

"My feet are killing me." Carol stood in the doorway of the dress shop changing room.

"Just a minute." Mary took off a white satin bolero jacket and handed it to the shop assistant. "It fits perfectly."

"You want it delivered today?"

"No," said Carol, "she'd rather get married in a gunny sack."

"Carol." Sometimes, Mary thought, my best friend should keep her mouth shut. "Pay no heed to her. She's got a headache." Mary slipped into her blouse. "Yes, please, and the attendants' outfits too."

"Come on, Mary. I need to take a cure."

Mary laughed. "You'll get your hair of the dog in a minute. Too much rum last night." She slipped on her raincoat. "Do you really like my outfit?"

"White, full-length sheath, jacket. 'The bride was lovely in white.' " Carol smiled. "Of course I like it."

White. With the satin lingerie underneath. "And the bridesmaids' dresses?"

Carol puffed out her cheeks and pushed her glasses up her nose with one finger. "They're all right for the others. I'll look like a lollipop in pink and white candystripes."

Mary laughed. "Come on, Carol. You'll be smashing." Although, in truth, Mary thought, Carol was a bit on the plump side. Perhaps she had been a bit selfish picking the other dresses to make hers stand out. "Brian's best man will rupture himself when he sees you."

Carol looked a bit dubious. "Tom? I don't know."

"Of course he will." Mary hugged Carol. "He doesn't know what he's missing."

Carol drooped an eyelid. "I'd keep that lad's slippers under my bed."

"Come on. I'll buy you lunch." Mary was hungry. "Where do you fancy?"

"Next door?"

Mary shook her head. " 'The Causerie'? That's where Brian proposed to me. It's sort of—our place."

"What about the 'Abercorn'? They've great oysters." Carol winked again. "I hear they're an aphrodisiac."

"Maybe you should give some to Tom, then," said Mary, quite unable to resist a little stab at Carol.

"You're rotten," said Carol, but she was laughing.

Mary linked her arm through Carol's. " 'The Abercorn' it is. Your poor feet up to the walk? It's not far from here. Just up Church Lane and around a couple of corners."

Mary speared a lettuce leaf with her fork as she watched an obviously bored security man searching other patrons coming into the bar. "I wish they wouldn't do that. Look." The man was running his hands over the swollen belly of a black-haired, very pregnant woman. Judging by the foul look the girl gave the security guard, she didn't think much of it either.

"Fact of life in Belfast," said Carol, pushing away her empty plate. "Cheers." She took a long swallow from her glass of wine. "God, that's better."

Mary watched her friend. Carol loved to pretend she was a woman of the world, but in fact she was a bit immature. Still, she was great fun, and they went back a very long way. Right to kindergarten.

Carol rolled a sip of wine round her mouth, swallowed, and said, "That's not a bad drop."

Mary looked over the rim of her own glass. "Did I tell you about the wine the night Brian proposed?"

"No." Carol sat forward.

"Memory's an odd thing. I can remember every detail. The napery, the cutlery arrangement in the place settings, the rose on the table—"

"The gypsy violins."

"What?"

"Get on with it. Did he go down on one knee?"

"Don't be so impatient. I've to tell you about the wine first."

"Go on then."

"Brian asks the waitress, 'What's a really nice white wine,' 'The Pooly Fussy's lovely, dear,' she says. Brian gives me one of those cross-eyed looks but says nothing till she's gone. 'I think she means Pouilly Fuissé,' says he. I don't know why we thought it was so funny, but the pair of us laughed so much I cried."

Carol imitated a thick Belfast accent. "I bet you near took the rickets."

"I did indeed. Anyway, there's me laughing away and suddenly Brian says something. I didn't hear him the first time. I just shook my head. I couldn't figure out why he looked so glum. 'What?' says I. 'I asked you to marry me.' I just about fell off my chair." Mary paused, remembering the solemn look on Brian's face.

"Go on."

"I said, 'Yes.' Just like that. Well, you know how quiet Brian usually is?"

Carol nodded.

"Doesn't he leap up and roar, 'Oh God, you will?' and nearly scares an old man at the next table to death."

"I don't believe it. Brian?"

"Brian." Mary looked into the middle distance thinking of him. "We never had the 'Pooly Fussy.' The waitress gave us a bottle of champagne on the house." She felt Carol's hand covering her own and looked at her friend.

"I'm happy for you. You're a very lucky woman."

"I know, Carol. Thanks. And thanks for being here today." Carol laughed and held up one hand summoning the waiter. "My good man, two glasses of Pooly Fussy."

"Right, dear."

Mary saw Carol's huge grin seconds before her own laughter pealed across the room.

"Oh Lord, Carol. I've laughed so much, I need a pee. I'll be back in a minute."

The pregnant woman who had given the security man such a scowl was leaving the toilet as Mary went in. She looked uncomfortable, waddling along, sway-backed. Mary smiled and was rewarded by a surly grunt as the woman hurried by. Poor lass.

Siobhan stood on the street. She felt ridiculous, and she wanted to hit somebody. Anybody. As if it hadn't been bad enough, what with Kieran driving her into town, hardly able to watch where he was going for trying to look at her. She knew bloody well what he wanted. That was his problem. She had a job to do. She had been curt with him when he had parked the car outside the iron security railings and apologized because she'd have to walk the rest of the way. She knew as well as he did that no cars were allowed in the city centre.

He'd tried to wish her good luck, putting his pockmarked face close to hers, all the concern in the world in his eyes. She had leant away from him. "I know. 'The Abercorn.' You wait here. I'll only be gone twenty minutes."

She looked at her watch. Half an hour already. It was hardly her fault she had not been able to pull the lid off the lavatory. The washroom had been crowded, and it would have looked bloody funny, her going into another stall. She knew she should have waited, but some fey feeling had told her to leave.

She put both hands on her belly, as pregnant women do, but she was shifting the lower edge of the swelling that pressed uncomfortably against her stomach. She began walking along Anne Street, past Johnston's, where a small, golden umbrella over the entrance advertised the shop's wares. She turned into Church Lane. Four shops down there was a restaurant and bar. Kieran wouldn't be too pleased about her decision to leave the bomb in a different pub, but the results would be the same. To hell with him and his cow eyes. She pushed through the glass-fronted swing doors.

"I don't believe it." Mary rummaged in her handbag.

"What don't you believe?"

"I must have left my wallet in the dress shop."

"Cheep," said Carol, flapping her elbows like a bird. "Cheep cheep."

"I am not cheap. I will pay for your lunch." Mary bridled. "I must have left it behind at the dress shop."

"A likely story." Carol opened her own bag and counted out the money. "Come on. Stop looking like you've lost a pound and found a penny. It's just around the corner. We'll go back, get your purse, and you can pay me back."

"Bless you, Carol."

"Never mind the blessing. Just get the money. I'm skint until next payday."

Siobhan closed the door of the tiny bathroom. This was better. These smaller places usually only had one room for the Ladies. She could take her time in here. She tried the cistern lid. Great. It came away easily. She manoeuvred it onto the linoleum floor. Now, let's get this damn contrivance off. She wriggled out of her dress and the supporting straps and put the carrier beside the cistern-lid. The floor was becoming crowded.

Now to get this bomb set and get to hell out of here. She lifted the plastic bags and the device from their foam nest and looked around. Nowhere to put the bloody things. She blew out her lips. Take your time. She managed to squeeze everything onto the top of the lavatory seat, leaving them there as she kicked the carrier aside. She'd have to put it on again before she left. Otherwise she'd have a hell of a job explaining to the few people in the restaurant how she'd managed to go to the bogs pregnant and come out looking like Twiggy.

She lifted the bomb. Funny how light it was. Good. She moved back one step to give herself room to work. Now, Paddy had said to strip the tape from the metal plate on the top of the clock. Gently. Gently. Done.

Siobhan released her breath in a low whistle.

She held the device even more gingerly now it was live and looked at it. Waterproofing it was going to be trickier than she had anticipated. She could hear Kieran and his, "Be very, very careful when you put the bomb into the bags." Jesus Christ. Just because she hadn't had as much to do with explosives as him didn't mean she was stupid. She knew damn well it wouldn't do to push the hammer against the plate while she was wrapping the thing in the plastic bags.

She leant forward slowly to place the bomb back on the seat. Her hands were steady as rocks, and she allowed herself a small smile of pride at how well she was in control of herself. The toilet bowl was not quite in reach and so she pushed the cistern lid away with her right foot, never taking her gaze from the Semtex. Now she had room. She moved forwards but her left foot became entangled in the straps of the foam-rubber carrier. She staggered and her hands glanced against the wall, moving them together, pushing the hammer against the plate.

The blast demolished the bathroom and ripped through the wall between the restaurant and the dress shop next door.

Siobhan, Carol and Mary were killed instantly. More martyrs for old Ireland.

1972

On January 30, several hundred Catholics gathered on the Creggan Estate in Derry intending to protest the government's policy of internment without trial. Soon more than 15,000 marchers were heading for the city centre. Soldiers of the 1st Battalion of the Parachute Regiment were sent in to disperse the crowd. It is not known who fired the first shot. By the end of Bloody Sunday, the Parachute Regiment had fired 108 rounds. Thirteen civilians were wounded. Thirteen men were dead.

On March 4, the Abercorn restaurant in Belfast was bombed by the Irish Republican Army. No warning was given. Janet Bereen and Anne Owens were killed. Rosaleen and Jennifer McNern, Irene Arnold, and Jimmy Stewart each lost both legs. Rosaleen McNern also lost her right arm. At least 130 people were wounded.

On March 20, a "no warning" bomb in Belfast left seven dead and more than 100 injured.

On July 21, Bloody Friday, members of the Provisional IRA detonated 22 bombs in Belfast. Nine people were killed and at least 130 wounded.

On July 31, the town of Claudy, County Londonderry, was hit by three large car bombs sent in by the Provisional IRA. Ten died.

1972 Dead 467   **Total Dead 679**

NEIGHBOURS

". . . Yoke not thyself equally with the unbeliever. Have no truck with the Antichrist in Rome, nor his disciples." The speaker, bull-like shoulders hunched forward, prognathous jaw jutting, glared over the Belfast congregation of the Free Protestant Church of Ireland. He held the edge of the pulpit firmly, taking his weight on his outstretched arms. "Our fathers and our forefathers said," he growled as he admonished the crowd with his right index finger, "'Not an inch. No surrender.' Verily, brethren I say unto you; we must remain true to our Protestant heritage. Not an inch. No surrender." He waved a heavy Bible above his head before putting it on the pulpit's rim, opening the book with a flourish. "Yoke not thyself equally with the unbeliever." He slammed the book shut. "That, brothers and sisters, concludes my sermon for today." The self-styled Moderator of the Free Protestant Church bowed his head, eyes screwed shut. "Thanks be to God. Amen, brothers and sisters, amen." He was gratified by the volume of the responding "amens."

"'Love thy neighbour'? I know most of us think it was Jesus who first said it, but the same can be found in the Book of Leviticus, Chapter 19, Verse 18. 'Thou shalt love thy neighbour as thyself.' Why, I wonder, do we here in Ulster find this so hard to do?"

The Reverend Jack Wilson looked down from his Belfast pulpit. At least, he thought, there's a fair turnout today. About three-quarters of the pews in the centre of the nave were filled. The benches to the sides were empty, but that didn't surprise him. The fluted pillars that supported the arched roof were pleasing to the eye as they marched in two rows from the front hall of the church to the altar, but they effectively screened the pulpit and apse from the view of anyone sitting to their sides.

He looked up to the gallery, past the long, octagonal lights that hung on metal chains from the vaulted ceiling. He could see his friend, sitting well to the back. He smiled to himself. One thing you could say of Hugh Conlan, he was a man of his word. Sweeping his gaze back over the congregation, Jack Wilson continued.

" 'Love thy neighbour.' The Old Testament did not say, 'Love thine Israelite neighbour,' Jesus did not say, 'Love thy Jewish neighbour.' Indeed He, as you well should know, preached love, *Agape*, to all mankind, Jew or Gentile. Would it be too much to ask that we Presbyterians stretch out our hands to our Catholic brothers and sisters?"

There was soft murmuring from the pews below, whether of approval or disapproval he couldn't tell. To say such a thing to a Belfast Presbyterian congregation in the early 1970s took courage. Ulster folk have long memories. When the Bible said, "A thousand years are but a day in His sight," Jack often thought wryly that even God Almighty must have some Ulster blood. Anyone in the church over the age of fifty—and, as in most congregations, the majority were— remembered Partition and the Troubles of the twenties as if they had been yesterday; to say nothing of the present idiocy.

"I know that for some of you the hurt is deep. I know that for three hundred years we of the Reformed Church and those who belong to the Church of Rome have had our differences. I know that to many of you what I am suggesting goes against the grain, but I will close with the text for today, the words of Our Lord to be found in the Gospel according to Saint Matthew, Chapter 6, Verse 27, 'Love your enemies, do good unto them which hate you.' Thanks be to God."

He came down the steps of the pulpit, which was mounted like a low crow's nest above the end of the choir stalls, and took his seat be-

low. He finished the rest of the service and pronounced the bene-
diction.

The choir rose. He looked with pleasure at their dark red robes,
the women with their hair demurely covered by soft shapeless caps
like those worn in academic processions by English dons, the men
bareheaded. Even robing the choir had been a struggle. Some of the
more conservative elders had thought it had smacked too much of
popery when he had first suggested the idea several years before. He
had won that battle. It remained to be seen if he could win this one.
Although the congregation did not know it, this morning's sermon
had been his opening salvo.

The organ played the first notes of the recessional hymn, and as
the choir began to sing and file out of their stalls he took his place at
their head, smiling as for the thousandth time he marvelled at the
majesty of the music and the cool beauty of his church. He stepped
through the multicoloured pool of light thrown by the sun's rays
through one of the stained glass windows, turned left past the lectern on which the great Bible lay, and passed into the vestry. He just
had time to hurry to the front door to greet the members of the congregation as they left.

As he arrived, he saw the back of his friend disappear around a
street corner. Well, they would meet later at the manse. The first of
the worshippers was coming through the doors.

"Powerful sermon, Reverend, powerful sermon. Gives us something
to think about."

"Thank you, Dr. Irwin. I hoped you might like it." The doctor and
his wife moved on and the rest of the congregation followed. Some
smiled and nodded, one or two shook his hand. Most refused to meet
his eyes, whether from a sense of guilt or more likely from disapproval.
He suspected the latter.

Bringing up the rear of the exodus was the clerk of sessions, the
Presbyterian equivalent of a deacon, and a small knot of elders. They
were all middle-aged, or older, all dressed in rusty black suits. And
all had looks of distinct displeasure.

"We'd like a word with you, Reverend Wilson," the clerk began.

He was a small man, small of stature and, as Jack well knew, small of mind. His face was lined, his thin lips permanently set at twenty past eight, and on those rare occasions when he smiled his mouth moved, but his eyes did not. "If you'd just step into the porch."

Jack Wilson agreed, and the little crowd moved back inside the church.

"Now see here, it's about your sermon," the clerk continued, "it's just not what we'd like to hear from a Protestant minister." The other elders nodded their agreement. He blustered on. "Now we know that you come here from London, but still and all you're Ulster born and Ulster reared. You know the score. We'll have no more of this pope-loving in this church." Three or four of his companions had the decency to look away in embarrassment, but the rest murmured their assent.

Jack saw the folded arms, the hunched shoulders, the stony glares.

"What seems to be upsetting you, Mr. Johnston?" Jack enquired politely, ignoring the others. "Does the idea bother you that people who worship in a different way, but still worship the same God, are our neighbours?" If his faith meant anything, it was just that. He'd be damned if he would cave in to this sanctimonious little man. "When I accepted my calling to this church, I met with you all and told you that some things would change. You accepted it then. Accept it now." His voice had risen. He inhaled a single breath, deeply, forcibly. He was furious. To avoid making a scene he turned and left. As he did so, he heard Johnston call after him, "You've not heard the end of this." He took some satisfaction from knowing that neither had Johnston and his ilk.

Jack walked swiftly round the side of the church to where his wife and two daughters were waiting in the car. Climbing into the passenger seat, he slammed the door. "Home," he said tersely, hoping that Norah, his wife of twenty-five years, would as usual read his mood and let the hare sit. He was not ready to talk about his recent encounter. When the time was ripe, he would tell her what was troubling him, but just for the moment he wanted to be alone with his thoughts. The girls, he knew, would follow their mother's lead. The family drove home in silence.

By the time they reached the manse, he had calmed down enough to make an attempt at conversation with Kate, his younger daughter, a student teacher at Stranmillis College. They were discussing the vagaries of the "new math" curriculum, which Jack secretly thought was a load of rubbish, as the car turned into the driveway.

The manse sat in a small garden flanked by prunus trees and rose bushes. The house itself was representative of the Ulster character, foursquare and uncompromising, with no frills or decorations.

Norah let herself out of the car, followed by the girls. She nodded her head in the direction of a rusty Ford Prefect parked on the other side of the road. "There's that terrible banger of Hugh's."

Jack waved and watched his old friend walk towards him. "Go on in, Norah, girls," he slammed the door of the car. "I'll wait for Father Hugh."

Norah and the girls went into the manse. Jack waited for his guest, clasped him warmly by the hand, and ushered him in.

"Good to see you, Hugh. Good to see you." This man always restored Jack's spirits. Hugh simply smiled. They went into the bright living room and sat in armchairs on either side of the fireplace. The room was redolent with the fragrance of a huge bunch of roses Norah had picked that morning from the garden and arranged in a bowl on a wooden plinth. Close by it was an old wooden music stand. Jack smiled fondly, remembering his younger daughter's awful attempts to master the violin. Above the fireplace hung a reproduction of a painting by some old master. It was of a young man drinking sherry.

Hugh looked at it and said wistfully, "Now there's an idea." His brogue was soft, County Cork, and gave counterpoint to the harsher tones of his Ulster companion.

"So it is true what they say about Catholic priests, Father Hugh Conlan. You are a drink-soaked lot." Both men laughed as Jack opened a cupboard and took out a tray of glasses and a bottle of Harvey's Shooting Sherry. He poured two glasses, handing one to his friend.

Jack Wilson leant against the mantel, glass in hand. "Now, get outside that, Hugh, and tell me, what did you think?"

The other sat forward, both hands wrapped round the small glass.

"The words were fine, Jack. The words were fine, but," he paused and lifted his shoulders slightly, "sitting where I was, right at the back there in the gallery, it was impossible to tell how they went down." He raised his eyes to Jack, cocking his head slightly to one side. "What do you think?"

It was Jack's turn to shrug. "Do you know, I just don't know. I got what I expected from the session clerk. That man would not know the meaning of Christian charity if the Archangel Gabriel himself gave him lessons. He went for me immediately after the service. I had to listen to his carping and face his cronies, every one of them with a look like last year's rhubarb." His smile was impish. "Good Lord, if he'd known there was a Catholic priest in the balcony he might have had apoplexy." Jack shook his head, the smile fading. "It was unforgivable. I nearly lost my temper with them. But Mr. Johnston and his happy band of pilgrims won't stop us." He set his half-empty glass on the mantel and pulled a small, well-used briar from his trouser pocket, lighting it and enjoying the taste of the Erinmore Flake.

The door opened and Kate came in, pulling a face as she sniffed the clouds of tobacco smoke. "Yeugh, Dad, that stuff stinks, and you look very fierce." She put her arms round Jack and smiled at Hugh Conlan. "And how are you, Father Hugh?"

"All the better for seeing your lovely self."

"Thank you, sir." She looked up at her father. "What were you two plotting?"

Jack freed himself from her arms. "Do you remember when I asked you, a while back, how much you knew about Catholics?"

She frowned. "Yes."

"Well, Father Hugh and I here had the notion to ask a priest to come to our youth club to explain what the Church of Rome is all about."

He watched her take a moment to digest what he had just said. "I think that's a terrific idea." Her eyes widened. "So that's what the sermon was about this morning."

Jack nodded and thought, Smart girl, my Kate. "Aye. Father Hugh's said he'll come."

Kate's frown returned. "And now you're having second thoughts because Mr. Johnston didn't like your sermon." She chuckled. "Did he call you an apostate again?"

It was Jack's turn to laugh. "Not quite." He became serious, looking at Hugh for confirmation. "Kitty, I think young Presbyterians need to know more. We've got to start breaking down the barriers if there is to be any hope for this country." He was not surprised to see Hugh nodding support.

Kate looked to Father Hugh. "And you've been recruited as the sacrificial lamb."

Hugh's laugh rumbled. "You know your dad. Once he gets his mind made up." He rubbed his nose, which was bent and misshapen. "He did this to me twice, when he and I went to different schools." He held up an index finger. "Once playing rugby,"—a second finger was extended—"and once boxing."

Jack used his pipe to give emphasis to his words, poking the stem at Father Hugh. "You'll see. Once you show them that your people are just like us, the young folk are bound to come round. Mind you, I can't hold out much hope for the older ones, the bitter ones, but it's the young folk I'm after." His left hand clenched. He looked directly into his friend's eyes. "You will do it, won't you, Hugh?"

"So you still want to go ahead?" Father Hugh enquired, the tone of his voice telling that he knew full well what the answer would be. "You still want me to do my Daniel in the lion's den impersonation, in spite of your clerk of sessions?" He smiled and sipped his sherry. "Of course I will. My bishop has given his approval, so there's nothing to stop us. All you have to do is name the day."

"We don't want to give them too much time to think about it. I'll make the announcement next Sunday. The youth club meets on Tuesday night, doesn't it, Kitty?" She nodded. "Right. That's when a priest of the Church of Rome will explain to a bunch of young Presbyterians what the differences are between us, and where we can overlook those differences and start coming together." He stabbed with the briar again. "If we can just get them to talk, first to you and then maybe to some of your young people, they'll see, Hugh, they'll see. It's only a small start, but it's a start."

Jack watched as Hugh looked at him for a long minute, pursed his lips, and shook his head slowly. "You really believe it's going to work, don't you, Jack?" He said it as he might have to a favourite nephew who had just protested his undying belief that Santa Claus was coming tomorrow—worldly-wise sorrow tinged with great hope that it might really be so.

Jack laughed, a great rolling laugh. "That's a great word Hugh, 'Belief.' Are not you and me in the belief business? I know it's not going to be easy, I'm not that much of an optimist, but we've been round these houses too often before. Yes, Hugh, it will work."

Kate looked from one man to the other. "I think if anyone can do it you two can."

And Jack looked fondly at his daughter, seeing what he hoped fervently was the future. He held out his hand to the priest. "Come on, Hugh. If we're not in the dining room before the Yorkshire pudding, Norah and Sheilah will make us both Christian martyrs."

While the meal continued at the manse, Johnston and his supporters were still meeting in the vestry. Johnston had his hands jammed in his trouser pockets. "Your man Wilson's astray in the head if he thinks Protestants and Catholics are going to get on together."

He was pleased by the approving nods.

"I tell you. We beat the Fenians at the Boyne, aye and Derry, and Aughrim and Eniskillen."

A heavy-set man standing to Johnston's left said, "Bless King William of Orange of 'glorious and immortal memory.'"

A small man, near the back of the group, coughed and asked, "Look. Do you not think Reverend Wilson means well?"

Johnston felt the heat rise in his face and turned on his questioner. "Means well? Don't be daft, Huey. I called him an apostate before. He is. He's forgotten 1689 and '90 and '91. Good Ulster Orangemen sent the papish King James to France, to exile, and we've had Protestants on the throne of Great Britain ever since." Spittle flew as he spoke.

"Don't you forget, Ulster's still a part of Great Britain. Means well? Wilson? Do you want Ulster ruled from Rome?"

"Sorry, Mr. Johnston."

"Aye, well. Let Wilson keep at it and that's what you'll get." Johnston still directed his remarks at the dissenter. "We can't let him away with it. There's no way. We should've never had him here in the first place." He spoke now to the rest. "Look at what he's done, would ye, just look. I never seen a minister dress up in robes, or have the choir dressed up either. This morning was enough. The next thing you know he'll be saying the Latin Mass. 'Love thy neighbour' indeed. I've no Catholics for neighbours." He was encouraged by the way one of the men close to Huey gave the little man a nudge, and by another round of nods from the rest of the audience.

"What do you think we should do, Sammy?" one of them asked.

"I'll tell ye. I'll tell ye. We'll call a meeting of the presbytery and we'll just tell him it's got to stop. Got to stop. Enough's enough."

"What'll ye do if he says he won't?" another man enquired.

"He'll do as he's bid. It's his bread and butter."

"I'm no' so sure, Mr. Johnston. Yon Reverend Wilson's a very proud man."

"Proud is he? And what does the Book of Proverbs say, Chapter 16, Verse 18? 'Pride goeth before destruction, and a haughty spirit before a fall.' Do you think he knows the Old Testament?"

The question produced a few snorts.

"He's been riding for a fall long enough. He's going to get it, and we're going to see to it."

He had no difficulty persuading the group that a full meeting of the presbytery should be called, and Johnston already knew that with this current collection of elders he could carry the vote. *Presbuteros*, the Greek from which the church took its name, meant literally, "rule by elders," and Johnston meant to exercise that rule to the full.

The meeting broke up. Johnston left and walked the half-mile to his home. Along his way he thought about his coming triumph. Love dirty Fenians indeed. Why should he? He had his own reason to hate

Catholics. His father, a soldier discarded when the Great War was over, had fought with the Black and Tans in the twenties.

Johnston knew rightly it was men like his da that had helped stop all of Ireland being given to the Romans. Back then Ireland had almost won independence, save for the six counties of Ulster. British then. British now.

He did not notice the softness of the day, the sun through the young leaves of the plane trees dappling their trunks, and blackbirds singing sweet as boy trebles.

Da had been right to hate the Taigs with their ambushes and bombings and senseless killings of the Civil War. He'd told his son about it often enough.

He turned onto the towpath of the Lagan Embankment where the tired old harridan of a river flowed slowly, her cheeks caked with the clotted smoke and grime of industrial Belfast. Even whores can wash their faces. The wind was making little runs of ripples that reflected the blues of the sky. Two eights from the university rowing club slid silently over her surface, the pools from the oars shining softly. Today the old girl was wearing her best string of pearls. He hawked and spat into the water. A haughty spirit, he thought. Well, we'll see. He had more up his sleeve than just the will of the presbytery.

He let himself into a public phone box and pulled a small diary from his pocket. He found the number he wanted, lifted the receiver, inserted the coins, and dialled. The voice at the other end of the line was deep, honeyed. "Hello."

Johnston spoke quickly. "Hello. Your Reverence?"

"Yes. Who is this?"

"Look. You don't know me, but I've a problem."

"'Come unto Me, all ye that labour and are heavy laden, and I will give you rest,' sayeth our Lord in the Gospel of Saint Matthew. What can I do for you?"

It was hot in the cramped booth. Johnston felt himself start to sweat. "Like, our minister, Reverend Wilson—"

"Reverend Jack Wilson?"

"Aye. Him."

"I know of him."

"Aye, well. He's been going on about loving Catholics." Johnston waited, but there was no response. "I'm going to call a meeting of the presbytery. But if he won't back off—will you help us?"

"Love Catholics? Oh dear." There was a pause. "I'm sure your senior ministers will be able to take care of things."

"Aye, but if they're not?"

"Call me." Johnston heard emphasis in the words just before the line went dead.

He left the phone booth. All right, Reverend Wilson. All right.

The next Sunday was raw. The rain, like shoemakers' knives, was driven by a biting wind from the northwest, whipping the trees and driving old papers and leaves along the glistening pavements. Jack Wilson wiped the raindrops from his spectacles as he entered the vestry. He glanced at his watch. Fifteen minutes until the start of the service. He opened the cupboard that held his robes and was just about to put them on when there was a knocking at the door.

"Come in."

The door opened. Johnston entered.

"Good morning, Mr. Johnston. What can I do for you?"

"You can do nothing for me. There's a meeting of the presbytery after service. Be there." He thrust his face forward. "D'ye hear me now? Be there."

Not even the courtesy of a "good day." Jack let that pass. "But of course, Mr. Johnston, as minister of this congregation it's my duty to attend any meeting of the governing body. Of course I'll be there. Would you care to tell me what this is all about?"

"You'll find out soon enough. After service now. In the vestry."

Jack stood motionless as he watched Johnston leave. Could he have underestimated so badly the intense depth of feeling which his remarks of the week before must have provoked? It was not unusual for lay members to request that meetings be held, but to do so without the simple decency of notifying the minister well in advance smacked of conspiracy. He inhaled deeply.

It's not just a matter of getting my own way, he thought, drawing his hand over the coarse black stuff of his robe. Am I being stiff-necked or is Johnston? I don't need to prove to him who's the better man. My faith may be simple, but it's deep. If men of God, a term used with derision by the bulk of the populace, could not work with their people towards reconciliation then who could? He smiled wryly, muttered, "Into Thy hands, oh Lord," and thought, At least I still have my sense of humour. He finished robing quickly and went into the church, suddenly eager as he had been as a theological student to face his final examiners.

As the choir sang the opening hymn, he took a few moments to collect his thoughts. Perhaps it would be impolitic to announce his plans to the entire congregation, but, damn it, not to would already be a small victory for Johnston. Still, it didn't matter who won the skirmishes, as long as the war was won.

He looked around at his church. His church. It was a Victorian building of red brick with a classic needle-pointed steeple. The interior, though well enough lit, was pleasantly dim. The ceiling was constructed of soaring wooden arches like the medieval cathedrals of England, but on a much smaller scale. The history of the church was there. Stained glass windows carried the names of their long dead donors, brass plaques adorned the walls. The font was of carved sandstone, the pulpit of polished mahogany. It was a place of peace, a place of love. Surely, he thought, surveying the worshippers, surely they can feel that.

When the service had ended, he waited in the vestry. The elders and the ministers of the adjoining parishes filed into the room. They sat around an old oak table, the senior minister at its head, Jack at its foot and Johnston, the elders, and the other clerics at opposite sides. The senior minister, the Reverend McKinnis, was a bespectacled man of indeterminate age. He sniffed, a moist sound, called the meeting to order and led them in a prayer for the good of the Presbyterian Church and for guidance in their deliberations.

". . . we beseech Thee, oh Lord. Amen." The bowed heads rose.

"Mr. Johnston, you have called this meeting. Would you be good enough to tell us your concerns?" the senior man asked, blowing his nose into a large handkerchief.

Johnston looked at Jack insolently for a long moment, glanced at his supporters, and turning to the head of the table, began. "It's very simple your Reverence. That man there," he pointed an accusatory finger at the foot of the table, "that man there has forgotten how to be a Protestant so he has."

The elders nodded. Two of the younger ministers present stiffened. The senior cleric sat back in his chair, whipped his glasses from his nose and polished them furiously with his handkerchief. "Dear me." He carefully replaced his glasses. "Come now, Mr. Johnston, that is a very serious charge. In what way has the Reverend Wilson transgressed?" He sniffed and looked sympathetically at Jack.

"Enough ways. Robes for himself and the choir and that's not the half of it."

"But surely, Mr. Johnston, you must remember that the General Assembly approved that measure three years ago?"

"I remember well enough, and no harm to ye, but I have a copy of the minutes here." He waved a sheaf of paper, pointing at the typed words with a quivering index finger. "It says, 'Robes can be worn by minister and choir with the approval of the local presbytery.' With-the-approval." Jack heard the emphasis on every word. "We never approved it, so we didn't."

Jack did not let Johnston's unexpected preparedness bother him. He interrupted mildly, "I hate to contradict you, Mr. Johnston, but you did know, the vote was taken right here and—"

Johnston spat back, "Aye, when me and six of these men weren't here. I didn't approve then, and I don't approve now."

Jack stole a glance at McKinnis. Good. Johnston's choler over what was really such a trivial issue seemed to be irritating the senior man. The look he was giving the clerk of sessions was distinctly unfriendly.

Johnston bored on. "Anyhow, that's not the half of it. Last Sunday that man had the brass neck to stand up in a Presbyterian pulpit and preach love of Catholics."

Not so good. As a student Jack had been forced to sit through some of McKinnis's sermons. Like many of his generation, his preaching had called down hellfire and damnation on the heads of the Romans.

McKinnis asked, "What exactly was said?"

Time to seize the initiative. "I took Matthew, 6 and 27, and Leviticus, 19 and 18, as my text. I suggested to these men of goodwill that perhaps it was time to start healing old wounds. Correct me if I am wrong, but I thought that was a minor suggestion of our Lord, or have my years at theological college been wasted? I distinctly remember Jesus saying 'Love thy neighbour.'" His gaze never left the senior minister's face. He paused. His voice took on the edge of knapped flint. "Of course, the early Christians did not have to concern themselves about internecine warfare. All they were was Christian."

He had, over the years, learned to control his temper, but, in truth, the advice of his own father, given when he had caught Jack and his brother wrestling, still lived like an unruly imp in his character. The old man had said while pulling his squirming children apart, "You must agree boys, but to tell you the truth—fighting's more fun." Jack Wilson, a man of peace, had never and would never shrink from a fight for a cause he believed to be just.

One of the younger ministers started to rise from his seat. "That's it? That's all there is to it?" His tone was querulous. "Mr. Johnston, I have some difficulty understanding why you are so tried about this."

"Aye, but there's more," Johnston snarled. "We hear that he's going to bring a priest—a Catholic priest—to the youth club." He turned to face Jack. "Could you not just invite Satan while ye're at it?" Naked hatred flew with every word.

The minister, who had begun to rise, presumably assuming that the issue had been resolved, sat heavily and looked at Jack as McKinnis enquired, "Is this true, Reverend Wilson?"

Jack caught his breath and clenched his fists. How had Johnston found out? Worry about that later. Defend yourself. Jack took a deep breath, controlled himself, sighed and said softly, "That was my plan, yes."

Every man at the table sat bolt upright.

Jack looked from face to face. No comprehension. No sympathy. He could tell what they were thinking. A priest, a Catholic priest in a Presbyterian church? Never!

Jack watched as Reverend McKinnis rose ponderously. "Reverend Wilson, I cannot find it in my heart to censure you for what appears to have been a well-intentioned sermon, but I cannot, and I am sure that I speak for everyone here, I cannot condone your desire to invite a Catholic priest into this church."

Jack heard the pronouncement and knew that each word had been weighed in the balance, just as he had been. But he had been found wanting.

McKinnis sniffed and said, "As the moderator of this meeting of the presbytery I do have the right to make a ruling without taking a vote. This suggestion goes beyond the bounds of brotherly love. It smacks of apostasy. You will not now, or ever, allow a priest across the threshold of this church." He punctuated this pronouncement with an enormous snort into his handkerchief.

It was very clear to Jack, from the still-astonished looks of the rest of the clergy, and the sneers of grim satisfaction on the faces of John-ston and his lay supporters, that there would be no objections from the floor.

Jack bowed his head in submission. He was not done yet. "I will of course abide by your ruling. I have no choice." He looked round the table. "But you are all wrong in this. Absolutely wrong." The edge in his voice softened, replaced by a supplicatory questioning. "Does the whole ecumenical movement mean so little to you? What a shame. What a confession of the sorry state of our faith."

"We'll have nothing to do with papists, nothing," Johnston crowed, clearly savouring his victory, "and you'll mind your manners in fu-ture, Reverend Wilson."

Jack rose. His brows knit. The flint was back. "My manners to you, Johnston, my manners to you and your like? You vitriolic bigot, you narrow-minded little man." He let a suggestion of a smile start. "I have agreed not to bring the priest here. You have my word on it. But not you Johnston, not you Reverend McKinnis, not the Moderator of the Presbyterian Church in Ireland, nor the whole of the General Assemblies can change my mind on the right of what I must do and the awful, sinful wrong of you and those like you. Now, sir," he turned towards the senior minister, "if you have nothing further to say to me I'll leave, but before I go you should know that I have no intentions of letting this matter drop. A priest will speak to the young people, not on church property, but I will find a way. Good morning to you all." He left before the stunned group could think of anything to say.

As Jack made his way to the door, Johnston said deferentially to the senior minister, "Thank you, Mr. Mckinnis, sir, thank you very much. Now you see what we have to put up with."

Jack left the vestry, but still he could overhear the continuing discussion, Johnston saying, "Do you think he'll go ahead with his plans?" and McKinnis replying, "I have no doubt of it, Mr. Johnston. The Reverend Jack Wilson is a man of very strong, although if I may say so, misguided principles. He'll find a way, and to tell you the truth, there is very little that you or I or anyone else can do to stop him."

Jack felt a chill when Johnston snapped, barely hiding his contempt. "Is there not? Aye, maybe you can't—but I can, and I will."

"What can I do for you?" The Moderator of the Free Protestant Church of Ireland answered his phone while looking with self-satisfied admiration at his framed Doctor of Divinity degree. He was sure he recognized the voice.

"Look, I'm sorry to bother you, sir, but it's awful important."

"Bother, it's no bother. A soul in despair can always call on me, and if you'll forgive me, you do sound troubled."

"Look, you've got to help us. Our minister, Reverend Wilson, wants to have a priest talk to our young people. Now we're not members of your flock, nor nothing, but everyone knows that you'll have no part of the Fenians."

"True." He knew now it was the man who had called last Sunday. The Reverend Doctor smiled. He glanced again at the certificate on the wall. Some people, not the ones who said his DD was from a postal diploma mill, recognized him as the true keeper of the faith, scourge of the Church of Rome, and defender of civil and religious liberty for all. Of course he would help.

"Obviously you are a man of the real faith, sir, a man who would keep this country of ours free from the dictates of Rome. Have no fear sir, have no fear." The Moderator slowly shook his head. "That man Wilson has been a thorn in our flesh. He will be dealt with, and dealt with by the righteous wrath of God. Goodbye to you, sir, and thank you." The Reverend Doctor sat back in his chair, steepled his fingers and became lost in thought. He knew his hatred of the Antichrist in Rome was justified. He thought sanctimoniously of his crusade to keep Ulster Protestant, and he thought with no little pleasure of the discomfort he and his followers were about to visit on Jack Wilson and his family.

It had been a miserable day, and even now, in the small hours of the next morning the wind and rain hammered against the windows of the study where Jack sat. What was he going to do? Bad enough that McKinnis had sided with Johnston, but that little man's parting shots had been vicious. What had he meant, "I can and I will?"

Norah had tried to help. It had been her suggestion that he go and have a word with Hugh Conlan at his home. Jack smiled ruefully. She had even arranged for the assistant minister to take the evening service.

Hugh had been understanding, loyal. He had listened to Jack's heartfelt outpouring as he had described the events of the morning.

"Hugh, you wouldn't believe it. They actually forbade me—forbade me—to bring a priest onto church property."

Hugh, bless him, had tried to make light of it. "So Torquemada wasn't the only one to run an inquisition?"

"Inquisition. That's about the height of it." He looked at Hugh and saw compassion in the priest's eyes. "Now don't you start feeling sorry for me."

Father Hugh laid a hand on Jack's shoulder. "Jack, I am sorry, but not for you. You're big enough and ugly enough to take care of yourself."

Jack had to smile. "Who are you sorry for then?"

"This poor benighted country."

Jack saw the pain in his friend's eyes. Felt it himself. "But, Hugh, if we don't try to do something who will? I know I'm right. Aren't I?"

Hugh Conlan put a finger to his lips. He always did that when he was considering what to say. "Yes, Jack. Absolutely. I know you want to work for a better Ulster."

"You don't think I'm just being stubborn?"

"That too. You've been stubborn as long as I've known you," he said, fiddling with the belt of his cassock. "But my old father, God rest his soul," he crossed himself, "would have called you 'a good gentleman.'"

"Thanks, Hugh." Jack put his own hand over Hugh's where its warmth was comforting, there on Jack's shoulder. In this moment of self-doubt, he needed Hugh's solidity.

"So, what do you think we should do?"

Father Hugh's face tightened. "I reckon we should back off for a few weeks."

Jack saw the set of his friend's jaw as Hugh said, "Then we'll do what you said. We'll find a venue and, by God, we'll do it anyway."

Jack stood and hugged the little Corkman. "You're right, Hugh. We'll do it."

Sitting in his own study now, he was not quite so confident. Still, Hugh had cheered him. Jack decided to sleep on it. He rose from his chair, looking at his watch. Two a.m. It was well past time for bed. The phone rang twice before he even recognized its shrill double ring. Who could it be at this hour of the night? Jack blew out his lips, knowing that the pastoral work of any minister is no respecter of nine-to-five and hoping that he was not going to be called out. Not tonight.

He picked up the receiver. "Wilson here."

There was a long silence, just a long silence.

He repeated, "Wilson here. Hello?" The line went dead. He hung up, hoping that whoever had called a wrong number had not disturbed his family. Ah dammit, Jack, he thought, you're not going to puzzle this one out tonight, but—he cast back to Hugh's advice—bide patiently. They would find a hall and the rest would fall into place.

The phone rang. This time there was a rough voice at the other end. All it said was, "Apostate." The line went dead again.

Jack stood for a long minute looking at the receiver. He wondered should he perhaps not replace it in its cradle. He had heard of this tactic of intimidation but had not expected to be the recipient. No. Damn it. He'd not let them scare him. He hung up.

The voice of the phone was as startling as the venom in the mouth of the man who had called moments before. Jack grabbed the receiver. "Now listen here." He got no further.

A man laughed at the other end of the line. "Fucking Popehead." The click of the other telephone being replaced echoed over the wires, mocking.

"What is it, Jack?" a sleepy woman's voice asked from upstairs.

"Nothing, dear. Go back to bed." This time he did leave the receiver on the desktop. That at least would hold them until the morning. In the morning he would decide what was to be done.

There was little sleep for Jack Wilson that night, or for him and his family for many nights to come. Any man, no matter how strong, has his Achilles' heel. Jack's had been found. While he cared not for himself, the sight of Norah in tears, and the anger and hurt of his daughters, made him pause. Despite the women's willingness to put up with the calls, calls that the authorities seemed powerless to stop, he and Father Hugh were forced to decide that, for the time being at least, discretion *was* the better part of valour. The priest never did get to speak to the young Presbyterians.

For the next two years the phone would ring at any time night or day. The messages, taken by Jack or his family, were as often as not obscene. Death threats were made. For two years, a constable of the Royal Ulster Constabulary mounted guard over the manse at dusk and did not leave until the daylight had come. Two years it took of his wishing that the spiteful, bitter, mean spirited Christians would leave him alone.

He knew he was becoming bitter himself and it hurt. He was a man of goodwill. All he wanted was peace.

Father Hugh had done his best to keep Jack's spirits up but even the priest's own faith seemed shaken as the two men sat in Jack's study in the evening of a clear spring day.

Father Hugh had declined his usual sherry and had pulled a small pocket tape recorder from his pocket and laid it on the desk.

"You're not going to like this, Jack."

"What is it?"

Father Hugh grimaced. "You remember one time I hid in the back of your church?"

"Aye. Two years ago."

"I did it again."

"Where? When?"

"On Sunday. I went to hear the Moderator of the Free Protestant Church."

"What?" Jack's voice rose. "You're mad."

Father Hugh shook his head. "Not me. Him. Jack, I was terrified."

"I'm not surprised. A Catholic priest in that man's church."

"No. Not of him. Of what he is. What he stands for." The priest was nearly in tears. "Jack, that man's another Hitler. He's a born orator. A demagogue. Listen."

Father Hugh Conlon pushed a button on the recorder. The Moderator's rasping tones, made harsher yet by the tape recording, filled the study.

"Yea verily Brethren, yea verily, the good book is right, Matthew 6 and 27, 'Thou shalt love thy neighbour as thyself.' "

Jack stood riveted, the hairs on the back of his neck starting to bristle.

For a moment there was no sound but soft whispering as the tape ran. Then there was a crash, as if a fist had smashed into the pulpit's edge, and the question, "But, bretheren, who is thy neighbour?"

1973

On March 8, car bombs were detonated in London. Four vehicles had been hijacked by the Belfast Brigade of the Provisional IRA, repainted, filled with explosives, and taken by ferry from Dublin to England. The explosions left one man dead and 180 people wounded.

On March 28, a five-ton shipment of arms destined for the Provisional IRA was intercepted on board the vessel *Claudia* off the coast of Waterford. It is believed that by this stage of the Troubles, Colonel Muammar Qaddafi of Libya had given $10 million to the Provos.

By December, political moves had led to the formation of a power-sharing executive to administer Northern Ireland. Representation was to come from both Loyalist and Republican quarters. The final agreement was signed in London on December 9. The following day, the major Loyalist paramilitary organizations announced the formation of the Ulster Army Council, specifically to resist this initiative.

On December 18, the Provisional IRA expressed its view of the power-sharing executive by detonating three bombs in London. Sixty-three people were wounded.

1973 Dead 250   **Total Dead 929**

1974

On February 4, explosives on a coach carrying familes of servicemen from Manchester to Catterick, Yorkshire, killed nine soldiers, a woman and two children. The Provisional IRA denied responsibility.

(continued)

On May 17, car bombs, probably planted by the Ulster Volunteer Force, killed 22 and wounded at least 100 people in Dublin. More car bombs exploded in Monaghan, killing five. Sammy Smyth of the Ulster Workers Council commented, "There is a war with the Free State and now we are laughing at them."

On October 5, bombs in two pubs in Guildford, Surrey, killed five and injured 54.

On November 21, the Birmingham pub bombings killed 21 and injured 182. The Guildford and Birmingham attacks were part of the Provisional IRA's campaign on the mainland of Britain.

On December 10, talks were held between Protestant clergymen and the IRA.

1974 Dead 216   **Total Dead 1,145**

THE SURGEON

He crawled to semiwakefulness, summoned by the telephone. The dim face of the alarm clock on the bedside table said 2:25. He shook his head and fumbled for the receiver.

"Dr. Sloan? Can you come at once, sir? There's been another riot. We need all the surgeons."

"Right. On my way." Cursing softly, he hung up. This was the second time in two days. He'd come home four hours ago after operating for twenty hours straight. The bombing campaign was heating up. Beside him his wife stirred and mumbled something.

"Go back to sleep, love," he whispered as he tucked the eiderdown over her warm shoulder. She pushed her head against the pillow and muttered again.

John Sloan stood looking at her for a moment, envying her her warmth and her sleep. He groped for his clothes and carried them through to the bathroom next door, dressing quickly, quietly so as not to disturb her. He went downstairs to the garage, climbed into his car, and started the engine. It should take him about thirty minutes to drive to the Royal Victoria Hospital.

The hospital, sited at the junction of the Falls Road and the Grosvenor Road, was not far from where Sandy Row crossed the Grosvenor. Of all the sectarian ghettoes in Belfast, the Falls was the most defiantly

Catholic, and Sandy Row vied with the Shankill Road as the most staunchly Protestant. The Royal had squatted, red-bricked, slate-roofed, Edwardian-solid for seventy years in its no-man's land between the factions, consistently rising above such considerations, treating Protestant and Catholic alike.

The Royal Victoria Hospital, Belfast, was opened on the 27th of July, 1903, by His Majesty King Edward VII. It was not unreasonable for him to have done so. Queen Victoria after all had been his mother. In that year, Ireland was still an integral part of the United Kingdom of Great Britain and Ireland; Harland and Wolff's shipyard launched the largest ship in the world, the *Baltic;* and 140 million yards of linen were exported from the port of Belfast. The Royal, as the hospital soon became known, was hailed as a "revolution in hospital design," which was only right and proper for an institution in one of the United Kingdom's most prosperous cities.

By 1973, the old lady was no longer the epitome of modern hospital design. The wards were overcrowded, the once pristine red brick stained with the smoke of factory chimneys, pitted by the cold rains of Belfast. The Royal, like the city itself, had fallen on hard times. The linen industry was all but gone, the previously bustling shipyards' slips lay empty. Unemployment was endemic and, for some of the out-of-work, the Troubles gave reason to vent their frustration under the guise of Irish nationalism or British patriotism. Being a freedom fighter was more exciting than being an unemployed riveter.

At least it was exciting for three young men. None of them was actually a member of any organized body; rather they made their protest by providing petrol bombs to the mobs that nightly roamed their home territory of the Falls, taunting the police and the bewildered British soldiers.

The security forces were caught up again in a riot on a rainy night among the mean little houses that lined the streets off the Falls Road. The sickly neon streetlights, those that had not been smashed in earlier battles, flickered weakly through the downpour and the haze of smoke and streamers of gas.

A petrol bomb, a Molotov cocktail, is very simple to make. All that is needed is an empty bottle, petrol, and water in the right proportions, some sugar so that the blazing fluid will stick—with any luck to human flesh—and a fuse. In the early days, the fuse was simply a rag stuffed into the neck of the bottle. Then some unsung Einstein had discovered that a woman's sanitary tampon was the ideal material for fuse making. The cylinder neatly fills the neck of the bottle, the string burns most satisfactorily when lit.

The three young men sat on wooden chairs in the small back scullery of Des and Sean's house. Fergus poured the premixed solution from a large drum into a funnel that Sean held over the necks of a succession of bottles. Once each was full, Des jammed a tampon into the neck and placed the finished product into a rapidly filling beer crate. From time to time a man would skulk into the room and leave with a full crate.

Tonight had started like many nights of the past few years. Women in shabby dresses and calico pinafores had been gossiping from doorway to doorway of the tiny terrace houses. They were the first to notice the approach of an army patrol. In an instant, they began banging loudly on dustbin lids to warn of the approach of the troops, screaming insults that would make a navvy blush.

A crowd had formed, knots of sullen youths, foulmouthed and angry. The little groups coalesced until a mob—a vicious, many-eyed, many-armed abortion—was spawned. The soldiers had formed a flying wedge and charged in fruitless efforts to disperse their tormentors. Soon they were facing a barrage of flying rocks, broken glass, and any other projectiles that came readily to hand, and all the while the women beat out a fierce tattoo of stick on bin lid.

The security forces were driven back until their commanding officer ordered his men to fire rubber bullets and CS gas cylinders. When these measures failed, he called up the armoured vehicle that carried the water cannon. High pressure jets of water can bowl men off their feet and lessen their ardour. Stones will just bounce off the armour, but a well-thrown petrol bomb will set the great rubber tyres alight.

John Sloan reversed the car onto the street outside his home, changed gears and began to drive to the Royal. God, but he was tired, and it was not simply from lack of sleep. He stopped at a red light, fingers drumming impatiently on the steering wheel, willing the light to change. He knew from bitter past experience that minutes could count and God alone knew what carnage might be waiting. He accelerated through the amber, not waiting for the green. He stopped at a junction, made sure his way was clear and turned onto the M1. Should be a clear run now to the back gates of the hospital. There was no oncoming traffic.

Had he really amputated six legs yesterday? Four singles and a double? The double had been a particularly bad case. The brave Irish—that was how he sarcastically thought of the bombers. He no longer even cared if the perpetrators were Loyalists or Republicans. All he knew was that the bombers had traded that young man's tomorrows, all of them, for some vague political goal that John Sloan doubted the bastards even understood. He used the back of his left hand to wipe condensation from the inside of the windscreen.

There really had been no choice about the victim's left leg, which was barely recognizable as a leg at all. The right one hadn't looked quite as bad. He had hoped he might be able to save the upper part of it.

He wiped the window again and turned up the heater. Save the leg? Damn it, that's why he had spent those extra two years training in reconstructive surgery.

A car was approaching from the opposite direction. He dimmed his headlights until it passed, silently cursing the other driver, who had neglected to observe the courtesy.

I should be used to bright lights, he thought. The glare of the operating room overheads on the green sterile drapes, ochre-painted flesh, scarlet blood and nacreous white bone, the femur rasping as the saw bit.

Reconstructive surgery. Putting things right, making them work, not like the bastards of either persuasion. Their specialty was destructive surgery, butchery. John hated amputations. It really had been a pity about the right leg. Although the shin and foot had been beyond redemption, he really had thought he could manage to salvage the knee joint. That would make a great deal of difference to the young man's eventual return to some degree of function. John sighed. He should have known better. He had started to operate before the X-rays of the right knee joint were ready. The youngster had lost so much blood it was imperative to stop the haemorrhage and it was obvious that nothing could be done for his left leg. By the time it was gone, looking like a badly butchered hindquarter, hurried from the operating room carelessly wrapped in a green towel, the pictures had arrived.

And that, thought John Sloan bitterly, had been that. The X-rays told of total disorganization of the knee joint. Another mid-thigh amputation. Bugger it. He had chosen reconstructive surgery because it suited his temperament. He liked to fix things. He liked to fix people, but lately he was beginning to feel no better than one of the hewers of limbs of the Napoleonic era.

The car tyres made a grinding noise over the road surface, not too different from the sound of a bone saw. Sloan held the steering wheel tightly. He grunted angrily, imagining the stumps he had created, blood vessels neatly ligated, flaps accurately sewn in place over the severed ends of the femurs. No doubt about it, he'd done another technically skilful job, but for what? He thought of an old Irish anti-war song, "Johnny I Hardly Knew You." "You haven't an arm, you haven't a leg, you're an eyeless, boneless, chickenless egg—you'll have to be set with a bowl to beg," and wondered what the future could hold for the patient with no legs. At least, unlike his predecessors in the nineteenth century, the poor bastard was unlikely to die of gangrene. Sometimes John wondered if that was necessarily a blessing, if there might not be a greater kindness than crippled survival. His eyes felt gritty, and his heart heavy in him. No wonder he was tired and irritable.

He saw the end of the M1 ahead and the back wall of the hospital grounds. Ahead, picked out by the headlights, someone was waving frantically. John Sloan slowed down and could just make out a huddled figure lying at the edge of the road.

The riot had been in full flight for several hours before John Sloan had been called from his bed. The rubber bullets, CS gas, and, most of all, the water cannon had taken their toll. The security forces were slowly gaining the upper hand. The mob was being broken down into smaller pockets of resistance. One such group, in a frantic effort to destroy the armoured car, sent a runner to collect another load of incendiaries. A quick-thinking corporal of the Black Watch spotted the would-be bomber leaving the house with his load, felled him with a rubber bullet, and called the sergeant.

"Over here, Sarge. I think I've found the bomb factory."

The sergeant immediately rounded up half a dozen other soldiers.

"Right then, Corporal, you first. The rest of you lot after, and I want the bastards in one piece. They'll go down for fucking years if we catch them at it."

Barely hesitating, the corporal smashed the butt of his rifle against the flimsy lock. Two burly squaddies put their shoulders to the door.

Three men leapt to their feet as khaki-clad figures crammed into the small room. The corporal led, FN rifle covering the suspects.

Sean had barely time to mutter "Oh shit!" before the soldier smartly reversed his rifle and belted him in the stomach with its butt.

"Shurrup, you Paddy bastard." Sean fell to his knees, supporting himself with one outstretched hand as the other sought the pain in his gut. He gasped for breath.

"Right, you," the corporal gestured at Des, "yes, you, you bloody bogtrotter. Get him up."

Des stooped to help Sean to his feet. As he did so, one of the other soldiers fetched Des a fierce kick in the backside, sending him sprawling. Fergus started forwards only to be roughly restrained.

"All right, that's enough." The sergeant had arrived. He turned to the corporal. "Get these men out of here, and you two," nodding at two other soldiers, "you bring the evidence. One crate'll do." He shook his head in exasperation as the two privates fumbled with their rifles and tried to lift a crate. "Sling your bloody muskets and take one end each."

The three bomb makers were hustled out into the dimly lit street. The sergeant formed his squad to surround the captives, Sean still labouring for breath and supported by Des, Fergus sullenly lagging a few steps behind. The two soldiers carrying the crate of firebombs walked behind the group. The pavement was strewn with lumps of rock. Here and there spent CS gas cylinders still leaked thin trickles of white vapour.

Fergus stumbled over one of the lumps of rock and pitched forwards onto the sodden pavement. The soldiers halted. Sean and Des turned to see what had happened. One of the soldiers bent down to drag his prisoner to his feet.

Fergus brushed his hand away, his face screwed up in pain. "Leave me be. I think I've broke my fucking ankle." He half sat, both hands nursing his left leg.

The sergeant, who had come back to see what was going on, bent over. "Let's have a look."

As he bent lower, Fergus lashed out with his boot, catching the sergeant full in the face, smashing his nose. The sergeant clapped both hands to his injury, trickles of blood already appearing through his fingers.

Fergus rolled sideways, pulled a Zippo lighter from his coat pocket, flicked it open, lit the wick, and hurled the flaming lighter into the crate of petrol bombs. One of the men carrying the crate sprang back, dropping his end, grabbing for his slung rifle. Three bottles fell to the pavement and smashed, spilling petrol, which exploded into flame and enveloped the other soldier in a halo of pain. He screamed.

Immediately his mates rushed to his aid.

Fergus was on his feet. He yelled to Sean and Des. "Run, you stupid buggers." His words were barely audible over the roaring of the flames and the shrieking of the burning soldier.

All three took to their heels, heading for a nearby back alley. Once in the maze of lanes and small streets that are at the core of Belfast they had every reason to hope they could escape. Sean was lagging. He was still winded.

Des and Fergus disappeared into the mouth of the alley.

A private, perhaps more alert than the rest of the squad, dropped to one knee and loosed off a single shot at the backs of the fleeing men. The bullet fired from his Belgian FN rifle was 7.62mm, lead-cored, copper-jacketed, and travelled much faster than the speed of sound. Sean did not hear the report.

Because of the spin imparted to the projectile by the lands and grooves in the rifle barrel, its trajectory is flat. When it hits human flesh it will pass straight through, unless it strikes something solid, in which case the bullet will start to tumble, tearing through anything in its path.

Sean was punched in the right flank by a force that spun him in a half circle before he collapsed.

The bullet glanced off his tenth right rib and smashed the bone into fragments, which themselves became instant instruments of destruction, puncturing his right lung. The tumbling bullet penetrated his diaphragm and put holes in three loops of the small bowel. It finally came to rest, tucked into the fold between the aorta and the vena cava, a jagged piece of torn metal jacket hooked round the great blue vein.

Sean was barely conscious as he watched Fergus grab Des and pull him into the darkness.

The corporal had already called for an ambulance for the sergeant and the horribly burnt private. When it arrived, it was only a matter of a few more moments to load Sean in with his enemies. Siren howling, the vehicle left for the short trip to the Royal.

· · ·

John Sloan pulled up just short of the man who was waving. The surgeon rolled down the window and yelled, "What seems to be the trouble?"

"My mate's been knocked down."

John remembered the car that had failed to dim its headlights. No wonder the driver was in a hurry if he had been involved in a hit and run. John climbed out. "Let's have a look—" He got no further. His right arm was grabbed and forced up into the small of his back. "What the hell?" He was surprised that he felt no fear, simply astonished outrage that he, a senior surgeon, was not being treated with the respect his position usually commanded.

"Shut the fuck up."

John winced as his arm was forced higher. He saw the other man rise from the ground and dust off his hands, then scurry to obey when John's attacker yelled, "Don't just stand there. Get in the fucking car."

Dr. John Sloan felt a ferocious shove in the middle of his back and staggered into the ditch, tripping over rough grass tussocks and sprawling onto his face. Instinctively he tried to protect his hands from the gravel of the roadside. By the time he managed to rise to his feet, all he could see were the taillights of his car fading into the dark distance of the M1. The buggers must have driven over the median and were now heading back in the direction from which John had come.

He was trembling. How dare they steal his car? It wasn't as if he valued the vehicle, the insurance would take care of it, but God dammit, he was a surgeon on an emergency call. Bastards. Bastards! John Sloan paused for a moment to examine a rip in his right trouser leg before deciding that whatever waited for him in the hospital was more important than the loss of his car and the hurt to his pride. He turned his coat collar to the rain and began to walk.

The ambulance arrived at the Royal casualty department and the attendants unloaded their patients. The sergeant was led stumbling to the nearest cubicle, where a junior doctor took one quick look at his face, scribbled "broken nose" on a history card, and yelled for a nurse to take the man to the fracture room.

The morphine given by the ambulance man had dulled the pain of the soldier's burns—dulled, but not obliterated. A young student nurse took one look at his charred face, hands like white sausages from the huge blisters, and quietly burst into tears. The sister hurried her away. The casualty officer rapidly assessed the severity of the injuries, immediately started an intravenous in a vein that had been protected by the man's sleeve, and told the sister to get him to the plastic surgery ward at once. He would survive, but his future held pain, scarring, skin graft after skin graft, and more pain. He might never use his hands again.

Sean lay facedown on a stretcher. The wound in his chest was making liquid, sucking noises. His lips were blue and he was struggling to breathe. Normally the pleura, the membrane that surrounds the lungs, is a closed sac. The entry wound had opened it to the outside air. With every breath, air was being sucked into the cavity, collapsing the lung and slowly suffocating Sean. The casualty officer slapped a large dressing over the entry wound, at least stopping the inflow of air. He called for chest tubes. When inserted, these would allow the air that was trapped in the chest cavity to escape, permitting the collapsed lung to re-expand. The first life-saving steps had been taken.

Between them, the sister and the young doctor manhandled Sean from his prone to a supine position. He groaned weakly, his groans becoming more pronounced as the doctor palpated his abdomen. The anterior abdominal muscles were as rigid as boards, the body's response to inflammation of the peritoneum. Leaking bowel contents were already setting up peritonitis. There was no sign of an exit wound. The bullet must still be somewhere in the body.

It was. The moving of Sean's body had shifted the bullet's serrated tip into the vena cava. Venous blood began to seep from the torn vessel.

"We'll have to open this one, Sister," the doctor said. "You let Dr.

Sloan know as soon as he gets here, I'll arrange the X-rays." He went to the telephone.

"What the fuck are we going to do, Fergus?" Des begged. Fergus was the oldest, and Des and Sean had always followed his lead.

Fergus concentrated on driving. Now that they had a car, he needed to think. He wished Des would shut up. Their run through the alleys had brought the two men to the back of the Royal. He had already decided that they had to get as far away as possible. His first thought had been to try to thumb a lift and so he had walked to the start of the M1, Des straggling behind. Only one car had sped past, away from the city. When Fergus had seen the headlights of another car approaching from the opposite direction, he had acted on the spur of the moment, crossing the road, ordering Des to play wounded. It had worked.

"Sean's shot." The younger brother, who had thought of their efforts as one big joke, had been shot. Des's voice cracked. "Sean's shot. He could die."

"Pull yourself together, Des. They'll take him to the Royal."

"Aye. Like enough he'll be all right." Des nodded his head, as if by agreeing with himself it would make things right for Sean.

Fergus hoped to God that he would be all right, but that of course would lead to further complications. If Sean survived, it would not be long before the security forces were in possession of the names of the other two men involved. To make matters worse, if the burnt soldier died they could be facing murder charges.

"We'll have to get down to the Republic. Now. Tonight." He saw the big blue sign pass by, glaring in the car's headlights, "M1 Lisburn 6 miles." Shit. He must have missed the first turn to The Border.

"If you say so, Fergus." Des sniffled.

"Right," said Fergus, touching Des's arm for a moment. "You just keep quiet now 'til I see if I can find a turn to Newry." He concentrated on his driving, relieved that Des had shut up. What mattered now was to get to hell out of Ulster. He'd worry about Sean when he and Des were safely across The Border.

John Sloan passed under the archway of the back gates of the Royal. His right leg was beginning to stiffen. He must have bruised it when he was thrown to the ground. He was soaked and worried and was going to be much later than he had expected. John lengthened his stride purposefully, ignoring the ache in his knee. The walk from the gates to the hospital was another three-quarters of a mile.

The wall of the vena cava is less than a few millimetres thick.

It took John Sloan ten more minutes to walk to the back entrance of the hospital.

It took just slightly longer for the small tear in Sean's vena cava to extend into a one-inch rip, a rip through which the venous blood ran in a silent torrent, filling the space behind the peritoneum, bleeding him to death.

1975

On April 5, a bomb was thrown through the window of McLaughlin's bar in Belfast, killing two Catholics. Three hours later the Mountain View Tavern on the Shankill Road was hit. Five Protestants died. The combined toll of wounded for the two incidents was seventy.

On July 31, the van in which the Miami Showband was travelling was flagged down near Newry, County Down. Members of the Ulster Volunteer Force made the musicians dismount and shot and killed three of them. Two UVF men died when the bomb they were trying to fit into the van exploded prematurely.

On August 13, the Bayardo Bar on the Shankill Road was bombed, killing five and wounding forty.

On November 27, Ross McWhirter, co-editor of the *Guinness Book of World Records*, was shot to death by members of the Provisional IRA.

1975 Dead 247   **Total Dead 1,392**

1976

On January 4, masked gunmen shot five Catholics to death in Whitecross, County Armagh, and at Ballydugan, County Down.

On January 5, in King Mills, County Armagh, in retaliation for the previous day's killings, ten Protestants were taken from their bus. The Catholic bus driver was told to stand aside and the Protestants were lined up and executed.

(continued)

On August 10, a wounded gunman's car crashed into Anne Maguire and her four children as they walked through Andersonstown. Two children died immediately and a third the following day. Mrs Maguire was seriously injured.

On August 11, Anne Maguire's sister, Mairead Corrigan, and Betty Williams founded "The Peace People."

On August 21, 20,000 people attended a peace rally in Ormeau Park in Belfast.

On September 4, 25,000 attended a Peace People rally in Derry.

1976 Dead 297   **Total Dead 1,689**

1977

On March 11, after a long trial, 26 members of the UVF were given sentences totalling 700 years.

On May 2, the Reverend Ian Paisley, right-wing Protestant, Moderator of the Free Presbyterian Church, pre-eminent Loyalist leader, called for a general strike. Trade Union leaders were able to convince their members to remain at work.

On May 3, Chuck Berry gave a concert in Belfast.

On July 27, a feud between the Official and the Provisional IRAs left four dead and 18 injured. On October 18, Betty Williams and

Mairead Corrigan were awarded the Nobel Peace Prize and received their awards in Oslo on December 10. The Unionist-dominated Belfast City Council decided not to honour the two women with a civic reception.

1977 Dead 112   **Total Dead 1,801**

THE DRIVER

All Freddy had to do was drive. No one asked him to think. He did not even have to know the men he ferried from one street to another. He liked driving, a skill he had acquired in the days when he had a job and a small second-hand car. Of course he hadn't worked for years and the wee Mini was long gone. The politicians were so bloody keen to creep to the Catholics that the bastards got all the jobs now. Changed days from the times when the papishes knew their place.

It was a good thing he'd joined. The Ulster Defence Association always slipped him a few quid—not a lot, mind you—but enough when added to his dole money for a packet of cigarettes and a few pints on a Saturday night.

And all he had to do was drive. Freddy'd done that, when summoned, these three years, ever since the stranger had come to the door. He thought about that day as he sat behind the wheel of a big old Vauxhall, parked in a dimly lit sidestreet of Belfast.

It had been a Sunday. He had not been pleased when his doorbell rang. When he answered, he saw a big man, tweed cap, blue raincoat, scuffed shoes, standing on the sandstone step.

"Freddy McMaster? I'd like a word."

"And who are you?" Freddy stood, arms folded, blocking the narrow entrance.

"That's no matter. You don't need to know me." The man's eyes were cold. "We know you."

Freddy stepped back as the stranger leant forward, putting his fleshy face too close to be comfortable. "I think you and me should maybe chat"—he glanced furtively up and down the street as if looking for something—"inside."

"Inside." The man took Freddy by the arm and pushed him backwards, closing the door behind them. "There's nothing to be scared about. I just want to ask you a few questions."

"What questions?" Freddy felt his palms start to sweat. He knew he had run off at the mouth last night in the pub. The talk had turned, as it inevitably did, to the shit being dumped on the loyal Protestant citizens of Northern Ireland. Could this man be from the IRA? The stranger marched Freddy through the hall and into the kitchen. Freddy, like a cornered animal, frantically looked for a way out.

"Sit down." The big man had taken off his cap, revealing a bald head with a mottled strawberry birthmark to the left of the crown. He pulled out two kitchen chairs, lowered his bulk into one, and motioned Freddy to the other. Freddy sat, as obedient as a well-trained springer spaniel. He could smell his own fear.

"Now look, if it's about what I said last night . . ."

"Aye. It is."

Freddy felt his legs start to tremble. He knew only too well what happened to people that the Provos decided to use as examples.

He heard the man say, "We could use a man like you, a loyal Ulsterman."

"What?" Freddy blinked. Could use him? "What?"

"Aye. There's a lot of us out there you know. The British don't seem to understand that we are true to Her Majesty, and want no part of the Antichrist in Rome." The stranger stuffed his cap in his coat pocket. "Last night in the pub one of our people heard what you were saying. He reckoned you might be useful to the organization."

"What organization?" Thank God. He wasn't going to be shot.

"We'll not worry too much about the name. The less you know the better. You'll not see me again." He unbuttoned his raincoat. "We keep it tight so that no one can give anyone away to the army or the peelers." He shook his head, lips pursed. "It's daft—fucking daft. Here we are on the same side as them, and what we do is illegal." He shrugged. "We keep it tight." He leant forward. Freddy smelled onions on the big man's breath as he asked, "Now. Are you in the Orange Order?"

"No."

"You're a Protestant?"

"Aye. Presbyterian. But I don't go to church much." Freddy looked in his interrogator's eyes for some sign of approval but found none.

"Are you true to Ulster?"

"Sure if your man heard what I was saying last night you should know that."

"What a man says with drink taken doesn't mean a whole hell of a lot." Freddy dropped his eyes. He could not meet the man's black stare. The next words were given individual emphasis. "Are you true to Ulster?"

Freddy sat straight. "I am indeed, so I am. And proud of it."

"Have you a record?"

"Not at all. I don't even have a gramophone."

He watched as his interrogator shook with silent laughter. Bloody hell. What a dumb mistake. The man must think he was soft in the head. Freddy let a smile start. His stupid answer had broken the ice a bit. Mebbe this chap was decent enough after all. "No. I've no record."

"Fair enough. Can you drive a motorcar?"

"Aye." Freddy waited to see if he had pleased the man.

"Can you keep your mouth shut?" The stranger's eyebrows went up, wrinkling his forehead and the birthmark above. "You were in brave voice last night."

"Look." Freddy leant across the table, one hand in front of him on the Formica top. "I know what side my bread's buttered on. I can hold my tongue just fine if I have to."

"If we sent for you to do a job—it would just be driving, like—would you come?"

Freddy jerked his hand back towards him, "Driving where?"

"That would be for us to know," the stranger lowered his head slightly, "but you'd be in no danger, and you'd be doing it to keep the

Fenians down." Freddy heard the same passion that had been there when the man had asked about loyalty to Ulster. The next words were flat but Freddy listened. "There'd be a few quid in it for you."

"I'd like that, so I would." Freddy smiled.

"Freddy McMaster, I think you're our man." The stranger held out his right hand. Freddy extended his own and completed the handshake.

The big man opposite released his grip, but not the way his eyes fixed on Freddy's.

"Before we go any further, I'll tell you right now, if you take the oath, you're in for life. The only way out is feet first." He paused. "Am I making myself clear?"

Freddy felt himself shiver, but stilled the small fear inside. He did not avert his gaze.

"You are." He tapped himself on the chest with one nicotine-stained finger. "I'm just as much a Loyalist as you are. I've had it with the fucking IRA, and it would suit me just fine to get a dig at them."

The stranger stood up and rummaged about in an inside pocket of his raincoat. He produced a small revolver and a tattered, leather-covered Bible. He put the Bible on the kitchen table, the revolver on top of the book, and, taking Freddy's right hand, set it on the gun. Freddy took the oath, swearing allegiance to the organization, Her Royal Majesty Queen Elizabeth the Second, her heirs and successors, and the Protestant faith. When it was done he felt a certain pride.

The big man replaced his icons, buttoned his coat, set his cap on his head, and started to leave. Just as he entered the hall he spoke.

"When we need you, we'll phone. Someone will tell you to be at a certain street corner. You'll be met by men in a car. You'll drive them to where they want to go and drop them off. They'll tell you where to pick them up. When you see them again they'll take the car and you'll get the bus home." He laid one index finger alongside his nose. "What they were doing is none of your business."

Freddy thought of Al Pacino in *The Godfather* and almost laughed, but he did not miss the rest of his instructions. "All you have to do is

drive. Be in the pub every Friday at seven. You'll get your money then."
He shook Freddy's hand. "Good to have you with us. Ulster needs all
her loyal sons." The man let himself out.

Even now, three years later, Freddy could remember his fear, his relief, and old blotch head's parting shot. "What they were doing is none
of your business." Bloody right it wasn't. He lit a cigarette and looked
at his watch. Christ. It was two in the morning. What was keeping
them? The buses had all stopped running. He would have a long, cold
walk home. He knew now that these jobs were always unpredict-
able. He'd done enough of them. He opened the window and flicked
the end of his smoke out into the night, closing the glass and trying
to keep some warmth in the car. There wasn't a whole hell of a lot to
do as he waited.

He thought back over the last three years. It had been almost six
months after the man with the strawberry mark had paid his visit before Freddy had his first call. By then his excitement about being recruited had worn off, and he had begun to wonder if he had been
forgotten.

Then it had started. Always the same. His phone would ring. A
voice, and rarely the same voice, would enquire, "Freddy McMaster?"

"Aye."

"Donegal Road and Lisburn Road. Seven." Or, "Dublin Road and
Bruce Street." He was always sent to a different spot.

He would repeat his instructions. The line would go dead. It was
up to him to get to the meeting place by the appointed time. There he
would wait, smoking—he hunted in his coat pocket for another
cigarette—and wondering where he would be going.

The routine never changed. At the agreed time a car would pull
up to the side of the road. A complete stranger would get out from the
driver's seat and beckon to Freddy, who would take his place. The man
would climb into the back seat and another stranger, sitting in the
passenger's seat, would tell Freddy where to go and where to take the
car and wait, after the passengers had gone.

He inhaled deeply and remembered the first time. The pickup had been at midnight. There had been only two silent men who had asked to be driven to a small street in the warren of Turf Lodge, a notoriously Republican stronghold. He was to pick them up one hour later, about half a mile away. He had sat in the car, barely able to control his impatience until the two reappeared.

"How did it go?" he began.

"Mind your own fucking business. Out. Leave the keys. Get yourself home." The answer came from the older of his two companions of earlier in the night. The younger man was vomiting in the gutter. Freddy bashed his head on the door frame in his haste to get out. He left the driver's door open.

"Get a hold of yourself and get in the fucking car. We haven't all night." The older man grabbed his companion and roughly bundled him into the back seat, then turned to Freddy. "Mind what you were told. You saw nothing. You know nothing. Now, away on home." The car had driven off, leaving Freddy to walk the four miles.

He had slept late the next morning. Why not? He'd no regular job to go to. He glanced at the columns of the *Belfast Telegraph* as he waited for the kettle to boil. The second page carried a story about a known Republican sympathizer who had been gunned down in his Turf Lodge home, sometime in the early hours of the morning. The report said that the police suspected the work of a Loyalist group but apparently had no clues. Freddy wondered dimly for a moment, then he knew, he knew that the men he had ferried had been involved. He rapidly dismissed the thought—none of his business—turned to the horse-racing page and put the events of the previous night out of his mind.

Freddy had lost track of the number of times he had sat and smoked in a strange car on a strange street, waiting for the return of a group of strange men just as he was doing now. He wriggled down into the car's worn seat, tucking his neck into the collar of his overcoat. He coughed. Fucking cigarettes. He stubbed out the smoke in the ashtray, nipped the end, blew through the filter, and stuck the butt behind his ear.

He no longer wondered about the news and only bought the *Telegraph* for the racing form, studiously avoiding any reports on the front page. He hunched his shoulders and rubbed his hands together rapidly. What the eye doesn't see, the heart doesn't grieve over. All Freddy had to do was drive.

1978

On February 17, the Northern Ireland Collie Club and the Northern Ireland Junior Motorcycle Club were among the groups attending functions in the La Mon House, an hotel between Belfast and Comber,
County Down. There were more than 300 people in the establishment
when two firebombs, set by the Provisional IRA, exploded. The blasts
created a fireball. Twelve people died and twenty-three were horribly
burnt. A warning, which was to have been given by telephone, was
delivered too late.

October 18, there were riots in Derry. Sixty-nine members of the RUC
were injured—sixty-seven of them by Loyalists.

On November 30, the Provisional IRA announced it was preparing for
a "long war" and detonated firebombs all over the Province.

1978 Dead 81   **Total Dead 1,882**

1979

On Februrary 20, eleven members of a Loyalist gang, the "Shankill
Butchers," received life sentences for committing nineteen murders.
The gang had been active since 1975 and was led by Lennie Murphy,
known as "Murphy the Mick" because of his Catholic surname. The
group was renowned for driving into a Catholic area, kidnapping a victim, and brutally torturing him before slitting his throat.

On March 2, the methods of interrogation used by the security forces
were probed by BBC reporter Keith Kyle on the programme "Pan-
orama." This report ultimately led to an investigation by the human
rights group Amnesty International.

On August 27, Lord Louis Mountbatten's boat was blown up off Sligo by a radio-controlled Republican bomb. Lord Louis, aged seventy-nine, his grandson, aged fourteen, and a fifteen-year-old crew member, Paul Maxwell, died. The Dowager Lady Brabourne died the following day. Lord and Lady Brabourne were seriously injured. On the same day, the Provisional IRA detonated a bomb in Warrenpoint, County Down. Six men of 2nd Parachute Regiment died. The rest of the squad took shelter under a stone archway. When a second bomb exploded there, another twelve were killed.

1979 Dead 113   **Total Dead 1,995**

BELFAST
1979

Perhaps the letter would come in the afternoon post. Pat closed the file of a house conveyancing, stood up, and moved two steps across the tiny office to stand by the window. Past rows of damp slate tile roofs and stands of brick chimneys, the domes of the Belfast City Hall bulked against the October sky, the patina on their copper coverings the green of unripe onions.

He watched a small flock of pigeons, dingy as the city they inhabited, wheel round one of the cupolas before dipping beneath the line of the rooftops and out of view. He exhaled slowly against pursed lips. Good thing it was Friday and he'd be out of here soon.

He heard the door open but did not bother to turn when a woman's voice said, "Here's your mail."

"Thanks, Joyce. Get away on home, now. Go on with you." He smiled. His secretary worked far too hard, and he wondered what he would do without her. He heard the door close.

He was keen to look at the post, but dark against the grey sky the pigeons swirled high over the roof line again, whirling like wind-tossed leaves, distracting him. He let his thoughts soar with the birds above the city, into the clouds.

He had to pretend the civil war didn't exist; otherwise he'd never come into the city to go to work. But it was only a pretence, and he knew it. The evidence was all around. Bombings, murders, Saracens on the streets. No progress on the political front either. Pat sighed. He had hoped that the arrest in February of a prominent IRA man, Gerry Adams, might have been a signal that the security forces were gaining the upper hand. They hadn't been able to get their hands on many top Provos. Now Adams had been released. A glimmer of hope snuffed. Would Maggie Thatcher's ousting of Harold Wilson in the general election last May bring any fresh perspective on how to find some resolution? Pat doubted it.

Last year over in England, Mrs. Brown had given birth to the world's first test-tube baby. This year the Provos had killed four policemen with a one-thousand-pound bomb. Modern science was a wonderful thing.

Ach, well, he'd get away for a day tomorrow, down to Strangford with Neill.

He turned back to his desk. A pile of letters, done up with a rubber band, sat on a broad blotter waiting for his attention.

Pat pulled off the band and rapidly sorted through the envelopes. Damn. Nothing with a Canadian postmark. He chucked the pile in an untidy heap in the "in" tray. If he was going to have to wait until Monday to hear, the rest of his correspondence could wait with him. It would only be the usual, boring details of a solicitor's daily work.

Pat tipped his chair back on two legs, hoisted his feet onto the desk top, and locked his hands behind his head. The law. It had all seemed so logical, sane, reasoned, when he had been a student. From the Magna Carta and Habeas Corpus on, British common and statute law was based on acts of parliament or on precedents handed down by learned judges, codifying and formalizing the ethos of the nation. What had his old professor of jurisprudence called it? "The majestic panoply of *Lex Britannicus*." Fat lot of use it was these days. All the rules of civilized behaviour, written and unwritten, were overturned daily, and the police and all the lawyers and judges and courts unable to do a damn thing about it.

Poor Humpty Dumpty Ulster. Not even all the Queen's men—or at least those regiments stationed here to try and maintain order— could put the pieces together again. Was it even worth trying?

The chair thumped on the thin carpet as he swung his legs back onto the floor and stood. Bugger the law. He was to meet Neill in the Crown Liquor Saloon on Great Victoria Street. They would have a jar together and finalize the plans for tomorrow's wildfowling. It would be good to leave the law office, to leave the city, and return tomorrow to the wild sanctuary of Strangford with Neill.

Where was his pen? He was fond of the trusty Parker. Neill had given it to him as a graduation present. He found it and clipped it into his inside pocket, then shuffled through the envelopes once more just in case. But there was nothing from Toronto.

He took his raincoat from a peg behind his frosted-glass panelled door, shrugged into the Burberry, and left the office, taking the stairs two at a time, skipping over the bare wooden treads worn concave by the daily up and down trudging of the nine-to-five brigade—a battalion, he recognized ruefully, to which he belonged.

He looked at his watch. He'd still have time to nip down to the bookstore on Royal Avenue and see if he could find the new Graham Greene.

The air on Bedford Street smelt of diesel fumes, but it was at least better than the dusty dryness of the office. The few clouds he could see in the gap of sky between the tall commercial buildings seemed to be moving to the north. Perhaps tomorrow would bring good fowling.

Nearing the City Hall, he waited impatiently in the queue at the security barrier—tall iron railings, coiled razorwire on top—for his turn to be frisked and permitted to enter the downtown streets. He watched the flak-jacketed RUC men, Sten guns slung, revolvers in hip holsters—hard-eyed men, alert, taking their jobs seriously. The majestic panoply of *Lex Britannicus* personified. More like Dodge-bloody-City with the marshalls in modern combat gear instead of cowboy boots and ten-gallon hats.

He made his purchase, left the security area, hurried to Great Victoria Street, and went into the Crown. He'd read somewhere it was John Betjeman's favourite pub. He looked along the length of the marble-topped bar. No Neill. Probably in their usual cubicle.

Pat opened the batwing half-door to the booth where he and Neill met. No one was waiting. It wasn't like Neill to be late for anything.

Perhaps he had been held up at work, but Pat could not quite avoid worrying. It was an inescapable part of life, the uncertainty of living in a community where nobody was immune to the daily acts of violence.

The pub was filling up. Yes, the IRA targeted pubs, but people were not going to stop living and hide. Pat shrugged and entered the booth, taking for granted the ornate gilt carvings of leaves and animals adorning the door posts and the etched glass windows on top of the dark wooden partition between this and the adjoining cubicle. Neill had remarked on the décor the first time they had come here, seven or eight years ago, when he had left his job in Bangor for a more senior position in the advertising section of the *Belfast Independent*. Now the garish ornaments were like the old ruined sheep-pen on the Long Island. Simply there.

Pat sat on the red leather bench that ran in a semicircle round the small central table and unbuttoned his raincoat. He wondered if there would be any pubs like this in Toronto. The whole business of enquiring about the possibility of his working there had been Phyllis's idea. Well, she'd just have to wait until Monday to find out. And Phyllis did not like being kept waiting—the way he was waiting for Neill now.

Phil was pretty decent about not minding him and Neill having a pint every Friday night and heading off on their outings most Saturdays, but she did get a bit shirty when he was late home. Even before she'd agreed to marry him, she'd liked him to be on time. She had cheerfully accepted his longstanding dates with Neill for Friday night drinks and Saturdays' expeditions—provided he didn't arrive home late. She could be a real harpy if he did.

Pat chuckled. It had been close once, when she had waited, done up to the nines for him to take her dancing. That had been a bitterly cold day on the Island. Neill had reckoned just one quick hot whiskey in the Mermaid on the way home. One had turned to two, two to three and then he had lost count.

Phyllis, polite Phyllis had greeted them like the wrath of God at her front door. "You can come in, but your drunken scutter of a friend can bugger off. Now."

She'd shut him up, sobered him up, and put him up for the night.

She'd been very calm the next morning. Icily calm. Yes, she loved him. Yes, she wanted to marry him, but no, she was not going to be like her mother waiting on the pleasure of her lord and master.

From now on, Saturdays would be for him and Neill, provided he arrived home when he said he would. Sundays were for her and, when they arrived, for the kids. That's the way it had been ever since. He loved her for her fairness as much as for her wicked laugh and, he felt a tightening in his pants, her delightful depravity in bed when the kids were asleep.

She knew how much he loved Ulster, but lately she had begun to say, forcibly, that it was no place to rear children. And she was right. Maybe he could get used to living so far away.

Neill really should meet someone like Phil, he thought, particularly if we decide to leave. Perhaps he would broach the subject tonight. Pat looked at his watch. Five-twenty-five. What the hell was keeping the man?

Pat opened the booth to have a look for Neill and nearly collided with Joe, the barman.

"Hold your horses, Pat. I'll not let you die of thirst."

"You'd better not. I could sue you for that." Pat laughed.

Joe did not. "That was a good one the first time. It's got whiskers now. The usual?"

"Please. Have you seen Neill?"

Joe shook his head and went to pour the pints.

Where the hell was he? Maybe ordering the drinks would bring him. Just like meteors brought ducks.

The drinks and Neill arrived simultaneously. He waited until the straight glasses were set on the tabletop, then squeezed past the barman and sat heavily on the bench seat opposite.

"You're late." Even as he spoke, Pat realized that his words were more harsh than he had intended, probably from relief that Neill had finally come. Pat paid Joe who left, closing the door of the booth behind him.

Neill did not reply. He grabbed his glass, took a healthy swallow, and set the drink back on the table. Pat could see his friend was flushed and just a little short of breath. His black hair, as always, looked as if Neill had run through a hedge backwards. Neill said coldly, "I got stopped by an Army patrol."

"Oh. Mistook you for a crazed bomber, did they?" Pat looked at Neill, hoping to see the start of a smile.

Neill took another pull of his stout and wiped his upper lip with the web between his thumb and forefinger.

"Come on, mate. Cheer up, it's Friday."

Neill muttered, "These bloody Troubles are going to cost me my job."

"Sure, and the Pope's going to become a Presbyterian. I'd have thought that all the excitement here would sell newspapers."

Neill shook his head and jabbed his index finger onto the tabletop. "It does, but it doesn't sell advertising—I lost another account today— and that's my job." He drank again. "At least it is for now."

Pat lifted his glass. This anger was not like his friend at all. This was definitely not the time to talk to him about Canada. He looked at Neill over the top of the glass. Neill had always been the serious one. Maybe he wasn't always quick to see the fun of a situation, but he usually responded good-naturedly to having his leg pulled.

"Perhaps I could put you in touch with one of my clients. I prepared his brief yesterday."

"Why?" Neill's voice was flat.

"He's onto a good thing. He sells window glass. He's put up his sales a hell of a lot in the last few years by getting his Provo brother to tip him the nod when bombs are going to go off near places with lots of windows. Business is booming, and I mean booming, literally."

Neill shrugged. "So?"

"I thought you could sell him a few inches of advertising, you know, something like—'Think you don't need windows? We know you will. Book now and avoid the rush later.'" Dammit. Not even a hint of a smile: What was eating Neill?

"Sometimes, Pat, you're not that funny." Neill held his half-empty glass in both hands and looked directly at Pat.

Time to back off. It hadn't happened often in all the years they had been friends, but once in a while the Celtic part of Neill's heritage seemed to get the better of him.

Fortunately, his black spells did not last long. Pat held up both hands, palms outward. "Right. I'll say no more."

Neill inhaled deeply. "It's just not funny. You know as well as I do people get hurt in these bombings. I don't think we should be joking about it."

Was it Neill's basic seriousness or was he really worried about losing his job? He could always be counted on to laugh at a typical Belfast joke. "Two IRA men in a car. The one in the passenger's seat says, 'Paddy, the bomb in me lap's going to go off,' and the driver says, 'Don't worry, there's a spare bomb in the boot.'" That kind of thing. Gallows humour. The sort that had helped the Londoners through the Blitz. But not today. Pat leant forward, touching Neill's hand with his own. "What's up, mate?"

Neill jerked his hand away. "Just leave it." He swallowed the last of his pint and stood. "I won't be going shooting tomorrow. I've to work." He snorted. "I've half a mind to leave this benighted country."

Pat called after him, "Hang on a minute." He tried to rise but Neill forestalled him. "I told you I have to work tomorrow." With that he pushed through the swing doors and thrust his way past the crowd in the bar.

Something really was getting to Neill, Pat thought. His friend had been offered a damn good job in Australia a few years back and had turned it down flat. He'd never leave Ulster. Would he? Would I?

The man could be taciturn, but this was the first time he had completely refused to talk about something that was bothering him. Pat had at least considered talking about his thoughts on emigration. He hadn't even had the chance. Obviously Neill had been in no mood to discuss anything rationally.

Indeed, the more Pat mulled over what had just happened the less he liked it and, if he was honest with himself, he was becoming angry too. Neill was upset, but there was no need to be so bloody rude, and—Pat swallowed the last of his pint, the stout bitter in his throat—tomorrow was ruined. It would not be the same going to Strangford without Neill. To hell with it, and to hell with Neill and his temper tantrums.

He looked round the busy bar, packed now, full of lads on their Friday night after work. Powerful crack in here, except Neill had gone and Pat had no desire to make idle chitchat with some of the other regulars. There wasn't much point hanging about. He might as well catch the corporation bus to the station and take the train home to Bangor. Neill had been going to give him a lift, and damn it, he'd left his season's ticket in the pocket of his other suit. He would be late now and Phyllis would not be pleased. He'd phone her before he left. "The soft word turneth away the blow," he thought, trying to remember the Biblical source.

He caught the diesel train to Bangor. Old Bangorians reckoned the locomotive had a mention in the book of Genesis. "And the Lord made all creeping things." It certainly was creeping tonight.

Pat let himself into the bungalow.

"I'm in the kitchen."

He shrugged out of his coat, hung it on a peg, and hurried through.

Phyllis sat at the kitchen table. The light from a neon strip above the counter played on her chestnut hair. He saw the curve of her neck, a small shadow at her throat, the little cross of Saint Bridget hanging there. He'd bought that last month, for their fifth anniversary. He bent and dropped a small kiss on her forhead.

"Sorry I'm late, love."

"You're forgiven," she said, "but supper's ruined."

"My fault." He bent to the oven, opened the door, and, slipping his pullover sleeve over his hand, pulled out a plate of steak and kidney pie. "Looks all right to me." He carried the plate to the table. "Kids in bed?"

She nodded. "Anne went out like a light, but Colin played his pins for a while. He's over now."

"Good. Tell you what. I'll not be shooting tomorrow. Why don't I take them out in the morning?" The steak and kidney was a bit dry, but it was still tasty.

"All right. Colin could use a new pair of shoes. He's going around like a steam engine now he's up and walking." Phyllis leaned back, watching him eat. "Is Neill all right?"

Pat heard the concern in her voice. He stopped chewing and laid his cutlery on the plate. "I don't honestly know. You know he can get a bit moody, but this was different. He was fit to be tied."

"So. Why don't you give him a ring after supper?"

Pat picked at a piece of dried-out steak stuck between his teeth. "Maybe."

"Come on, Pat. I'm sure he'll have calmed down by now."

"Maybe. I think I'll let it sit until tomorrow."

"Well. If you're not going to call him, try to put it out of your mind." She put her elbows on the table and rested her chin on her folded hands. "No letter, Neill's in a snit, and you're going to sit there, chewing your dinner like an old lion with toothache."

"Well."

"No 'well' about it. Neill and you've been friends since you were kids. He'll come around. It's a shame about the letter, but it'll be there on Monday."

Pat nodded. "I suppose so."

"Look, I'm the one that wants to go to Canada. I can wait for a few more days to hear."

"I thought you'd be disappointed."

"I am, but I'm not going to let it ruin the weekend." She rose, walked round the table and stood behind him, massaging his shoulders. "And I'm not going to let it spoil yours."

He put a hand over hers. "All right." He could feel the softness of her breast against his back. "I'll take the kids in the morning if you'll do the afternoon shift. Do you think your mum would take them in the evening?"

"I'll ask. I'd a half-notion to pop over and see her tomorrow any-way."

"Great. We could go to Balloo House for dinner. Just you and me."

She bent and kissed him. "You never know what that might lead to."

He returned the kiss, tasting her, wanting her. The desiccated steak and kidney, his concern about Neill, and the letter from Canada could all keep.

Pat waved at Phyllis and the kids as the mini pulled out of the drive-way. Now, he thought, I know why I like my Saturdays with Neill. Much as I love the sprats they kept me going this morning. Anne was no bother in her pram, but Colin had run round like a whirling dervish. He had nearly fallen into the lake at Ward Park this morn-ing. Took after his dad. He had been trying to get at the ornamental ducks.

He sniffed at the southerly wind sensing that it would have been a good day on the Lough and missing it. He wondered if Grouse had missed going out too. Probably. Even though the Labrador was get-ting on now he was still game. What the hell was eating Neill? Pat found himself trying to decide if he was disappointed or worried by Neill's behaviour. Neill couldn't be in any real danger of losing his job, could he? Only last year he had won the award for best salesman. If he put as much effort into his work as he did into his hobbies, he must be a fine worker. It had to be something else.

Another romance gone sour? Poor Neill never seemed to be able to understand that women were not prepared to play second fiddle to his outdoor pursuits. Pat had lost count of the ones who had given Neill the ultimatum: "The ducks or me."

That made it worse. If Neill had a family of his own, Pat would not have felt so badly about thinking of emigrating.

He went back into the house, lifted the telephone, and began to dial. He couldn't let this rift go on. No reply. Of course, Neill would be in Belfast now. He'd said he had to work today. But he would call, prob-ably this evening, before Pat took Phyllis to "Balloo."

But what if Neill didn't call? Pat paused as he walked towards the kitchen. He remembered his own father telling him years ago that a man was lucky to be able to count his true friends on the fingers of one hand. And Neill was a true friend. At least Pat had thought so. Knew so, dammit. Pat looked at the telephone. Could he reach Neill at work? He shook his head.

From where he stood in the hall, he could see through the kitchen window. Not a bad day. It seemed a pity to waste the sunshine, watery though it might be in late October. Usually he and Neill would not start getting *Gannet*, Pat's fourteen-foot dinghy, ready for the sailing season until February when the duck shooting was finished, but he might as well wander round to the yacht club. After a week stuck in an office in Belfast, making a start on stripping last year's paint would do him good, and when he'd had enough of that there was sure to be some of the sailing crowd in the clubhouse. Just one with them, of course. Phyllis was expecting him home for five.

Pat enjoyed the short walk round to Ballyholme where *Gannett* lay under a tarpaulin in the dinghy park. It did not take him long to pull the cover back and get to work. The rhythm of the sanding soothed him and he lost track of time.

He straightened up, holding a piece of coarse sandpaper wrapped round a block of wood in his right hand. He rubbed his brow with the back of his left hand. Despite the coolness of the day and the soft wind blowing in from Belfast Lough, he was sweating. His hand came away smeared with perspiration and white paint dust. He knew he must look like an Apache warrior in full war-paint.

The little wooden-hulled boat lay upside down on trestles. Her white-painted bottom, stained and scratched after last year's sailing, was almost down to the planking for about a third of its length. The job was taking forever. No task seemed so arduous when Neill was giving a hand.

Pat looked at his watch. Good Lord, it was three-thirty already. The flight from the River Quoile would be starting about now. No question. He'd rather be down on the Long Island, waiting for the ducks.

He smiled. Bloody Neill. Pat was able to think with less rancour now. The physical effort of sandpapering had lifted his mind from yesterday's scene in the Crown. Neill must have had his reasons. Pat bent back to his task, one hand resting on the wooden hull, the other rasping the paper-covered block back and forth in short, firm strokes.

He'd call tonight before he took Phyllis out.

A shadow fell over the piece of hull he was working on. Pat looked up, seeing a familiar form dark against the disc of the low winter sun. "You're in my light."

"Sorry." Neill stepped to one side, standing stiffly, blue duffle-coated arms folded across his chest.

Pat kept on sanding. He waited for Neill to say something, knowing what it would cost the stubborn sod to apologize. He heard Neill cough. "Look. I'm sorry about last night."

Pat stopped scraping, stood, and looked directly at Neill and saw abject contrition on his friend's face, like old Grouse when he had been chastised by his master. Pat almost smiled. Not yet. Let him sweat. Pat had worried enough about Neill since last night. "I should bloody well hope so."

Neill's voice held no pleading. "Look, I've said I'm sorry. What more do you want?"

Pat smiled and cocked his head slightly to one side. "Care to tell me why you were so owly last night?"

Neill hitched his hip onto the end of one of the trestles, looked at the ground, and back to Pat. "He got to me, that's all."

"'He got to me.'" Pat leant one hand on the dinghy's hull. "Christ. Who got to you?" He was more than willing to listen. He just wished Neill would get on with it but knew that when something was bothering him, his friend could be reticent.

Pat glanced away, out across the shingle of the dinghy park to the waters of Ballyholme Bay, chopped by the wind, blue and slate-grey in the winter light—to the low hills of Ballymacormick Point on the far shore. A single gull swooped low over the waves, keening and mourning for something lost.

"I told you I might lose my job," Neill said. "You didn't give me a chance to tell you why." His tone was not accusatory. "Some stupid story about a glass merchant—"

"I was trying to cheer you up. I thought it was funny."

"I know. But it wasn't. I wanted you to listen."

Pat heard the cry of the gull and heard the pain in his friend's voice.

"They weren't going to fire me. I damn near quit. And I meant it about getting to hell out of Ulster."

"Quit? Good God. Why?"

"Because the junior sales manager said it was my fault that we had lost the account," Neill stood, looked straight into Pat's eyes, "and that I'd only got the job in the first place because the paper was bending over backwards to hire Catholics."

"What?" Pat dropped the sanding block. His voice rose to a higher register. "What?" He felt as though he had been slapped in the face. "Oh, Jesus."

"Aye." Neill nodded his head, once, slowly. By the way his lips tightened as he spoke, Pat realized that the junior sales manager probably didn't know how close he'd come to losing a few teeth.

"Jesus. What did you do?" No wonder Neill had been talking about leaving Ulster.

"Walked out."

Pat whistled. "That's why you looked like the wrath of God when you came in last night."

Neill shrugged. "Anyway. I went to see the publisher this morning." He ran one hand carelessly back and forth along a piece of recently sanded hull. "It's all smoothed out."

"How the hell can you smooth out a thing like that?"

Neill shook his head. "It doesn't matter. It's done."

"Dammit, Neill, stop doing your *Quiet Man* impression. What happened?"

Neill rubbed his thumb over his fingertips, making little flakes of paint dust fall. "I really did go in there today to quit, you know." Pat heard the edge. He did not doubt for one second that had been Neill's intention.

"And?"

"He's a very decent man." Neill lifted one shoulder slightly. "He said I couldn't resign until I'd told him why. I told him the story. He listened."

Pat accepted the unspoken rebuke and waited for Neill to continue. He saw a slow smile begin. "At least he listened for a while, then he said he'd heard enough." Neill grinned. "He said he'd never heard such claptrap in his life, that I was his best salesman, and that as far as he was concerned it didn't matter if I was a bloody Hottentot." Neill put one foot up on the trestle and leant forward, elbow on knee, chin resting on his hand. "He meant it. I've never seen him so mad."

Pat laid a hand on Neill's shoulder. "I should bloody well hope so." He tightened his hand and softened his voice. "I really didn't understand last night."

"Aye, well."

Pat heard the accusation in the words, then saw Neill's big smile. He was teasing. The bugger. Pat loosened his grip. "Come on. You didn't give me a whole hell of a lot to go on."

Neill stood straight. "No." He started to take off the donkey jacket. "I shouldn't have bitten your head off and stormed out like that."

"Forget it." For a moment his eyes held Neill's. "If it hadn't worked out, would you have left Ulster?"

"For a moment I thought I could." Neill took a deep breath. "No. I'll never leave."

They stood together in silence for a moment before Neill bent and picked up a piece of sandpaper, sighted with his craftsman's eye along the line of the grain of the wooden hull, and began sanding with slow, powerful strokes, pausing only to say, "Come on, you skiver, get on with it."

Pat hesitated, thinking of the letter to come on Monday, hoping that it would say that his legal qualifications were no good in Toronto. Hoping Phyllis would understand.

He looked out to sea. Two seagulls drifted down the wind, and as he bent to work he heard their hoarse cries chuckling in tune with the rasp of two men sandpapering a little boat together at the evening of a Saturday in October.

1980

On January 6, a landmine set by the Provisional IRA exploded beneath the Burren Bridge, killing four members of the Ulster Defence Regiment.

On May 5, the IRA blew up the north-south power link.

On June 26, Dr. Miriam Daly was shot dead in her own home.

On December 8, British prime minister Margaret Thatcher flew to Dublin to meet with the Taioseach (the Irish prime minister), Charles Haughey. This was the first time a British prime minister had visited the Republic of Ireland since partition.

1980 Dead 76   **Total Dead 2,017**

1981

On January 16, Bernadette McAlliskey, née Devlin, civil rights activist, youngest member of the British House of Commons, and committed Republican, was shot nine times by members of the Ulster Defence Association. Her husband was also badly injured in the shooting. They both survived.

On January 21, Sir Norman Stronge, aged 86, former speaker of the Stormont Parliament, and his only son, James, were shot to death by the Provisional IRA in retaliation for the McAlliskey shootings. The Stronge home, Tynan Abbey, was burned down.

(*continued*)

On March 1, Bobby Sands began the first hunger strike in the Maze Prison. In 1972, his family had been burned out of their home in Rathcoole, a Catholic district of Belfast, and Sands had joined the Provisional IRA. He was sentenced to fourteen years in 1976 for possession of firearms with intent. He took a leading role among the prisoners. On May 5, the sixty-sixth day of his hunger strike, at 1:17 a.m., he died.

In October 3, the Provisional IRA called a halt to the hunger strikes during which ten prisoners had starved themselves to death. Each death had been followed by rioting. Sixty-one people were killed in these riots.

In November, Lennie Murphy, leader of the Shankill Butchers, recently released from prison, was shot to death by the Provisional IRA. Murphy had become such an embarrassment to the UVF that it is probable that the Loyalists provided the Provos with the information that led to his assassination. His gravestone in the cemetery in Carnmoney carries this epitaph: "UVF. For God and Ulster. Here lies a soldier. Murphy."

1981 Dead 101   **Total Dead 2,272**

SHOULD OLD ACQUAINTANCE BE FORGOT?

". . . are forty shades of green." The big man in the tweed cap finished his song. Henry shook his head, feeling the damp of his jacket collar against the back of his neck. More like forty shades of fucking grey. He wanted to spit on the planks of the pub's floor. It's all very well for these yobbos to get pissed of a Friday, but this maudlin horseshit? He craned to look through the dirty window. The rain was still coming down in stair-rods. He shrugged and leant back against the bar counter. His habit of finding a corner where his back was protected had led him to the end of the bar. He had an excellent view of the small, crowded room. Typical bloody Belfast pub. Room enough to stand, but not enough to fall. He shook his head again, eyes never still, scanning the room and the men in it.

Tobacco smoke, beer stains, and mildew complemented the torn Guinness posters on the smutty plaster walls. There were about thirty poorly dressed men in the room. Henry recognized no one; not that he had expected to. He did not frequent this part of the city. He'd only come in here to get out of the unexpected downpour.

He turned to look at a clock on the wall behind the bar. Four-twenty. If the bloody rain would stop, he'd still have time to keep his appointment. Henry massaged one shoulder, feeling the tension in the muscles. He always felt this way when the call came, wondering what his next assignment might be.

Four twenty-one. It bothered him. He hated being late for anything, and yet, would it really be the end of the world if he did not show up exactly on time?

He leant on the counter, head turned, watching. All he could see were the featureless faces of middle-aged strangers who, he surmised, had collected their unemployment money and headed for the boozer. Now, having sunk pint after pint of stout, they were starting to sing. Jesus. He despised them, yet knew he was being unfair. If it weren't for the Troubles he'd be one of this mob, another unemployed man, useless, living off the handouts of the British Government.

Henry turned back, refusing to meet the barman's friendly look, and tried to ignore the raucous, off-key bawling of the cloth-capped idiot who was well into the second verse of "Come out ye Black and Tans."

Did these buggers know who the Black and Tans had been, the hated paramilitary of the British in the Troubles of the twenties? Some might, but most probably thought it was a drink made half of beer, half of stout.

Henry looked at the clock. Four-thirty. He looked outside. Still no sign of the rain ending. If he didn't leave soon he would be late. Ach, but sometimes he tired of putting everything aside for the cause. Why the hell should he get soaked for the sake of a few more minutes? Maybe when he did get to the rendezvous he'd ask for more money so he could buy a decent raincoat. Tell them he'd be less likely to be late in future if he wasn't worried about catching fucking pneumonia.

He took a pull on his pint. A heavy-set man was pushing his way past the group standing round the singer. Henry followed the stranger's progress by watching his reflection in a mirrored advertisement for Paddy Irish Whiskey that hung on the wall beneath the clock. Henry had no idea who the man was, but he seemed to be heading his way.

Henry felt the pressure of a body beside him. He turned slowly, curling the fingers of his right hand into a tight fist.

"How's about ye?" The man Henry had been watching had forced his way up to the bar.

"Are ye all right, oul' hand?"

The last thing Henry wanted today was to be noticed. Not meeting the man's eyes, he replied, "Fair enough." He began to turn away, but the stranger was not to be denied. Henry felt a hand on his arm. He started, involuntarily.

"Didn't mean to scare you." The man removed his hand, but carried on relentlessly, "Like, ah . . . I haven't seen ye in here before. Live round here?" He was as insistent as a puppy that wants to have its tummy rubbed.

Henry looked into the man's eyes. All he saw was friendly curiosity, the easy familiarity so often found in Belfast pubs. His fingers relaxed. This man was no member of the security forces, just an inquisitive local. Even so, to ignore him might be to cause offence. The words were just so slightly slurred, and Henry knew from long experience that the would-be friendly Ulsterman can turn vicious with very little provocation, particularly if he's had a jar or two. Henry smiled with his mouth. "No. I'm just in out of the rain." The thick bastard would remember nothing by tomorrow if they chatted for a while. He'd remember forever if he thought he had been slighted.

"Right enough. It's fair lashing down."

Henry nodded. Keep it superficial. Talk about the weather. The Irish have long memories—indeed wasn't that half of what was wrong with the country? Communal memories like elephants. "There's enough out there to fill the Boyne River," he said. Henry watched to see if the reference to the Protestant victory of 1690 would have any effect. He had guessed from the songs being sung earlier that this was unlikely to be a Protestant bar, but you never could tell.

The face before him—round, big, ruddy-cheeked—split into a great grin. "Aye, and the Lagan as well." The man picked his nose, rubbed his finger under the nostrils, sniffed, and asked, "Will you have a pint or a wee half? The name's Joe Galvin, by the way."

"Just a glass. I have to be getting on." He had only intended to have one pint. Men in his line of work with a weakness for the drink didn't last long. Still, now he'd half-made up his mind that a few more minutes didn't matter, what would he lose by having a jar with this Galvin?

Henry did not offer his name, not that it would have mattered. He had plenty to choose from. He waited and was not surprised by the next question.

"Where're you from then?"

Less subtle than, "Where did you go to school?" less blunt than, "Are you a Catholic or a Protestant?" but just as searching. Perhaps the remark about the Boyne River had not gone unnoticed after all. Henry paused before answering, sipping his pint and deciding to give the name of a town where the communities were so mixed it would be impossible to infer a man's political affiliations. "Bangor. I'm just in town for the day."

"Right enough? You could've picked a better day. You're soaking, so you are."

Henry shrugged. He swallowed the last of his Guinness. "They keep the stout in good order here. Mebbe I'll look in again."

Galvin jerked his head sharply to one side and lowered his voice. "Look. It's no business of mine who you are, but just so you know, this is a Republican bar." He leaned back watching Henry's face.

Henry did not allow any surprise to show. He had no need to. He had been with the Provos since he was sixteen. He had killed three men, if you could consider members of the Ulster Freedom Fighters or informers to be men. He had to be careful. Even someone so seemingly simple as this Joe Galvin could be an informer. Henry decided to take a chance. "Up the Republic." He smiled at Galvin. Henry realized that by now, if asked, he could describe his new companion's features. If the name came up in conversation, he would be able to put a face to the name.

Henry preferred not to notice faces. It was easier that way. He looked at the clock. Now he was late. The fresh drinks had just arrived, Galvin's pint and a half-pint for Henry. He sipped his. "Cheers." He set the glass on the bar top. "I just have to make a phone call."

"Away on. Phone's in the hall." Galvin hoisted his glass, smiled his simple smile, a mole on his upper lip whitened by the beer suds.

Henry turned to walk to the hall. Republican bar. Jesus Christ. How many men in here had killed or kneecapped for Ireland? How would Galvin like to drive a power drill through the patella and into the knee joint of a man, listening to his screams, watching his tears, ignoring his sobs, ignoring his face or who he was? Henry had lost count. Was his score twelve or fourteen? He found the telephone, mounted on the wall outside the lavatory. The smell of stale urine and puke fought a losing battle with the thickly wreathed cigarette smoke. Henry inserted the coins and dialled his number. Puke. It didn't bother him. He'd smelt men's vomit before. Twelve or fourteen times.

"Hello. Look. Tell Liam I'll be late. What? Who the hell do you think it is? Just tell him I'll be fucking well late. About an hour." He hung up and looked at the receiver. Let them wait. He was tired of jumping like a performing flea. He forced his way back to the bar. Joe Galvin had not moved. He grinned again as Henry reappeared. Galvin lifted his glass.

"Get through all right?"

Henry nodded.

"Lettin' the missus know?" The man's curiosity was limitless.

"No, I'm not married."

Galvin's grin faded. "Nor me." He drank deeply before continuing. "The wife died six years back."

Henry could see the man's eyes beginning to mist. He muttered a conventional "Sorry."

"That's all right. I'm over it now." The pain in his eyes belied his words. He picked his nose, sniffed, and brightening somewhat remarked, "Still, I've Sammy."

"Sammy?"

"Aye. He was twelve when his mother died. He's eighteen now." Galvin began to fumble in his inside jacket pocket. He pulled out a wrinkled photograph. He handed it to Henry, pointing with obvious pride at the figures frozen on the cracked, glossy paper. "That's me and that's Sammy holding the mackerel. He was about fourteen then."

The boy was shorter than his father. Open-faced, grinning. He was wearing a calliper-brace on his left leg. Henry returned the photo. "You like to fish?"

Joe Galvin smoothed the picture before slipping it back inside his jacket. "Oh, aye. So does Sammy. He's daft about the fishing." He drank. "He's had a bad leg since he was wee, couldn't kick a ball like, but the leg doesn't stop him going on a boat." Galvin thrust his head forward.

"He's a game lad. Him and me's got very close since his mother died."
Galvin turned to the barman. Before Henry could protest, the big man
had ordered two more drinks. He winked at Henry. "One more won't
hurt, and my Sammy sees me right. He's workin' too. Has been for
about a year now, and he gives his dad a few quid on Fridays."

Henry finished his drink and lifted the fresh half-pint. This Galvin seemed to be a decent enough fellow. Damn it, his appointment
would keep. When was the last time he had just stood in a pub, having a quiet jar, chatting, just like ordinary men? He winked at
Galvin. "Thanks, Joe."

"Drink up." Galvin touched his glass to Henry's. "Do you fish?"

"I haven't. Not for a brave few years." Keeping ahead of the security forces was sport enough.

"Me and Sammy go every Sunday. Every Sunday. Donaghadee. We
go out on one of them boats."

Galvin was in full cry and Henry was happy enough to let him talk,
occasionally contributing to the conversation. By the time his glass was
almost finished he was wondering, only half cynically, when the pair
of them would start to belt out "The Town I Love so Well" with the
rest of the drunken skitters. He reminded himself that pleasant though
this unexpected interlude might be, he still had an appointment. He
glanced through the window. "Look, Joe. The rain's over and I have
to be getting along. Mebbe I'll drop in again. I owe you a couple."

Galvin, swaying a bit now, draped one arm loosely round Henry's shoulders. "Aye. That'll be grand. Don't forget. The name's Joe
Galvin. Joe. Me and Sammy live up the back of Roden Street." He
pulled his arm away and punched Henry lightly on the shoulder. "If I
don't see you through the week, I'll see you through the window."
He began to smile at his own wit, shook Henry's hand, and was still
smiling good-naturedly as Henry left the bar.

The pavement was wet, with empty cigarette packets and discarded
fish-and-chip wrappers stuck here and there or wadded in the gutter. The rain had stopped but a raw wind tugged at the tails of his
coat. He pulled the peak of his cloth cap down and turned up the collar of his jacket. Just like James fucking Bond, he thought as he strode

rapidly, not yet considering what he was going to be asked to do, but letting his mind dwell on his recent meeting with Joe Galvin.

The bloody man wouldn't know a real Republican if one bit him; and yet Henry had enjoyed the interlude with nothing to talk about but fishing and Joe Galvin's son, Sammy. Sammy. Henry knew that until the struggle was over he would not be having any sons of his own to take fishing at Donaghadee. He found himself envying his recent acquaintance's obvious deep affection for his lame boy. Joe Galvin thought the sun shone out of his youngster's arse. Henry turned a corner. He could envy Galvin. Just a bit.

A Saracen armoured car drove slowly past, great rubber tyres rumbling over the damp street. Two young British paratroopers stood in the tailgate, FN rifles at the port, slowly quartering the road behind them. Shites, Henry thought, as he turned reflexively with head lowered to gaze into a shop window until the enemy had passed.

He stepped sideways to avoid a lump of dog shit. Filthy city. Saxon oppressors. British Bastards. How often had he said or thought those words? The occupying power. Sure he meant them, but today they sounded tired. As tired as he was. They'd just come as automatically as his hiding his face.

Perhaps it was the Guinness he had just consumed, perhaps it was the lingering pleasantness of the conversation, a chat that had nothing to do with killing, that made him pause. Were those two kids on the Saracen—were they really the enemy? In truth he no longer knew. He wondered if he even cared. The enemy was a cipher, a faceless man, an anonymous job, like the one he would hear about as soon as the commandant had identified the target. A job that kept all those like himself and the commandant one better than the men who had filled that pub, and the hundreds of men like them, in other pubs and betting shops and welfare offices all over the ghettoes of Belfast.

He turned into one of the countless, narrow back streets, streets of grimy terraces that run like rat trails through the slums of the city. He followed the numbers. Finding the door he sought, he knocked. A stringy-haired youth, who, like the hall in which he was standing, smelled of mould, opened the door.

"You're late."

Henry stared at the young man, slowly, piercingly, and with ill-concealed contempt.

The boy lowered his eyes. "Look, I'm sorry. All right? Liam's fit to be tied."

Henry stood. Immobile, silent.

The boy's lower lip trembled. "Aw, would you for God's sake come in off the street and let me get this door shut." He glanced nervously up and down the narrow thoroughfare. Ignoring the youth, Henry slid past. He heard the door slam as he walked down the dimly lit hall and into the scullery.

An older man sat at the kitchen table. He did not rise but just looked up wearily and took another drag on his cigarette. "Decent of you to phone, Henry." His voice was flat, his face impassive.

"Fuck you too, Liam. I'm here. You didn't die of old age waiting for me." He sat down at the table across from the older man and helped himself to a Woodbine from the packet on the table. He lit up. "So? What's it to be?" The smoke was raw in his throat.

Liam reached under the table, straightened up and silently handed Henry an old Webley .38 revolver. He took it and stuffed it into his coat pocket, not even bothering to inspect the weapon, wondering if the target was to be maimed or killed. "Well?"

"We've found a grass. A fucking informer." Liam's voice was acidic with disgust. "This bugger's been feeding the Brits for the last year. We want him stopped." He looked at Henry coldly. "Permanently." Liam crushed out his cigarette. "It's set up for Sunday morning, early." Henry relaxed. A killing. At least it wasn't tonight. One more faceless man. Henry waited.

"He lives round the back of Roden Street. His name's Galvin." Henry stiffened, his mind racing. Galvin. Jesus Christ. Not half an hour ago. Henry could picture the big man's ruddy cheeks, the mole on his upper lip, the way he picked his nose. Christ, he had shaken Joe Galvin by the hand.

Henry barely heard Liam continue. "You'll have no trouble identifying the fucker. He's one leg in a brace."

1982

On March 16, an eleven-year-old boy was killed and 34 people were injured by a bomb in Banbridge, County Down. No warning was given.

On July 20, the Provisional IRA carried out two bomb attacks in London, one in a bandstand in Regent's Park where an army band was playing. Eight British soldiers died immediately and three other people died later.

On November 9, outside the Lakeland Forum in Eniskillen, Detective Constable Gary Ewing and a civilian were killed by an explosive device attached to their car.

On November 11, the Royal Ulster Constabulary in Lurgan, County Armagh, shot dead three unarmed Provisional IRA men.

On December 6, over 150 people, many off-duty members of the Cheshire Regiment, were attending the Razzamatazz disco at the Droppin' Well pub in Ballykelly, County Londonderry. The explosion of a bomb planted by the Irish National Liberation Army brought down the concrete roof. When the rescue efforts were over, twelve soldiers and five civilians had been found dead. Sixty-six people were injured.

1982 Dead 97   **Total Dead 2,369**

THE VIKINGS

Jean Swanson sat at her desk and looked out over the children in her fourth-form history class. She considered herself lucky to have secured this position as a history mistress at Bangor Grammar School. Most of her youngsters, fourteen- and fifteen-year-olds, were well behaved.

"Stop that, Michael." Most of her charges were well behaved. Not all of them.

"Yes, Miss."

Michael was a little devil, a red-haired, freckle-faced boy who had just used a bent plastic ruler to fire a wad of chewed up blotting paper at his favourite target, Nonie Ferguson. He'd missed.

"Put that ruler down and pay attention."

Not only were most of the children in this class well behaved, they were also keen to learn. She thought of some of the horror stories she had heard from friends who tried to teach in Belfast schools. As if working with a bunch of little savages from the slums wasn't enough, they had to face the constant threats and daily dangers of the city.

She hoped this morning's lesson would really interest her pupils. It was about Bangor. She turned and glanced at the clock above the blackboard behind her. Time to get started.

"Now. Settle down."

She waited for the fidgeting and chatter to stop.

"Today we are going to learn more about the Dark Ages in Ireland."

She opened a book. "I thought we would do things a bit differently today. We won't be using our textbooks. I'm going to read you a story."

Michael was playing with his desk-lid, opening and closing it.

"Michael, I think you'll like this one. It's about the Vikings."

She waited for him to close the lid and sit up straight. It gave her time to wonder if she had made the right choice of subject. She admired the way the tale described the peace of Ireland then showed how violence could shatter the idyll. She wanted to see what some of the cleverer children might recognize. Problem was some of the scenes were a bit grisly. She just hoped the gory bits would help her make her point, as well as hold the attention of Michael and one or two others.

"Ready?"

"Yes, miss," said the girl who had been the target of Michael's missile.

Jean smiled at Nonie. She was a bright little button. "Good. Then let's get started." She began to read.

A longship swam through the still waters. The mists parted before its arched dragon prow and clung to the masthead in long, ragged pennants. Oars dipped, pulled, and rose as one. Their looms were wrapped in sheepskins to muffle any sound that they might make against the tholes, and each blade as it cleared the water left nothing but the turbulence of its passage. The ship was the only thing that moved on the surface of the long, dark lough. They had lowered the great square sail as they rounded the islands at the mouth of the lough, and each man, save Ragnar their captain, had taken his massive oar, as a child might take a fishing rod, and with seemingly as little effort as the same child casting, had rowed for eight miles. They were Norsemen out a-Viking. What was an eight-mile row to a Norseman?

Matins, the first prayers of the monastic day, held in the chill, dark, small hours, were over and the drowsy monks were now leaving the refectory. Life was simple and peaceful at Bangor Abbey set on the shores of Belfast Lough in the northeast corner of Ireland. After matins the monks ate a simple breakfast and then turned to the tasks of the day. Most of the monks worked on the farm, helped by the *manaig*, married laymen who lived on the estate and laboured with the monks. Seven of the brothers retired to the scriptorium, where they lit their oil and rush lamps and lovingly uncovered their works, painstakingly illuminated copies of the *Caltach*, the "book of battles" of Saint Columba, so called because Irish soldiers of an earlier time had believed that if it were borne around their army before a fight it would ensure victory. The original had been written in the early part of the seventh century, more than two hundred years ago, and it was the pride of the monks of the Abbey that they were privileged to have one of the first copies from which to make their own.

The bow wave gurgled back along the clinker-laid strakes of the longship's prow. She was tightly built, broad enough in the beam to weather the sea passage from her home fiord in Norway, yet narrow enough to slice through the water as her crew rowed on. They had covered another mile and were nearing their destination. The stroke oar, on a grunted command from Ragnar, quickened the pace. Ragnar knew that they must reach their intended landing place soon if the boat was to be beached and concealed, and the raiding party sent off overland well before dawn. Complete surprise in the attack was worth two more longships' crews in any battle, and Ragnar and his men were no strangers to battle. Beside each oarsman on his thwart or at his feet lay his great two-bladed axe.

Brother Columbanus, named for the ancient Irish saint, moved his lamp closer—it was not yet light enough to see clearly—and carefully studied the intricate spirals on the page he was to transcribe. Even after eight years of continuous work on this task, he was still in awe of the artists who had created the original book. The *Caltach* was quite extraordinary. It had been written before the Irish scribes had begun to borrow artistic ideas from their Northumbrian colleagues. The decorative motifs were all of the la Tène school, the pure Celtic form. There were trumpet patterns, peltas, and spirals lovingly etched into the parchment with goldleaf and scarlet. He knew his copy must match the original exactly. He had joined the Abbey thirty years earlier and had progressed from farm worker, to scribe, to being their most skilled illustrator. He dearly loved the peace and the timelessness of the rhythm of life in the Abbey. Day ran seamlessly into day as canonical hour followed canonical hour. His life pursued the easily charted path from matins in the chapel to compline in his cell at night.

The bows of the longship slid into the sand of a small cove, and immediately eight of the oarsmen leapt over the shield-hung gunwales into the low surf and began dragging her further ashore before the momentum of her final rush towards the land was lost. The rest of the crew rapidly followed them into the water and by their combined efforts soon manhandled the craft above the high-water mark. Working with long-practised precision, the men stowed their oars and unloaded their weapons. The eight who had been first ashore seized their axes and silently disappeared into the gorse-covered dunes that surrounded the cove. As the guards took up their positions, the rest struck the mast and began to cover the now low-lying hull with gorse branches, careless of the thorns that ripped into their callused hands. Ragnar watched, quietly satisfied, thinking pleasurably of the day's work ahead. The task was completed rapidly. Ragnar hooted twice like an owl, and four of the eight guards rejoined the rest of the crew. It was time. They had landed about a mile as the raven flies from their destination but Ragnar wanted to take a roundabout route. He knew it would take about an hour to cover the distance. The false dawn was just beginning to touch the eastern sky. If nothing untoward happened, his timing should be perfect.

Brother Columbanus looked up from his work. Already the darkness, held at bay only by the small circle of light from the gently flickering flame, was softening. He paused. By now the field hands would be leading the cattle from the byres to the pasture behind the Abbey, the cooks in the kitchen would be waiting for the yeast to make the dough rise a second time before putting the loaves in the ovens. He bent willingly to his task.

Ragnar's raiding party silently climbed a small rise. They had made excellent time. Before they reached the crest, Ragnar motioned for them to halt. He dropped to his belly, covering the last few yards prone so that his silhouette would not break the skyline. The Abbey lay below him. Between the small hill where he crouched and the walls of the outbuildings was an open field. To the left of the field ran a ditch with overgrown banks. The ditch curved gently round from the hill and disappeared behind the rough-hewn rock walls. Dawn was breaking. Their route had brought the Norsemen to the west of the Abbey. Any defenders would be limned against the light of the watery sun that even now was breaking through the thin cloud cover. In the field below, Ragnar could clearly see a herd of shaggy cattle, watched over by a solitary cow-herd. Ragnar turned, pointed at two of his men, and beckoned. When they were lying beside him he simply pointed to the ditch, pointed to the cow-herd, and drew his right index finger sharply across his throat. As he did so he smiled.

The first weak rays of the rising sun spilled over the window ledge and fell upon Columbanus's desk. The goldleaf of the trumpet he was just completing sparkled like the ripples of a trout stream. He wanted to extinguish the lamp, but a cloud passed over the sun's face and the gloom returned. He sighed resignedly and continued working. Sounds of a cheerful conversation from the courtyard below rose through the window. Columbanus smiled.

The cow-herd looked up sharply as the beasts began to run to the far corner of the field. Before he had time to wonder why, a rough hand was clamped over his mouth, dragging his head backwards as a knee was jammed into the small of his back, thrusting his body in the opposite direction. The blade bit from ear to ear and crunched into a vertebra. The two Vikings, crouching low, hurriedly dragged their thrashing victim into the ditch, holding him above its scum-covered surface until he was quite limp. They silently lowered the bloody corpse into the water. For the second time that morning an owl hooted.

Columbanus lifted his head. He had heard the owl. He took great joy from the birds that lived all around and had made some study of their habits. Not often had he heard an owl after the sun had risen. He was filled with simple wonder. He had been hoping that now the great work was almost finished, after eight long but satisfying years, the Abbot would allow him to start on a project he had secretly cherished for

quite some time, an illuminated rendering of the great Gospels. But it
was to be a departure from the earlier style. Instead of the usual old
Celtic serpents and the recently introduced Vulgate symbols, the An-
gel for Saint Matthew, the Lion for Mark, the Ox for Luke, and the
Eagle for John, he dearly wanted to introduce some of the humbler
local animals. Perhaps this was a sign that the Abbot would approve.

The Norsemen burst over the wall, Ragnar in the vanguard, each
roaring his ferocious battle-cry, each bound for honour in battle or
Valhalla, though how much honour was to be gained from butchering
these meek men of the mild Christian God remained to be seen. The
monks in the courtyard tried to flee, scattering like a flock of teal
when the hunter flings his net, and with as little success. It mattered
not whether they ran, fell on their knees in anguished prayer, or tried
to defend themselves with hoes or long, narrow turf spades, the great
axes rose and fell, cleaving through slane handles and skulls with the
same arrogant ease.

The Abbot rushed into the scriptorium where Columbanus and his
six terrified fellows crowded the window slits looking helplessly over
the carnage below. As they watched, one of the Norsemen grabbed a
fleeing monk by his cowl, rammed a dagger into his belly, and with
no apparent effort hurled the screaming man into the pigsty. Already
a knot of attackers was heading for the stairway that led to their room.
Frantically, the Abbot and Columbanus marshalled the other monks.
The copy of the *Caltach* from which they had been working and the
piles of completed parchments were hurriedly bundled together and
hidden in a cupboard in a corner where ordinarily the monks stored
their pens and inks.

The door was flung open. Ragnar stood at the head of his men,
bloody axe in hand, panting slightly from his exertions. The Abbot
fell to his knees, followed by the other monks. He began to pray.

"Pater noster . . ." was as far as he got before Ragnar seized him by
the throat and dragged him to his feet. Ragnar spoke no Latin but
had one word of Irish.

"*Ór*," he demanded, "gold." When no reply was forthcoming he
hurled the Abbot from him, grabbed one of the other monks, and

forced his head across a desk where moments before a parchment had lain. He raised his axe.

"Gold, gold."

When the Abbot failed to reply the axe swung down, decapitating the wretched brother and spraying the room with his blood. The Abbot vomited. Ragnar shrugged and motioned to his men, who fell upon their cowering victims. Columbanus was the last to die, and his despairing efforts to distract the savages from the cupboard only served to draw it to their attention.

One of the axemen opened the cupboard door, reached inside, and handed the piles of parchment to Ragnar, who glanced at them briefly before stuffing them into a large leather pouch that hung at this waist. Satisfied at last that the scriptorium contained no worthwhile booty, Ragnar's group returned to the now ominously quiet courtyard. Corpses lay pathetically where they had fallen. Some of the invaders were following dark trails to the places where the wounded had dragged themselves in futile attempts to escape. There was to be no escape.

A cry from the chapel brought Ragnar at the run. There, in the cool, dim light, stood his goal, the intricately patterned gold and silver altarware, the crosses, chalices, and silver plates. He roared out his approval. Carelessly scattering the leaves of parchment from his satchel, he greedily grabbed the nearest cross and jammed it in. In moments the chapel was stripped of all its finery. In the rush, the illuminated manuscript, the fruits of the labours of seven men for eight years, was trampled into shreds of gilded animal skin.

Jean Swanson closed the book and looked up at the class, searching the upturned faces to see if the murders she had just described had worried anyone. She could detect no signs of any concern and wondered for a moment if these children had become inured to killings.

"Well now, children," she said, "that's the story of our Abbey here in Bangor, and why the ancient history books of Ireland do not mention it from 839 till 871. It was during those years that the Vikings raided our coasts. What do you think of the story?"

Nonie held up her hand.

"Yes, Nonie."

"I think it's awful sad."

"Awfully."

"Yes. I think it's awfully sad, those poor monks like, all that work like, and them—"

"Those."

"Yes. Those awful Vikings." The child shuddered.

"They were awful, weren't they? Let's see what anyone else has learned from the story."

A boy in the back row held up his hand.

She nodded at him. "Yes, Peter?"

"Keep away from Vikings, Miss."

Several of the children laughed. Jean Swanson's own lips curled up in a little smile. "I think that would certainly be wise."

Nonie held her hand up again.

"Nonie?"

"Miss, did they kill everybody?"

"As far as we can tell, they did indeed kill everyone—and burn the Abbey down too." Jean watched the girl frown and hesitate before she said, "It's a bit like today, isn't it, Miss, like with the Troubles and the poor people getting blown up?"

"Yes, it is a lot like today. That's why we should understand that killing is wrong. The story tells us that this could be a beautiful country if only there was peace." She smiled. At least one of the children had noticed.

One of the boys held up his hand. Good gracious. Had red-haired Michael seen something too?"

"Yes, Michael?"

"Was them monks—?"

"Were those."

"Aye, were those monks Catholics?"

"Yes."

"Served them bloody well right."

1983

On January 16, members of the IRA shot Judge William Doyle as he was leaving Sunday mass in Belfast.

On June 9, in the general election, Sinn Fein took 13.4 percent of the vote in Northern Ireland. Gerry Adams was returned with 16,379 votes as the member for West Belfast.

On July 13, four Ulster Defence Regiment soldiers were killed in County Tyrone by an IRA landmine.

On August 5, twenty-two IRA suspects were convicted on the evidence of an informer, Christopher Black. The prisoners received sentences totalling more than four thousand years.

On November 21, gunmen of the Irish National Liberation Army shot and killed three people and wounded seven others, at Darkley Mountain Gospel Lodge Pentecostal Church in Armagh City. The sounds of the massacre were caught on a tape recorder being used to record the service.

1983 Dead 77   **Total Dead 2,446**

BALLYSALLAGH
1983

Neill changed gears to negotiate another turn in the twisty Bangor to Belfast Old Road. It was great to have Pat snoozing there in the passenger seat. It had been a while since he had lolled there.

Neill squinted as the rising sun spilled through the leaves, making it difficult for him to see. The road was straighter now. He changed up, driving under ageless elms that he had known since he had been a schoolboy. Their boughs arched overhead, roofing for a verdant cathedral.

The trees grew behind the low, moss-and-ivy-covered dry-stone boundary of the Clandeboye estate, hereditary land of the Marquis of Dufferin and Ava. Lord O'Neill. Descendant of the *Ui Niàll*, the clan that had ruled Ulster since before Neill's Spanish forebear had been washed ashore.

He screwed up his eyes against the glare. Something was moving on the road immediately ahead and Neill jammed on the brakes.

"What the hell are you doing?"

"Sorry." Neill leant back and let his taut seatbelt slacken. "Look." Three pheasants were crossing the road, two hens muted in their khaki pinafores, a green-headed cock proudly strutting in his white-collared morning suit, its maroon lapels and tan-and-black striped tails brilliant in a patch of sunlight. "Wouldn't mind a shot at that big fellow."

Pat harrumphed. "I wouldn't mind still being asleep."

Neill turned. "You all right?"

Pat grinned. "I'll live. Come on. I want to get a fly on the water before the morning rise is over."

"Right," said Neill, driving on.

Ten minutes later he turned the car into a familiar, narrow, rutted lane and jolted over the uneven surface until he reached the open banks of Ballysallagh Reservoir. "We're here." He opened the door and stepped out onto a wide grassy ride that ran down to the half-dressed, granite-block banks of the man-made lake. Neill filled his lungs. The air was fresh, clean, pine-scented from the surrounding conifers of a reafforestation scheme—and away to hell-and-gone from Belfast. He strolled to the rear of the car.

Pat was already fussing round the open boot, pulling out rod cases and creels. Neill stood and watched as Pat slipped two rod halves from their canvas sleeve. There was a pleasing symmetry to the long pieces of split-cane—brown, varnished, light, well balanced. Pat rubbed the brass ferrule of one end of the rod through his hair, still fair but thinner than when Neill had last seen his friend, lubricating the metal with natural oils. He slipped the ferrule into its socket in the butt end.

"Here," said Pat. "All you have to do is fit the reel and run the line through the guides. You haven't forgotten how?"

"Away off and chase yourself." Pat grinned and his blue eyes twinkled behind his spectacles. Those were new.

Neill laughed. It was good to have Pat back, if only for a couple of weeks. Neill finished assembling his tackle, slung his creel, tossed the rod case into the back of the car, closed the door, and turned to see Pat, rod over his shoulder, waiting.

Neill set off towards the water's edge, remarking, "Come on, Izaak Walton. What's keeping you?"

"Just getting used to the place again," said Pat, falling into step.

Neill halted near the bank and studied the surface of the water, grey where it lay under the streamers of mist, eggshell-blue beneath the summer sky, the great granite blocks perfectly mirrored in the water below, every fleck of flint and patch of lichen reflected in exact detail. In the far corner of the lake, a family of coots swam. Beneath each little bird its image in the water was blurred by the waves of the wake of their passage.

Pat pointed with his rod tip. Neill followed the direction, seeing a disturbance out in the middle of the lake, a small splash in the centre of a series of rapidly spreading rings. A rise. A fish had come to the surface. The ripples faded and only the dabbling of the coots disturbed the surface of Ballysallagh.

He turned to see Pat looking pensive. What was he thinking about?

"What flies do you reckon?" Pat asked.

Neill pulled a silvery fly-box from a pocket. "Take some of these." He pointed one blunt finger at rows of perfectly crafted caddis larvae imitations. He'd sat up tying them last night after Pat had gone early to bed, tired after his flight.

Pat helped himself to four, hooking the tips into the band of his tweed Paddy hat. "Thanks, Neill."

"My pleasure." Neill closed the box and continued, "If there's no surface feeding, the fish will be on the bottom. Try those nymphs on a sinking line." Neill suddenly realized that Pat was paying no attention. He stood there, head cocked to one side like a blackbird waiting for a worm. Was that the beginning of a frown?

"What's up?"

"Just listening."

"To what?" All Neill could hear was the far-off calling of wood-pigeons and collared doves. "I don't hear anything."

Pat smiled. "That's what I mean. I'd forgotten how quiet this place can be. It's wonderful."

"Aye," said Neill wistfully. "I know." He didn't feel like saying anything else, and stood there watching his old friend. Pat had put on a bit of weight. He'd always been one for a laugh and round his eyes indelible marks, little crow's feet, were half-hidden by the legs of his spectacles. It is quiet at Ballysallagh, Neill thought. Especially when you're out here on your own. "Well," he said, "we can either stand here all day listening to the sounds of silence, or we could try to catch a fish."

"Come on, then." Pat started to walk along the bank, long rod vibrating in his hand. Neill followed, striding over the grass, admiring the way the dew sparkled, thinking how transient the droplets were and how they would fade as the day moved along. Here and there tiny yellow flowers peeped through the taller blades.

Pat stopped and knelt. "Look at this. Pretty isn't it?"

Neill bent down to see a spider's web hanging between two benweeds, concentric, octagonal rings spread on silk spokes, the dew droplets on the threads making tiny rainbows of the sunlight.

"Unless you're an insect." He pointed to a corner of the web where a small grasshopper struggled against the gossamer chains. "He's not going to get out." He looked up and saw sadness in Pat's eyes. Was he thinking that his friend was like the 'hopper, stuck here in the web that was Ulster? Neill used his finger to part the strands that held the little green creature. "Go on. Beat it." He saw the spider watching him. "You'll soon have it fixed. You'll not miss one that got away."

Pat was smiling.

"Right." Neill straightened. "I'll stay here. You push on a bit."

"Tight lines," said Pat as he started off along the bank.

Neill waited for a moment, watching him go. How many times had they shared this stretch of water? He turned and looked across the lake. The mist was almost gone and the sun laid a golden swath across the blue underlay of the water. Still. Not a breath of wind. He would have liked a breeze, not strong enough to make casting difficult, but with enough force to raise ripples on the surface, ripples that would hinder a fish's abilities to detect the leader attached to the fly.

He looked along the bank. There was Pat, about a hundred yards away, rod in fluid action, a thin parabola of line arcing out over the water, drops falling, fly drifting onto the surface far from the shore.

What a great way to spend a morning. No time to dwell on weighty matters when all his concentration had to be focused on choosing the right fly, trying to read the water and the timeless rhythm of cast and retrieve, cast and retrieve. Neill cast twice in the same spot then moved a couple of paces to his right, following Pat who was slowly making his way round the bank.

The rod tip twitched and Neill struck. No. Missed that one. Never mind. Cast and retrieve. Cast and retrieve. He heard a faint splashing and looked to where Pat stood, rod angled high, tip bowed, taut line running to a flurry on the surface. A faint "Whoop" sounded over the water. Neill smiled.

Cast and retrieve. Cast and retrieve. No luck. It didn't really matter. The sun was warm on his back and the mist gone from the lake. Wood-pigeons called, liquid sounds from the beech woods over in the estate. He watched as the dragonflies, enamel-green and metallic-maroon—insect helicopters and deadly killers—hovered and swooped over the surface, murdering flies that had been lucky enough to escape the fish below. At least, he thought, you do it because you're hungry and it's in your nature.

He started as the silence was shattered by a harsh clattering overhead. He looked up to see an army Lynx helicopter beat its raucous way over the Holywood hills. Neill growled, "Bugger off," even though he knew that overhead security patrols did keep the number of attacks down. He preferred dragonflies.

He glanced along the bank to where Pat worked the water. Pat waved and Neill returned the greeting. He'd be damned if he was going to let the intrusion of moments ago spoil his day. It might be the last he'd share with Pat out here for quite some time.

Cast and retrieve. Cast and retrieve. Two steps to the right.

He heard a rustling behind him. He ignored his line, letting it drift, and sank slowly to his hunkers, watching.

A black, whisker-twitching snout poked from between the grass tussocks. It was followed by a pointed muzzle, jet eyes, tiny ears. The creature's nostrils whiffled, searching for danger, the eyes darted, never still. Neill waited until the otter humped his sleek body forward, running across the turf of the verge and down over the granite blocks.

The little animal's round, fat tail brought sudden, bittersweet memories of Grouse, companion of countless shooting trips to Strangford. The otter slid effortlessly into the water and began swimming alongside the bank. He must have seen the man there because he sank suddenly, leaving only a swirl on the surface. Neill smiled, looking at the wavelets. Grouse could swim as well but did not have the otter's ability to submerge.

Gone now, put to sleep when he'd developed a cancer as big as an orange. The vet had been right when he said you had to know when to let go. Neill looked along the bank again seeing Pat, his shadow foreshortened on the water. Aye, it is hard to let go. Neill stood and watched, scanning the water, and was rewarded with one more glimpse of the otter as the animal surfaced to breathe, out in the middle. Neill watched him, silently wishing the little creature well.

He had been so intent in following the otter's progress that he had failed to notice Pat's approach until he said, "So?"

Neill turned and saw Pat grinning as he held a fat rainbow trout for inspection.

"See the otter?"

"Aye. No wonder you're not catching anything. What do you think of this one?"

"That's a beauty."

"Not bad." Neill swung the creel off his shoulder. "Lunch?"

Pat sat on the soft grass. "As long as it's not cold sausages."

"Or curry." Neill joined Pat on the ground. He pulled ham sandwiches wrapped in grease-proof paper from the creel and set two bottles of Bass ale beside the packages on the grass. "Here, get stuck into that." He handed a sandwich to Pat. "You'll not get ham like that in Canada."

Pat's words were indistinct as he chewed. "You're right." He uncapped a bottle and took a huge swallow. "Nor a decent beer."

Neill wiped froth from his lip. "Are you glad to be back?"

Pat nodded vigorously. "Aye. I miss the place you know."

"You're away three years, now?"

"Aye. Doesn't seem that long."

It does to me. Neill kept the thought to himself.

Pat handed over his bottle. "Dead man. Have you another in there?"

"Sure. Here."

"Ta." Pat set the bottle on the grass and reclined, propping himself up with his arms outstretched behind his back. "I do miss the place.

I bloody nearly wept when the plane headed into Aldergrove airport. We flew up over Strangford Lough. I could see the Long Island. We were so low I could make out the sheep-cot. Do you ever get down there?"

Neill shook his head. "Getting too old. Can't take the cold the way I used to."

Pat laughed. "You're not that old. You should try the cold in Toronto in the winter. Minus forty."

"Minus forty?"

"Well. Minus twenty."

Neill shuddered. He could barely imagine how cold that must be. "Phyllis likes it there?"

"Took to it like a duck to water. Kids are doing well too. Colin's at school now. She didn't want to take him out of class. This was the only two weeks I could get off."

"She didn't mind you coming over on your own?"

"Not at all. She's in no raging hurry to come to Ulster."

"So," said Neill, "I don't suppose you'd think of coming back?"

Pat rolled over onto his belly. He stared down at the grass for a long moment. "I would," Neill took a short breath, letting it out as Pat continued, "but I'd need a good lawyer."

Neill frowned. "Sure you'd not need an immigration lawyer to get back in. You were born here."

Pat laughed. "No, a divorce lawyer. Phyllis wouldn't leave. Not now."

"Oh."

"Don't look so disappointed. You can hardly blame her. Nobody's shooting at her over there."

Neill folded his arms across his chest. "It's not as bad as the papers make out."

Pat hesitated before he said, "Really?"

"Aye. Well." Neill looked down. "That was a big one in Belfast last night." He raised his eyes. "But no one was hurt."

Pat put a hand on Neill's arm. "You don't really want to talk about it, do you?"

Neill let a sliver of teeth show above his lower lip. "Not much." He inhaled deeply. "You have to try to put it out of your mind. There's bugger all anyone can do anyway." He stood up. "Come on, let's see if we can get one or two more fish."

Pat handed over his empty bottle and Neill finished repacking the creel. He buckled it shut, busying himself. He heard Pat rise, felt a hand on his shoulder. He looked up straight into Pat's eyes.

"Neill, are you still mad that I left?"

Neill smiled. "Not at all. You just surprised me back then when you said you were going." He held out his hand and Pat took it, threw his other arm round Neill's shoulder and hauled him into an enormous bear-hug. For a moment he stiffened, then hugged back. "Come on, you daft bugger. Let's catch some fish."

"Thanks, Neill," said Pat.

Neill stepped back. "For what?"

Pat shook his head. "Just thanks. That's all."

Neill nodded and looked to the lake. "I reckon we should give the far bank a try. There might be a mayfly hatch over there."

"Lead on, MacDuff." Pat shouldered his rod.

Neill sent Pat on to one of the best spots on the lake. This would be his only day's fishing. He was flying back in two weeks and the pair of them had plenty to do between now and then. If the weather was decent tomorrow they were going to row the punt out to the Long Island. Just for the trip. Places to go. Old acquaintances to look up. And there was someone Neill wanted Pat to meet. Funny he hadn't got round to telling him about her. Too much catching up since the plane had landed yesterday. Neill watched Pat start to fish. Good luck. Neill knew he could come here to Ballysallagh anytime he wanted. If he wanted.

Cast and retrieve. Cast and retrieve. No fish but it didn't matter. Just being here was enough, Neill thought. Like old times, enjoying his own company, and Pat's at lunch, comfortable that his friend was just along the bank where he belonged.

Neill watched the shadows lengthen as the sun travelled round the firmament. He heard the quiet of the late afternoon broken by the evensong of the birds—blackbird and thrush, mellifluous in the little forest, homeward-bound rooks raucous, high overhead.

Something caught his eye, difficult to see, now that the sun was sliding down towards the far Antrim Hills, the light fading. Not far from the shore a tiny disturbance had appeared on the surface. He watched more closely. More rings, here, there, and everywhere, as if a fine drizzle had started, drops dancing on the lake, their footprints circles on the water. In the centre of each, a tiny insect, lace-winged, ephemeral, rested on the surface for a while before taking flight to search through the gloaming for a mate. Mayfly. A hatch.

Neill cupped his hands to his mouth and yelled, "Hatch. Hatch," and saw Pat's answering wave. "Get a dry fly on and a floating line." Again Pat waved.

Neill scrambled down the granite to the water's edge, scooped a handful, and peered intently into the palm of his hand, careless of the drips falling from his fingers. He held a tiny insect—erect, broad, lacy wings, two pairs, segmented body, three sharp hairs sticking rigidly from its tail. He fumbled for a fly-box, hurriedly comparing the natural imago with the rows of artificial ones inside. He selected carefully for both size and colour, matching the dun of the insect's thorax with wool of a similar hue on the dry fly. It only took a moment to tie the snell of the hook to the leader. His ears told him what he wanted to hear. Above the chorus of the birds there was a new refrain, played by a liquid percussion section of splashes as trout rose, all over the lake, sometimes arcing above the surface, feeding on the mayfly.

Neill stood alert, watching. There, about fifteen yards from where he stood, and again. Twice in quick succession a mayfly had been dragged below the surface, leaving a heavy swirl to show where the trout had risen. Again.

He lifted his rod, letting the line fly out behind so that its weight would bend the tip of the cane, storing energy in its flexible fibres to propel the line ahead when he brought his arm forward. He repeated the action again and again, methodically, patiently, never letting the cast touch the surface, gradually paying out more line, until he judged the tippet to be over the place the fish should be. Satisfied at last, he let the fly drift down onto the water, lightly, gently, like a single dandelion seed.

The surface tension held the little creation of wool and feathers and deerhair afloat, drifting slowly until suddenly it vanished. He felt the tug and struck, driving the barbed hook firmly into the fish's bony jaw.

The trout ran, stripping line from the reel. Neill heard the ratchets scream. He held the rod tip high, watching it bend, supple and strong, absorbing the shock of the pull on the fine nylon leader. The rays of the setting sun flashed from silvery scales and made the lateral stripe blaze with purple and indigo as the trout leapt and leapt again, churning the waters. And still the reel sang. This was a big fish.

He waited, letting the trout complete its run before starting to reel in. He recovered almost half of the line that had been taken before the fish ran again. You really want to go, he thought, but I'm not going to let you. He applied pressure again. The rod flew backwards, line hanging limply from its tip. "Bugger," he said and laughed at himself.

Neill stood in the gentle evening, softly chuckling at his stubborn belief that he had the skills to keep such a big rainbow, its mind set on freedom. He should have known better. He wished the fish Godspeed, while the velour dusk turned to velvet night.

Time for home. He walked along the bank looking up occasionally to watch the stars come out over Ballysallagh Reservoir. Gnats buzzed and the moths fluttered. Somewhere in the Clandeboye estate an owl hooted, mournful first cousin to the banshee.

"Well?" asked Pat.

Neill shrugged. "I'd a beauty, but I lost him."

Pat clapped him on the shoulder and laughed. "Never worry. I've three more. That's a pair apiece." There was no gloating in his voice. "But you can buy the beer on the way home."

Neill shook his head. "I've a better idea."

"Than a beer?"

"Yes. It's only nine o'clock. Let's take the fish round to Helen's place. We'll pick up a decent bottle of wine on the way and we can clean and cook the fish there."

"Helen? Who the hell's Helen?"

Neill thought of her. The first woman he'd met who didn't mind his outdoor hobbies. Divorced. Two youngsters about the age of Pat's. A slow smile and a deep laugh.

"I said, 'Who's Helen?'"

Neill took Pat by the arm and started to propel him towards the parked car. "Just someone I'd like you to meet. She's heard a lot about you."

Pat stopped dead, turned and said, with a huge grin, "You crafty old devil. I'd love to meet her. Anyway, I want her to hear my side."

1984

On March 14, Gerry Adams, president of Sinn Fein, the political arm of the Provisional IRA, was wounded in an attack by Loyalists.

On June 5, the RUC men accused of murdering three unarmed IRA members in Lurgan in 1982 were acquitted.

On October 12, The Grand Hotel, Brighton, site of the Conservative Party's conference, was bombed. The explosives had been hidden behind a panel in the bathroom of Room 629. The blast occurred at 2:54 a.m. Five people were killed and many more, including Norman Tebbit and his wife, who were buried for hours under the debris, were wounded. The Provisional IRA claimed responsibility and expressed regret that they had failed to kill British prime minister Margaret Thatcher.

1984 Dead 64   **Total Dead 2,510**

1985

On February 28, the Provisional IRA launched a mortar attack on the RUC station at Newry, County Down. Nine officers were killed, seven men and two women.

On May 20, the Provisional IRA bombed the Killeen customs post on the Ulster-Republic of Ireland border, killing four RUC men.

On July 12, in Portadown, County Armagh, an Orange parade commemorating the seventeenth-century victories of the Protestant King William over the Catholic King James, tried to march through the Catholic Obins Street and an area known as The Tunnel. Fifty-two RUC officers were injured when they attempted to interfere.

On August 19, Seamus McAvoy was shot dead in his bungalow in Dublin. He ran a company that had supplied portable buildings to the Army and the RUC.

On November 21, Kurt Koenig, a German who had worked as a catering manager for the RUC, was murdered in Derry by the Provisional IRA.

1985 Dead 54   **Total Dead 2,564**

1986

In March, a Catholic family was forced to leave its home in a Protestant area between the towns of Strabane and Derry, County Londonderry, and relocate to a Catholic suburb. They had been constantly harassed and had received letters with such messages as, "Get out, you Fenian bastards," and "Bottles today, bullets tomorrow." A Protestant friend of one of the boys in the family was warned by fellow Protestants that unless he severed the friendship, he would be kneecapped.

On March 31, riots broke out in Portadown, County Armagh, when the RUC banned a Loyalist parade.

On July 23, three RUC officers were shot to death by members of the Provisional IRA.

On the night of August 7,500 Loyalists crossed the border into County Monaghan, savagely beat two Gardai officers, and marched through the village of Clontibret.

On November 11, 2,000 Loyalists paraded through Kilkeel, County Down.

1986 Dead 61   **Total Dead 2,625**

THE GUN

"Away off and chase yourself, you're too wee to get into this." Aidan's big brother Val smiled as he tousled the youngster's hair. "Wait 'til you're grown."

Aidan knew better than to ask twice to accompany Val. When Val said, "No," he meant it. But Aidan doted on his elder brother—would have given his right arm for Val—and, with the fierce loyalty of a thirteen-year-old, wanted to emulate his hero's every action. Aidan wished he knew exactly what "this" was. But if Val was involved, it had to be right.

"Is it to do with the Prods again?"

The smile faded from Val's face. "Aye." He frowned. "I'm sick of them. Me and my mates is all sick of them. Orange bastards."

Aidan looked up at Val, the man who helped with his lessons, took him to the hurling matches and the Gaelic football games on Sundays, and slipped him twenty P every Saturday. Val looked very cross, at someone.

Aidan hurried to show that he understood. "I'm sick of them too, and I'm tired of them calling us Catholics 'Bloody Fenians,' or 'Micks,' or 'Taigs,' as if we were just some kind of dirt." He screwed up his eyes and tried to look as fierce as Val. "Why do they, anyway?"

"Because they hate us, and because they're scared of us."

Aidan recognized the serious tone in his brother's voice, the one he usually used when Aidan had been caught in some transgression, like not doing his sums.

"You mind what I've told you before. You keep away from them." There was a finality in the way Val spoke.

Aidan looked solemn and nodded his head.

"Good." The smile was back on Val's face. "Now, you get on with your homework. No going out to play until it's done. I'm away out." He spoke sternly, but Aidan knew his brother was joking. "Fifty lashes if you don't get all the sums right. I'll look at them when I get back," Val said as he walked into the hall, leaving Aidan alone in the cramped front parlour of the Belfast terrace house, the room where Da had decreed that his three children were to be given peace to study.

Aidan sighed. He wished his father had as much time for helping with their schoolwork as he used to before he lost his job four years ago. Da seemed more interested in going to the pub or the bookie's now. But Val cared.

Aidan hated maths, wanted instead to go to the shed at the back of the yard to examine his secret find, but knew he must do as Val had said.

The tortured face of Christ on his crucifix, hanging on the wall beside three plastic ducks, caught Aidan's eye. I know how you feel, Aidan thought, grinning. They probably made you do arithmetic too.

He carried his satchel over to the little table under the crucifix, his mind returning to the subject of the Prods. Val and his big friends certainly hated them and were working for the day Ulster would be free. On that day, Aidan secretly hoped, his da would be able to buy the bicycle that Aidan so desperately coveted.

He started to pull out his schoolbooks. Val had come home a bit the worse for wear the other night, battered like the old leather schoolbag, aye, and twice in the last year he had brought home a friend, bruised and bleeding. Whatever Val and his mates were doing seemed to carry a price. Aidan flipped his head back, tossing aside a fair cowlick that had fallen over his left eye. One day, one day soon, he would be old enough to help Val; indeed that day might be sooner than Val knew. Aidan had a secret.

It would have to wait. He opened his exercise book, grabbed his pencil, and started his homework. Get this done, and he could go and examine the treasure he had found on his way home from school this afternoon.

He hadn't quite finished the last question when the door to the room opened, and Fiona stuck her blonde head round the door. "Come on, Aidan. Supper's ready."

Sisters. Just because she was sixteen, she thought herself grown-up. Aidan ignored her and concentrated on dividing 946 by 81, which was the last step in the stupid maths problem about men digging ditches.

She raised her voice. "Aidan. Ma'll be mad if you don't come."

He put down the pencil and closed the book. "Right, your majesty." He stood up. "I'd not want to keep you late for the dance tonight." He ducked the slap she threw at him. Girls. All they ever thought about was clothes and dances. He had more important things to do. In the shed, after supper. Not long now.

He unlatched the back door of the kitchen, letting himself out into the tiny yard, a small concrete enclosure hemmed in by high, moss-encrusted red brick walls. He shivered. It was cold and gloomy. In the early summer evening, the sun's light was strangled by the smoke haze and blocked by the factory walls across the street from his home.

Aidan made his way quickly through the stored family cast-offs—an old pram, the cat's litterbox, untidy piles of old roofing slates, old motorcar tyres. He paused for a moment looking at the black rubber. Fat chance Da was ever going to buy a car. Val might though. Val was twenty-two and had finished his apprenticeship as a cabinet-maker. He brought home good money, and Aidan had made up his mind to be a cabinet-maker too, just like Val. Val wanted his young brother to study and try to get a scholarship to university. Aidan smiled as he thought of the number of times Val had told him that there was a better way to earn a living than with your hands. Val did all right with his hands. Aidan would too.

He had to push hard to open the door of the shed, a dilapidated construction of rusting corrugated iron where Val kept his bicycle and his carpenter's tools. Here, this afternoon, Aidan had hidden his find, hidden it in the darkest corner of the shed, buried deeply beneath a pile of old sacks and broken flowerpots.

The poorly fitting planks of the door scraped over the concrete, leaving white scratches on the floor. He closed the door. Only a pale light filtered through the single, cobwebbed window but it was enough to see by until he had rigged a makeshift curtain with one of the sacks from the heap. Only then did Aidan pull the string above his head to switch on the bare light bulb. He wanted no one to see what he was doing. He took a deep breath, blew it out slowly, and hurriedly pulled the potsherds and sacking aside.

The old revolver was still there.

Aidan lifted it with both hands, marvelling at the weight of it. He knew it must be old by the rust. It certainly wasn't in great shape. The handle looked very funny. He held the gun up to the light. In the movies, John Wayne's six-shooters had covers over the butt yet Aidan could see right through the frame of this one. There was a strange collection of levers and springs in there.

He laid the gun on the workbench and stood, arms folded, admiring his treasure and thinking about how lucky he had been to find it.

He'd been coming home from school, trailing his satchel. An open lorry had been held up in the heavy traffic. Aidan was no stranger to the Belfast street sport of stealing rides. He'd nipped over the tailgate and hidden behind the pile of scrap metal on the truck bed. Something sticking out from the heap of rusting iron bars and bent pieces of scrap had caught his eye. He'd seen enough Westerns to recognize the cylinder of the old revolver for what it was. Curiosity aroused, he had tugged the gun free, holding it in both hands. The last couple of inches of the barrel were squashed flat, as if someone had crushed the muzzle in a metal-press. It was a real pistol.

He'd looked around quickly, but no one was looking so he'd stuffed the gun into his satchel, rearranging his books to make room. The truck had stopped at a traffic light and the driver was coming round from his cab. He did not look happy to see Aidan, who knew that the price of a free ride could be a clout about the ears.

He jumped over the side and fled, hearing the driver yell, "I'll get you the next time, you wee bugger."

Aidan had run all the way home, heavy schoolbag bumping on his hip. Once in the safety of his own backyard, he had gone straight to the shed and hidden his new possession. He stood looking at it now, wondering if he could fix it. Maybe he could make sides for the butt. He could cut out the pieces in wood-working class. He turned the gun over. It shouldn't be too hard to saw off the flattened end of the barrel. When he'd done that he'd have something like the snub-nosed revolver he'd seen Humphrey Bogart use in *The Maltese Falcon*. He hardly dared to hope that he could actually get it to work, anyway he couldn't get bullets, but once it was fixed, he'd be the envy of all of the rest of his pals the next time they played Provos and Brits.

He picked it up again. It really was heavy. He tried to turn the six-chambered cylinder, but it wouldn't budge. He flicked his hair out of his eyes. Why wouldn't the cylinder move? He tried pulling the trigger. It only gave a little, but the cylinder started to turn. Right. The trigger made the cylinder move. He squeezed again, peering intently at the springs and levers in the butt. They seemed to want to work in sequence but were covered in red rust.

He put the gun back on the bench top and rummaged about in one of the drawers. He soon found the sandpaper and a can of 3-in-One oil he was looking for. He had no idea how to disassemble the firing mechanism and was scared to try in case he couldn't put it back together again. Instead he carefully dripped oil over the metal and, folding the sandpaper into a fine point, began working it back and forth over the most rusted parts.

The work was engrossing. He developed a simple routine—sand, examine, try to pull the trigger. It was helping. The more he sanded, the more easily he could pull the trigger. Now each time he tried, the hammer at the top of the butt began to move away from the body of the gun. At last, to Aidan's enormous delight, when he pulled, the hammer reached the full extent of its backwards excursion, the cylinder made a one-sixth rotation, and the hammer snapped forwards with a solid satisfying click.

He put the gun down, lifted an old rag, wiped the oil and rust off his hands, and thought of the looks of amazement that producing the gun would bring to the faces of his friends. Especially that smarty-ass Johnny Heaney.

He took the gun in the rag and began to polish it. Something was blocking the chamber that had been hidden before he had got the mechanism to work. The turn of the cylinder had exposed whatever was in there. He cleaned the place with the rag, squinting with concentration as he tried to make out what it was. He almost dropped the gun. Now that the dirt and rust were off, he could see a brass circle with a copper centre. Oh, Jesus.

Aidan set the pistol gingerly on the bench top and took two steps back, eyes widening, staring at the dull glint of the round. He crossed himself. "Holy Mary, Mother of God." This was a real gun with a real bullet in it. Now what was he going to do?

Maybe he should tell Val. Aye. Val. He thought about that for a while. No. No, he'd not tell his big brother. Not yet. Not until he finished the repairs. Then he would show Val a real working pistol. Johnny Heaney could just go and fuck himself. Making that wee skitter envious wouldn't be nearly as good as basking in Val's admiration.

Aidan stood savouring that thought and laughing at himself for being so scared a minute ago.

His pleasant daydream was interrupted by raised voices coming from his house. He started guiltily. He'd better hide the gun. He soaked the rag in oil, wrapped the revolver, and tucked the bundle under the sacks. He switched off the light and stood for a few moments in the dark before letting himself out into the yard. He must have been in the shed for a brave while. It was dark, and the streetlights were on. The kitchen curtains were drawn.

He waited, listening. Val and their da were having a row. Val must have come home while Aidan was so busy with the revolver. He could hear Da's voice raised in anger.

"For fuck's sake, Val, have you no bloody wit? What the hell do you and your Republican friends think you're going to do?"

Aidan could not hear Val's reply, but by the tone of Da's voice it had not been the right answer.

"Oh you are, are you? You and a bunch of toughs are going to teach the Prods a lesson. All ten of you are going to take on the whole bloody Orange Order." Aidan heard the sarcasm. "You'll likely scare them all to death."

"It's better than sitting in a pub, whining to your broken-down old friends about how unfair life is, how the Protestants get all the jobs and the houses."

"They do."

"I know. It's been like that forever. Do you think it's going to change if we do nothing?"

Aidan heard his father's derisive snort. "And you think that breaking a few heads will bring fair play to Belfast? Jesus. I suppose you believe in fucking fairies too?"

Aidan flinched. He'd heard Da get mad like this before.

Val's reply was weary, subdued, but spoken with great conviction. "I believe no such thing, but I do believe it's gone far enough. Anyway, when you heard me on the phone you got the wrong end of the stick as usual."

"What do you mean, wrong end of the stick?"

"Look. We've no notion of setting the world to rights. But we won't stand for what a bunch of fucking Prods did to my sister."

Fiona? What had happened to her? Aidan heard his father's gasp.

"What are you talking about?" His voice had lost its hectoring tone. He was obviously concerned. So was Aidan.

"Aye. Now you'll listen. Look. She was at that stupid dance, the ones Father Riley puts on so the young folks can get to know each other. You know, us Catholics and them Prods?"

"What about it?"

Aidan crept closer to the window.

"While our Fiona's dancing with this young lad from Sandy Row, one of his mates tried to put his hand up her dress."

"What?" Aidan could hear the outrage in Da's voice. "He never."

"He did. Now, fair play to the young lad, he told his mate to stop. The shite tells him to fuck off and pulls the front of her dress down."

Aidan closed his eyes and took a very deep breath. Fiona must have near died of shame. No wonder Val hated the Prods if they did things like that to a girl.

"Ah, Jesus, Val. That's rotten." Da sounded broken.

"It's worse. Do you know what he says? 'Them's Fenian titties'."

Aidan wondered why Fiona wasn't in the house now. Val's next remarks explained.

"Her friend Bridget took Fiona over to the McCallions. She's there now. I was having a word with Don McCallion when they came in. That's how I heard."

"Is she all right, son?"

"Oh, aye. She'll live, but that's why I came on home. The McCallions have no phone. You heard me talking to Brian about getting a few of the lads together and going round to teach that wee Protestant bastard manners."

Aidan heard the scrape of a chair on the floor. Da must have stood up. "That's dire. Hold on, I'll come with you."

"Not tonight, Da." Val's voice was calm. "Tonight I need to get away back up to the McCallions and keep an eye on Fiona. But we'll see to him soon. We know who he is and where he lives."

A shadow passed in front of the curtain, silhouetted by the light behind. "Good night, Da."

"Good night, son. Take care of your sister."

Aidan knew he had better go in.

When he entered the kitchen his father was standing, shoulders slouched, looking at the floor. He looked up when he heard the back door close. "Where the hell have you been? Your ma's away up to bed already. Go on. Bed."

Aidan could see that his da was angry and was trying hard not to take it out on his younger son. Aidan, who knew why, was only too pleased to obey.

"Goodnight, Da."

" 'Night, son. And listen." He was looking straight into Aidan's eyes. "You keep to hell away from those bloody Prods."

Aidan went upstairs. He was scared. Really scared. Val could get hurt. If he had the gun that would help. By the time Aidan was ready for bed he was more resolved than ever to fix the weapon and give it to Val.

Aidan dreamed of Val and guns and titties, and woke early, before anyone else was about. He dressed quietly and slipped downstairs. He took a pencil, some greaseproof paper, and a pair of scissors from the kitchen and went out to the shed. It was urgent now that he finish repairing the gun. He rapidly unwrapped it, laid it on the bench top, and used the pencil to trace the outline of the butt on the paper. It took only a moment to cut out rough templates with the scissors.

The revolver was rehidden and Aidan was sitting quietly at the breakfast table when Val appeared.

Val seemed his usual cheerful self.

"Toast and marmalade this morning, the bacon's all done for this week."

Aidan waited as Val made the toast, browning the white bread slices under the grill of the old gas stove. He wondered if Val would say anything about what had happened to their sister. His big brother took the pieces of toast and dropped them quickly onto a plate, blowing on his fingertips. "Hot," he said, flapping his hand.

"Fiona not having any?" Aidan asked, innocently, watching to see how Val would reply.

"No." Val finished spreading the marmalade. "Fiona stayed the night at the McCallions."

He handed the plate to Aidan. "Here. Get that into you."

Val was telling nothing. Aidan chewed his toast, thinking to himself. So that's the way of it. Away off and chase yourself. He smiled. Val would soon see that his little brother was not "too wee."

Aidan bolted his breakfast and ran all the way to school, hoping that if he arrived early, the morning would pass more quickly.

The first two classes, English and history, dragged. Aidan could barely wait for woodwork class. He helped himself to two pieces of ash, which he judged to be of about the right size. Using the paper patterns he traced out the shape he wanted and shyly approached the teacher.

"Excuse me, Mr. Kelly, could you cut these out for me?"

"Sure I will, Aidan, just a minute now. And what are they to be?"

"It's a surprise for me brother, sir."

"All right. Make sure it's a good one now." The teacher went to the band saw and soon returned with the shaped blocks of wood.

"Here you are, boy."

Aidan thanked him and returned to his bench. He used the templates to mark the places where he would need to make holes for the screws that would anchor the wooden handles to the butt. He used a brace and bit to drill the holes and a punch to deepen their tops so that any screw could be countersunk and not protrude above the surface. He didn't want the edges of a screw to hurt Val's hands. He carefully chamfered the edges of the new buttplates. He could do no more until he had tried them for size.

The rest of the day seemed to crawl. Aidan had trouble concentrating. He got yelled at in maths class for not paying attention, but how could men digging holes be as interesting as the way Val was going to look when Aidan gave him the gun?

And he thought of the shame of his sister. Aidan could still remember the day she had come out of the bathroom and he had seen her tits. Boy, she'd got angry. And last night a whole bunch of strangers had seen her—he hesitated even to think the word—breasts. No wonder Val and Da were so mad. Aidan reckoned that he was beginning to understand more about the Prods and why Val would see to them. No one was as strong as Val, and if Val had the gun . . .

At last school was over. Aidan didn't even stay to have a blether with Johnny Heaney and the rest of the lads who were hanging about the tarmac playground. Aidan was going straight home.

The house was empty. He used the door key that he kept on a string around his neck to let himself in. Hardly stopping to throw his satchel on the kitchen table, he ran to the shed. The revolver was waiting for him.

He oiled the insides of the butt for the last time, gently pulling the trigger to ensure that the mechanism still worked. The hammer rose and fell, smoothly advancing the chamber that contained the single bullet.

The wooden buttplates fitted almost perfectly. He found a couple of screw bolts which matched the threads of the sockets in the butt. It was the work of only a minute to fit them and screw them down snugly below the level of the wood. It took much longer to sandpaper the wood to a degree of smoothness that pleased Aidan.

Now for the barrel. He found a block of wood with which to support the butt and put the barrel into the jaws of the vice. It was convenient that whoever had crushed the metal had done so from side to side rather than up and down. The vice gripped the barrel firmly. Aidan lifted a hacksaw down from a rack. He chose his place carefully, far enough from the flattened piece that the circumference seemed to be a perfect circle. He took a deep breath and began to saw, slowly, deliberately, just as they had taught him in metalwork class.

The teeth of the saw bit, clean silver metal showing through the rust. Aidan sawed on, from time to time lubricating the blade with a few drops of oil. Before long, his action became easier as the blade entered the bore. He constantly checked to make sure the cut was true. The blade slowed as it re-entered solid metal at the undersurface. He paused. Just a few more strokes. He had to steady the butt as he finally severed the remaining sliver.

He examined his work closely. The new muzzle was rough to the touch, shining as he had seen newly cut steel do in metalwork class. He took a file and smoothed and smoothed away every last vestige of roughness. At last he was satisfied.

He held the revolver in both hands, looking at it from every angle. Not bad. He could tell that it was by no means perfect. The pale unvarnished wood of the new handles contrasted starkly with the rusty, pitted exterior of the cylinder and frame of the revolver. He turned it towards himself, peering closely at the muzzle. The bright new metal where the saw had cut was like a sparkling ring on the finger of a corpse. Aidan felt rightly proud of his work and he knew—he just knew—how proud Val would be. Now he had to wait for Val to come home and for the right moment to take him out to the shed and astound him.

He went into the house to find Ma sitting in the kitchen. She had her beefy, mottled legs propped up on a small stool.

"How are you, son?"

"I'm rightly, Ma."

"I'm done. Would you make us a cup of tea?"

"Aye, surely." He felt sorry for Ma. She always seemed to be tired. She never complained, but Aidan was sure that scrubbing other people's floors all day must take it out of her.

When the tea was made, he brought her a cup.

"Thanks. You not having any, Aidan?"

"Ach, no, Mammy. I've more sums to do the night."

"Go on then. I'll just have this in my hand and then I'll get the supper on." She smiled up at him. "You're a good lad, so you are."

His homework was done, supper over. Was Val never coming home? Da had left to play snooker at the pub. Fiona was out. She had refused to tell Aidan what she was so indignant about. Well, he wasn't going to let on that he already knew. He smiled inside, guessing that for all her mumping and moaning she was secretly rather enjoying her celebrity. Only Aidan and Ma remained, sitting at the table, Ma reading one of Fiona's fashion magazines and from time to time showing Aidan some pictures of skinny women in fancy dresses. As if he was interested in girls' stuff. And the prices. No one in this house was going to wear any of those clothes.

He fidgeted. What was keeping Val? Aidan stood up, ready to go out to the street to see if Val was coming when the front door opened with a bang. Val walked into the kitchen. Aidan flinched when he saw his brother's face. His right eye was closed and an angry welt burned on his cheekbone. He sat down heavily at the table, nursing the skinned knuckles of his right hand.

"Val. Have you been fighting?" Ma asked.

"I have, Ma. There's one of those Prod gits that won't be coming round to the dances here no more." He sucked his bruised knuckles and grinned at Aidan. "Now do you see why you'll need to grow a bit yet?" His grin was lopsided and he winced. "Aidan, would you get me a glass of water?"

The teachers had told the boys at Aidan's school the stories of Cu Chulainn and the Knights of the Red Branch, of their gallantry and prowess. Tonight Val was Aidan's Chu Chulainn and Finn McCool all in one. He went over and hugged his brother.

"I may not be as big as you, but I bet I could fight too."

Val's laugh was cut short by a heavy knocking at the front door. Ma went to answer it as Aidan moved over to the sink to get his brother the water.

Aidan heard Ma scream. Two big, angry men pushed her roughly out of the way and strode into the kitchen.

Val rose to meet them. He raised his fists. "What the fuck do you want? Get away to hell out of my house." Val half-turned, saying quietly, "Aidan, outside."

Aidan started towards his brother's side. Val cut him off.

"Out. Now. You'll not be a part of this." He pointed a finger at the two men. "I've just been sorting out one Prod bastard . . ."

"Our brother," the larger of the two said.

Aidan did not like the way the man was glaring at him. He looked back to Val. Could his big brother handle these two? They looked awful hard men.

"Get out, Aidan. You too, Ma. Run away up to the neighbours."

Ma tried to step past the intruders to where Aidan stood, but one of the men held out an arm and blocked her advance.

"You leave my lad alone." Ma said. "Come on, Aidan."

"Fuck off, dear." The smaller of the two shoved Ma, and she staggered as she was pushed away.

"You let him alone." Ma's voice was shrill and harsh. "Come with me right now, Aidan."

"I'm staying with Val." Aidan tried to sound brave.

"I'm not telling you again, missus. Fuck off."

Ma was crying as she left. Aidan watched her go along the hall. He swallowed. His throat was dry. Val was still there, but Aidan suddenly felt very small without his mother.

"Go on, bugger off like your brother told you," one of the strangers said softly. "We've no fight with babies." He stepped close to Val. "It's you we want, you Fenian shite."

Aidan could feel the hot tears starting, not tears of fear but tears of frustration because he could not think of what to do to help. The gun. It was in the shed, only a few steps away. The ugly looking Prod had said Aidan could go. He looked hard at his big brother, trying to tell him it would be all right. Not taking his eyes from Val's face, Aidan sniffed, blinked away his tears and said, with as much dignity as he could muster, "All right, I'm leaving. But if you hurt Val, I'll get you."

The other stranger laughed. "These bloody papishes are even poisonous when they're little. Piss off, you skitter."

Aidan left through the back door. He ran blindly to the shed, hurled back the sacks and unwrapped the revolver. It was there for him like an old friend. He tested the trigger. The cylinder moved slightly. The next squeeze would load and fire the bullet.

Aidan waited for just a little while until his rapid breathing slowed. He walked back deliberately, holding the heavy revolver in both hands in front of his chest. See how those two Prods liked this.

He almost let the gun drop as he re-entered the kitchen. One of the men was pinioning Val's arms as the other used him for a punching bag. Spittle flecked with blood flew from Val's puffed lips.

They were hurting Val. Bastards. Aidan held the gun out before him, no longer bothered by its weight.

"Let my brother go." His shrill voice cut at them. The puncher stopped in amazement.

"My God," he said, and Aidan took joy from the fear in the man's voice, "the git's got a gun."

"I'm not afraid to shoot." The barrel was pointed directly at the belly of Val's tormentor.

He looked at his companion.

"I think he means it," he said, backing away.

"I'm not for finding out," the other replied, releasing Val's arms. "Come on away to hell out of here."

Val staggered but remained standing. The strangers left.

God. Val looked awful. His already closed right eye was horribly swollen, his lower lip split, a trickle of blood running down his chin.

"Are you all right, Val?"

Val wiped the back of his hand across his mouth. "I'll live. Jesus, Aidan that was smart . . ."

Aidan's chest swelled.

". . . pretending you had a real gun."

"It is real. See?" Aidan held the revolver at arm's length. This was even better than he had dreamed. The lad who was "too wee" coming to the rescue.

Val's good eye narrowed. He took the gun. His mouth opened. "Jesus." He sat at the table, the old revolver dangling in one hand.

Aidan waited, hoping for more praise.

Val said nothing.

"It's got a bullet in it."

"What?" Val lifted his hand and squinted at the chamber. He shook his head and frowned.

Was he cross?

Val set the weapon on the table, muzzle pointing at the far wall. He spun towards Aidan. "You could have killed yourself."

He was mad.

"But I thought I'd done good."

"Och, I'll get over this," Val pointed at his face, "but I'd not get over it if you'd blown your silly head off. Why didn't you tell me?"

Aidan scuffed his toes on the carpet and drooped his head. He felt Val's hand on his shoulder and looked up. He saw the look on his brother's battered face. It was all right. Val wasn't really mad. Just worried. "I was going to give it to you tonight."

"Aye. Well. You were lucky you didn't shoot yourself." Val picked the gun up and examined it more closely. "Is there only the one bullet?"

"Aye." Aidan craned over to see what Val was doing. That stuff about the gun going off—he hadn't thought about that. Scary. But it was all right now. Val would know what to do.

Val was plucking at the bullet with his strong fingers. "I can't get it out."

"Does that matter?"

"It does indeed. We can't leave this thing lying around loaded."

"Could we not just throw it away?" Aidan was beginning to wish he'd never found the stupid thing.

"Not at all. Someone else could get hurt. What the hell am I going to do with it?"

This was getting worse. Aidan had never, ever seen his big brother at a loss. "Val, there's only the one bullet. Could you not just shoot the gun?"

"Aye. That might work." Val ran his tongue over his lip and winced. He pointed the revolver at the floor and gently squeezed the trigger.

Aidan pulled his head down into his shoulders and screwed his eyes shut. There was going to be a God-awful bang.

Nothing.

Val was saying something. Aidan opened his eyes.

"Don't look so worried. I was just testing it. It works all right. I could fire it."

Val did know what to do after all, thought Aidan. He felt guilty for having doubted his brother. "Where?"

Val rose unsteadily to his feet and headed to the back door. Aidan followed but Val said, "Wait you here."

Aidan watched through the window as Val set the gun aside and began to pile the old tyres one on top of the other. He was going to shoot into the rubber. That made sense. Aidan could hear the whine of the richochets of the bullets in the cowboy movies. Val thought of everything.

It was taking him a while to get the tyres just right. Aidan wished Val would hurry up. He wanted this over and done. His eyes misted again. It wasn't fair. All he'd wanted to do was please Val.

Val waved at the window. Short jerky movements. He wanted Aidan to get back. As he obeyed he saw Val pick up the revolver.

The crash was enormous. Much louder than Aidan had expected. What was that noise? An animal's keening, shrill and agonized, came from the yard. It went on and on.

Aidan rushed to the window. Val was on his knees. Head thrown back. He was howling. His left hand grasped his right wrist, which ended in a bloody mess of bone, tendon, and flesh.

Aidan stood, eyes wide, mouth agape. In front of Val lay the gun, or what remained of it, a twisted wreck of burst metal, the barrel split and a thin whisper of smoke drifting upward.

1987

On April 25, as Lord Chief Justice Sir Maurice Gibson and his wife, Cecily, were driving near Killeen an IRA car bomb exploded, killing them both.

On May 8, an excavating machine carrying a bomb in its bucket crashed through the outer wall of the RUC station at Loughall, County Armagh. Soldiers of the Special Air Services, who had been waiting in ambush, fired a total of 1,200 rounds, killing all eight of the Provisional IRA attackers and a passing motorist. The news of the deaths of the IRA men led to some of the worst rioting seen in West Belfast for many years.

On October 31, the vessel *Eksund* was seized off the coast of France. In her holds were 150 tons of arms and explosives, supplied by Libya's Colonel Muammar Qaddafi and destined for the Provisional IRA. The French government released evidence that suggested the *Eksund's* cargo was only one of five such consignments to be dispatched.

On November 8, an IRA bomb at the Enniskillen, County Fermanagh, War Memorial killed 11 and injured 63 during a service of remembrance for the dead of two world wars. Marie Wilson was among those slain. Her father, in an interview with Mike Gaston of the BBC, said, ". . . I have lost my daughter, and we shall miss her. But I bear no ill will. I bear no grudge. . . ."

1987 Dead 93   **Total Dead 2,718**

1988

On March 6, SAS soldiers shot Mairead Farrell, Sean Savage, and Daniel McCann on a road near the Spanish frontier in Gibraltar. All three, members of the Provisional IRA, were unarmed.

On March 16, the three Provisionals were buried in Milltown cemetery in Belfast. Loyalist Michael Stone attacked the funeral with grenades and a gun. Three mourners were killed before he was arrested.

On March 19, in Anderstown, Belfast, corporals David Howes and Derek Woods inadvertently drove their car into the IRA funeral cortège for Kevin Brady, who had been killed at the Milltown cemetery. They were dragged from the car and killed by a mob.

On July 23, an IRA bomb intended for a judge mistakenly killed a Hillsborough couple and their son.

1988 Dead 93   **Total Dead 2,811**

1989

On February 22, a soldier who was driving a school bus was shot dead by the IRA.

On March 20, Chief Superintendent Harry Breen and Superintendent Bob Buchanan of the RUC met in Dundalk with their opposite numbers in the Garda, the police force of the Republic of Ireland. Returning home from the meeting, the RUC men were ambushed near Jonesborough, County Armagh, and shot to death.

On September 7, the wife of a British soldier serving in Dortmund, Germany, was shot by the Provisional IRA.

On November 29, two men were murdered by members of the Ulster Volunteer Force at Ardboe, County Tyrone.

1989 Dead 62   **Total Dead 2,873**

FIVER

He was scared shitless. Eamon McCafferty, twenty-five, a baker by trade, a hanger-on to the fringes of the Republican movement, wished fervently that he was anywhere but in the dark with these silent, menacing men. And there was no way out.

Jesus. Only a minute ago he had been walking home from the bus stop after another unsuccessful night at the dog track; then, just as he had rounded a corner into a deserted street, the Land Rover had drawn up beside him. Two policemen dismounted, one in front, one behind, effectively hemming him in.

"Eamon McCafferty?" A coarse, harsh voice.

"Aye?" Slight defiance.

The nearside rear door of the Rover was open.

"In." No change in tone, just one, cold word.

He was seized by the collar of his shabby raincoat and pulled towards the car.

"Just get in, son and keep your mouth shut." The voice, obviously used to being obeyed, did not bother to add emphasis to a single word.

"Look. I've my rights." He tried to squirm free.

A stiff jab to the pit of his stomach rapidly disabused him of that notion. He was unceremoniously bundled aboard, one constable preceding him, one following. The door slammed and a sergeant, sitting in the driver's seat, half-turned.

"Sit still and keep your fucking mouth shut."

Eamon was too winded even to try to reply. The vehicle was driven off, through the city to the outskirts and on up into the darkness of the Cave Hill countryside. The Rover stopped. The rain rattled off the metal roof and streaked the windows. The condensation from the breath of four men steamed the insides of the glass. Eamon, a creature of the city streets, had lost all sense of direction. He might as well have been on the far side of the moon. By now he had regained his ability to breathe, but the rhythm was rapid. Despite the cold and damp, he was sweating.

The sergeant half-opened his window, drew a packet of cigarettes from his uniform pocket, took one out and lit up. Eamon would have given his immortal soul for a fag. The sergeant exhaled a cloud of smoke that drifted gently through the window to be driven down by the rain, drops of which from time to time splashed into the car, wetting Eamon's face.

"Now, Mr. McCafferty, what's it to be then?"

Christ, thought Eamon, trying to get his bearings, noting that the sergeant had a soft, Antrim accent. What's it to be? He didn't think the sergeant was offering a round of drinks. Better say nothing, because—

One constable clamped hold of Eamon's hand and viciously bent the little finger back. The pain began. He whimpered.

"What do youse want?" His voice rose as the pressure on his finger increased.

The sergeant's voice was soft, caressing. "Just a little cooperation, Mr. McCafferty." An edge began to creep in, "Just a little cooperation." The man's voice hardened, "Just a little help, or my friend there will break your fingers, one at a time."

Oh, God. Eamon's thoughts churned. Oh, God, and the fucker in the front had started to laugh.

"We're in no rush tonight," the sergeant added.

Beads of sweat stood out on Eamon's forehead. The pain in his hand was unbearable. He moaned and twisted, trying to relieve the awful rending feeling. The other constable slammed the heel of his boot into Eamon's instep, the crunch of hobnails on bone distracting him momentarily from the all-consuming agony of his finger. He felt his bladder let go, the damp spreading out in the crotch of his pants. He sobbed—tearing, racking cries, like a terrified, lost child.

"All right. That's enough for now."

On the sergeant's command, the constable released the pressure. The searing subsided into a gnawing throb. Eamon nursed his damaged hand and blubbered softly, only releasing the wounded extremity to take the back of his left sleeve and wipe the snot from his upper lip.

"Oh, Jesus, what do youse want?"

"We think that you can help us, Eamon. Here, have a fag." The sergeant reached over the back of his seat, put a cigarette between Eamon's lips and gave him a light. He inhaled greedily, pulling the smoke deep into his lungs, coughing as he exhaled—a dry, hacking sound. "What do you want me to do?"

The sergeant carelessly threw his half-finished smoke through the window. "McCafferty, we didn't lift you tonight because we thought you might like a ride up here."

Eamon cowered into himself, waiting.

The man in the front seat took Eamon's face in his hand. Eamon could feel the calluses on the fingers as they began to squeeze. He found himself being forced to look into a pair of deep-set, hard eyes.

"We know that you work with the IRA. We also know who borrowed two hundred quid three weeks ago from a certain tobacconist's shop on the Grosvenor Road." The pressure from the fingers increased. "As a matter of fact, we have a witness."

Eamon's lips were being forced into an obscene imitation of the pucker before a kiss.

"You'd have a lovely time in the Crumlin, with all those Protestant hard men, wouldn't you, son?"

Eamon felt his world shrink. He'd not last a month in the Crumlin Road Gaol, not if someone let it out that he was a Republican.

As the sergeant eased his grip, the constable took hold of Eamon's finger again.

"If you still need straightening out, we can do a bit more work on your fingers." The sergeant's tone was matter-of-fact, but he pulled

Eamon's face forward and said, slowly, deliberately, "What's it to be then?" just before pushing Eamon's face away.

Eamon drew a deep breath, took a pull on his still smouldering cigarette. "I don't care. What do you want?"

"Just a bit of help."

"What kind of help?"

The sergeant spoke as if addressing a not-very-bright five-year-old. "Information, son. Information."

Eamon's eyes widened. Turn informer. It could be the death of him. "Well?"

The constable gave Eamon's finger a sharp tug.

Eamon gasped. "All right. All right. For God's sake stop."

"Good lad. Here." The sergeant took the finished cigarette from Eamon and gave him a new one and a light. "And don't you worry about your friends finding out. We'll look after you."

Worry? Worry? Eamon knew that now he had crossed the threshold, he would never be free from worry. He sat smoking, head bowed, waiting.

"Just you do like I tell you. No one will know."

Eamon looked up. The sergeant was leaning over the front seat, bulky in his flak jacket, his peaked cap pushed back on his head. "Now, son, when you have what you think we would like—names, times, places—go to Dunmore." He laughed. "Aye. We know you like the dogs. There's a bookie there, John Rolston."

The sergeant's Antrim pronunciation with its long vowels momentarily confused Eamon.

The name sounded like "Rowlston."

Eamon interrupted. "Excuse me, I didn't get the name."

"R-o-l-s-t-o-n. Now don't you butt in again. You go to him, give him your name and put five pounds on a dog." The sergeant smiled with his mouth, eyes flat. "You should still have a bit left out of the two hundred. Put what you want to tell us on a piece of paper folded in the fiver. Have you got that?"

"Aye. Put a message in a five-pound note and give it to a bookie called John Rolston."

Eamon's Belfast intonation was flat. He was eager to please and desperately wanted to get his instructions straight. He just wanted to be set free.

"Good, son. Very good." The sergeant turned to his front, started the engine, and put the Rover in gear.

Eamon's terror began to ebb as the vehicle came out of the dark and into the familiar lights of the city. He recognized the back alley where they had stopped. "Can I go?"

The sergeant did not bother to turn round. "Just a couple more things. You give us good stuff, the next time you bet with Rolston you'll do very well—but, you give us shit," the sergeant's voice cut like a razor, "we'll remember the two hundred pounds." His tone softened. "And, son, we always know where to find you."

Eamon was dumped out into the rain. He stood in the alley, watching the taillights of the Land Rover disappear, feeling as though he had been discarded like the cigarette butt the Antrim sergeant had tossed carelessly through the window.

He trudged through the night, cold, aching, damp, terrified and ashamed. He let himself into his flat on Camden Street, locking the door behind him, shutting out the night, but not the fear that gnawed.

He slept little that night. The pain in his hand and the throbbing of his instep were enough to keep him awake. So was the worry about how to get the kind of information that would satisfy the sergeant; enough names and times and places to make the man go away forever. The chance of a payoff sounded good, but, Jesus, the risks.

How was he going to find out anything? He hadn't even taken the oath, for Christ's sake. It wasn't as if he was a member. His involvement with the Provos had been limited to delivering an occasional parcel to a safe house. He never asked what he was carrying, partly because he simply did not want to know, mostly because he knew very well that undue curiosity would be regarded with deep suspicion by the obsessively security-conscious men who skulked in the shadows of the city.

Once, and only once, had he been asked to drive a car. He could remember clearly being told where to be and when. Two men had appeared from a sidestreet and curtly told him where to go. At the destination they had left, telling him to abandon the car in the heart of a huge housing estate and make his way home by bus. He'd read about the Andersonstown police station bombing in the paper the next day and had put two and two together, but that had been afterwards. How the hell was he ever going to find out anything, and how was he ever going to find a way out?

He was still pondering these questions when he drifted into sleep, just as a watery dawn came to Belfast, outlining the gantries of the shipyards against a grey sky and wakening the starlings and pigeons from their roosts on the ledges of the green-domed City Hall.

As the same day broke, three men argued.

"I don't like it, Davy. Not one bit." The skinny young man who spoke stood leaning on the back of a kitchen chair.

Davy McCullough, mid-forties, ran a hand through his thinning, iron-grey hair. He looked up from where he sat, glancing briefly at another man, who was also seated, and was nodding his head. Davy smiled reassuringly before he spoke to the lanky youth. "Jimmy, it's your first job since you joined. It's only natural to be a bit anxious."

Jimmy stiffened. "I'm not scared. I just don't like last-minute changes. Nor does Bobby."

Davy turned to the third man, an old comrade. He'd been with Davy when they'd done the Anderstonstown RUC Barracks. Sound man, Bobby. "Well?"

Bobby shifted uncomfortably in his chair. He lowered his gaze. "Jimmy and me here have to go along with what you say, Davy, but . . ." he hesitated. "We both think it's bloody dangerous to bring in a new man at the last minute."

Davy pursed his lips and blew out his breath. His moustache, grey like his hair, bristled.

"None of us likes it, but the job's set for tomorrow. Rory had his appendix out last night and we need four men." Just the facts, stated flatly.

"We know that," said Jimmy, petulantly, "but where would we find someone we could trust?"

Davy ignored him and spoke to Bobby. "You remember the baker lad, McCafferty?"

"Aye." Bobby brightened. "Aye, right enough."

"I reckon he did all right the last time."

Bobby pushed three fingers between the buttons of his shirt and scratched his chest. "He'd not need to know all the details?"

"Not at all." Davy laughed, dryly. "He's not even in the organization. Just helps out, once in a while."

Bobby's brows furrowed for a moment, then he smiled. "You're right, Davy. Your man would do rightly. He's a good driver."

Davy noticed Jimmy open his mouth as if to speak, but again ignored the youth and said, "Good. You two'll need to steal the car tomorrow. I'll phone you after I've got McCafferty organized and let you know where to leave it. Be back here tomorrow at seven. You'll get the rest of the details then. I'll take care of McCafferty." He turned, smiling, to Jimmy. "For Christ's sake, stop looking so bloody worried." Davy rose to his feet and nodded his head towards the door. "It's going to work. Away on home, the pair of you."

Bobby stood. "Right, Davy. Come on, Jim."

Davy held the door and watched them leave, and as they went he heard Jimmy say, "I still don't like it—" and Bobby interrupt, "For fuck's sake Jimmy, when Saint Peter gives you your wings, you won't like them either."

He put on the kettle to make a cup of tea. God, he was tired. Tired of the killings, the destruction. Tired of having to carry the likes of Bobby and that little turd, Jimmy.

The kettle boiled and he made his tea, carrying the cup to the table, sitting, looking at two framed photographs hanging side by side on the far wall, above a small dresser. That was himself, Private McCullough, Royal Army Corps of Engineers, a much younger Davy with black hair, his arm round a pretty young girl. She'd not minded his joining the British Army back then. Of course, he'd only been eighteen and she fourteen.

The other picture had been taken when Maureen had turned eighteen.

He did not need to examine the fading black-and-white enlargement more closely to see her smile and her dimples and her long dark hair, done up in a saucy ponytail. God, but he'd been proud of his sister that day, shining in the sun in the courtyard of the Tower of London. He sipped his tea. She'd always been his favourite. He'd taken that snap when she'd come to stay with Paddy, the eldest brother, in London. Davy had managed a weekend pass and the three of them had done the town, celebrating her scholarship to Queen's University. He, from all the maturity of his twenty-two years had, like a father, revelled in her delight at the sights of the Metropolis—Maureen on her first, and only, holiday outside Belfast.

His tea was cold. To hell with it. He didn't really want it anyway. He rose and emptied the cup, rinsing it and leaving it in the sink. They used to wash the dishes together, when they were kids, Maureen and he, and she always teasing and pulling her big brother's leg. He just stood, fists on the edge of the sink, head drooping. She had not teased him on his last leave, back in '69. In fact she had called him a mercenary of the occupying power. He remembered being hurt, hoping that it was just some student nonsense that she'd picked up from her first-year classmates.

He grabbed a tea towel and began to dry the cup. It had taken him a week to realize that Maureen really meant what she said. That was the night she had sat him down and explained how the political system in the North of Ireland discriminated against the Catholics, like them, and how she and her friends in the Ulster Civil Rights Association were going to make a difference. She'd apologized for calling him a mercenary and he'd hugged her, forgiven her, and said he understood, although in truth all the facts and figures she'd showered on him had mostly gone over his head. No matter. She'd always been the smart one, and if she believed in what she was doing, that had been good enough for Davy.

He hung the cup back on its hook alongside its five chipped fellows and dried his hands on the tea towel. Maybe if he'd tried to stop her?

She'd gone to some rally to demand "One Man, One Vote." No one quite knew why but somehow things had got out of hand. The police had been forced to intervene and in one of their baton charges a truncheon had caught Maureen a fierce blow to the temple, crushing the bone and starting a haemorrhage—at least that's what they had told him when he arrived, breathless, at the neurosurgery ward of the Royal Victoria Hospital.

He hung the damp tea towel in its place and stepped over to the picture. Ach, Maureen. He had sat by her bedside for hours, waiting for her to wake up after the surgery. The nurses and doctors had been patient with him; he could see that now. He touched the glass, gently. The doctors had been right. Six months after he had returned to his depot, Maureen had died. She had never regained consciousness.

And your funeral, girl. Jesus, but it had been awful. Out of unthinking respect for her, he had worn his number-one uniform, corporal's stripes and all. The looks of undisguised hatred from the other mourners had rattled him.

He glanced at the picture of himself as a private, catching a glimpse of his own reflection, seeing the scar above his right eyebrow. He rubbed it. He'd been lucky that time when the detonator had gone off. Still, he had liked the army.

He shrugged. He might have made a career of it, but one little man in the funeral party, a stranger, had taken Davy aside after the service, and spoken softly. The man had extolled Maureen's commitment to her beliefs, and Davy had agreed, bewildered in his grief. The stranger had wondered, should someone not be made to pay? He said he'd be happy to talk to Davy again and gave him a telephone number. No more had been said. He'd not thought too much about it at the time.

Back with his unit in England he had tried to bury his sorrow under his day-to-day duties, but that man's question kept coming back. Should someone not be made to pay? Bloody right they should, and who was going to listen to a Catholic from the slums of Belfast? Nobody, unless he could force the faceless "them" to take notice, and who better to do that than a man who had spent most of his adult life learning about explosives?

He knew he had not made his decision quickly, but as the weeks passed Davy became more convinced of the rightness of his choice. He'd not paid a hell of a lot of attention to the priests at his school, but he still remembered one Old Testament phrase. "An eye for an eye. A tooth for a tooth."

When his enlistment was up six months later, Davy McCullough left the British Army. Two weeks after that he was a member of the Provisional IRA.

He felt the tears start and brushed them away with the back of his hand. He turned away from the photograph, forcing his mind to the things he must do next. The driver first, nip over to the City Hospital and have a word with Rory, let him know they'd found a replacement, tell the other two where to leave the car, then get things ready for himself and Bobby and Jimmy. Jimmy and his, "I don't like it." He'd better learn to like it. Davy knew well that, once in, there was no way out.

The insistent ringing of his telephone brought Eamon to his senses. Christ, his finger hurt. It couldn't be the peelers already. He got out of bed and walked gingerly to the telephone, the ache in his instep reminding him of the events of the night before.

"Hello."

"Eamon McCafferty?"

He thought he knew the voice but couldn't quite place it.

"Aye."

"You and me need to have a word. Do you know the back entrance to the Botanic Gardens?"

"I do."

"Good. There's a bench there under a big lilac tree, just inside the gates. Be there at twelve today." The line went dead.

Last night Eamon had known fear. Now, half-awake, he was terrified and confused. What little loyalty he might have possessed was with the IRA, but his sense of self-preservation was overriding.

Christ, he wished he could remember everything that had been said. He remembered his instructions, and the sergeant's parting shot, "We always know where to find you." But had the man just wanted information this once, or would he keep bleeding Eamon like a leech until he was sucked dry and useless to them?

Now this phone call. Did that mean the IRA had found out already? Eamon had no doubt whatsoever what would happen to him if they had. But if the voice on the phone was from the IRA, not showing up at, when, noon? would be as good as an admission of guilt. He shivered and looked at his watch. Ten-thirty. He had better phone in sick to the bakery. That done, it was time to wash and shave in the tepid water of his cracked sink.

The Botanic Gardens were only a short walk from Camden Street, say about fifteen minutes—past the "Club Bar," turn left at Queen's University, and a short right along Botanic Avenue. He had plenty of time for a cup of coffee and a smoke. He boiled a kettle and scooped the instant into a mug. The coffee was acid in his stomach, the cigarette of little solace. What the fuck—what the fuck was he going to do?

He looked out the window. For once it was not raining. He'd not bother with a raincoat. He dressed—old jeans, a blue shirt, socks, the left with a hole worn in the heel, old leather shoes. He stood for a while, deciding between a tweed sports coat or a denim jacket, the mundane chores of living temporarily distracting him from the nagging worry about what this day would hold. Damn it. The sports coat would do rightly. He shrugged it on.

Twice he opened the front door, each time closing it again, daunted by the prospect of this meeting. Finally, at eleven-forty, he steeled himself, left home, and set off for the Botanic Gardens.

He arrived at eleven-fifty. The bench beneath the lilac tree was empty. He sat down, lit another cigarette, and looked about him. At the end of the walk, a man was approaching him purposefully. There was no one else about.

Eamon recognized the new arrival as one of the two men he had picked up before the police station bombing. It was the scar above the right eye. Eamon smiled weakly but said nothing.

"'Morning." The man sat on the bench beside Eamon, looking round as if to satisfy himself that no one could overhear their conversation.

"Now, Eamon, you've done some work for us before."

"I have."

"I tell you what, I'll do the talking and you just listen."

Eamon flinched.

"We need you to do a job for us tomorrow night."

Eamon hurriedly nodded in agreement, unable to tear his gaze away from the hard eyes in front of him.

"It's simple enough, just a bit of driving, just like the last time. Remember?"

Eamon saw his past being held over him as no less a threat than the events of the previous night. It was more subtle, but the threat was there. He looked at the ground, his eyes searching for the escape that he himself could not find. He found no escape, just dead lilac petals.

He heard the man continue, "Tomorrow night at seven-thirty you leave home. If you look under your mat you'll find the keys to a car. Walk down to the corner of the Lisburn Road and Camden Street. There'll be a red car parked there."

Eamon felt the shake in his own voice as he asked, "What kind?"

"We don't know. We haven't borrowed it yet." The man grinned sardonically. "But it'll be a red one. Now you drive that car to the Divis Flats. There'll be three of us waiting on the corner at eight-fifteen. You'll recognize me."

Indeed Eamon would. Five-foot-eight or thereabouts, stocky build, forty, forty-five, thin grey hair, grey moustache, scar.

"Now just stop and pick us up. Then I'll tell you where to take us and where to drop us off."

"Can I go home then?" Eamon was pleading.

"No. We'll need collecting later, but you'll find out about that tomorrow night."

Eamon feigned hurt. "Do youse not trust me then?"

The man shrugged. His voice was tired when he said, "Eamon, we trust nobody. The less anyone knows, the less he can tell." He looked directly at Eamon, who averted his gaze.

Eamon was sure he was blushing. He blustered, "You can trust me, so you can."

"Do you think I'd be here now if I didn't think so? Now, do you understand what you've to do?"

"I do indeed."

"Tell me." It was an order, given by a soldier.

Eamon straightened his shoulders. "I've to get the keys of a car under my mat, pick up a red car at the corner of the street, and come for you and two of your mates at eight-fifteen outside the Divis Flats." He almost saluted. "You can count on me, sir."

"I hope so, Eamon, I hope so." With that, the man rose, looked at Eamon hard for several seconds, turned and walked away. After he had gone, Eamon realized that he still did not know the man's name. Why should he? He knew the rules.

The sun had gone behind the clouds, the all-pervading smell of the lilac blossoms seemed to fade with Eamon's fear. He sat on, just letting the time pass. He might as well go home. He sighed, stood up, and began to walk.

He passed the university again. Knots of undergraduates were lounging on the steps of the students' union building or lying on the lawn under the old sycamore trees. A young woman in a yellow dress ran laughing by him to catch up with her friends, careless and carefree. He envied her.

It was only one o'clock. He had to kill the afternoon. He reached the "Club Bar." He hesitated. Why not? One pint wouldn't hurt him. He went in through the front doors to the dimly lit public bar and ordered a pint of Guinness, waiting while the barman poured first from the barrel of old, flat stout, then from the new ale to build a pint neither too flat nor too high, the while scraping off the foaming head with a wooden spatula.

Eamon lit a cigarette and let his pint settle, the faint white rings ascending through the velvet black of the stout until the straight glass was ebony with a pure white collar of head. He took his glass from the bar, paid, and walked over to a table. Apart from himself and the barman, the room was empty. He took a deep drink, a pull on his cigarette, and looked around. Since he had moved into his flat in Camden Street, he had sunk a quare few pints in here. He wondered if after the next few days he'd ever get the chance for another one.

Sure it would be easy enough to slip a note to the bookie tonight. The police could lift the grey-haired man and his mates tomorrow night, but if Eamon wasn't picked up too it wouldn't take someone long to work out who had told the police. If that happened his chances of survival, or at least survival with intact kneecaps, would be slim indeed. On the other hand, if he was arrested with the others, no one would suspect that he had grassed, but how would he avoid a long jail sentence? The only hope he could find was that the sergeant had said the police would take care of things. Eamon crushed out his cigarette and finished the last of his pint. He prayed to Christ that the sergeant was right.

God, he'd love another pint, but he knew that he would have to keep his wits about him. He looked at the bar clock. One-forty-five. It was going to be a long afternoon. He might as well go home.

It took him ten minutes, dawdling, to reach his flat. He let himself in. His apartment was in a previously elegant terrace house, now converted into flats. It was on the ground floor, along a dim hall to two dingy rooms. A kitchen-cum-sitting room led directly to a bedroom and washing area. If he wanted to take a bath, which he did about once a week, or use the lavatory, he had to go to the communal facilities off the hall.

He went through to the bedroom. A pile of dirty clothes lay untidily on the single chair, last night's soiled pants among them. He looked at them, thinking that it was about time he made a trip to the launderette, but he was in no mood for everyday chores today. He'd had little enough sleep last night. He might as well take a nap now.

He kicked off his shoes, hung his jacket and trousers on a wall peg, crawled under the unmade covers, and drifted into a troubled sleep.

. . .

Eamon McCafferty woke. He took a few moments to collect his thoughts. For the second time that day, he washed perfunctorily, and dressed. He pulled out his wallet. Two five-pound notes were in there along with a few singles. He removed one fiver and went through to the front room. He found a scrap of paper and a pencil, but hesitated before he finally scrawled, "Job tomorrow night." He folded the paper into the banknote, looked at the thing he held before hurriedly replacing it and its message in his wallet, and tucked the wallet in his hip pocket.

Six o'clock. He'd better get a bite to eat. He was in no mood to cook. He grabbed a cap and his raincoat and left, walking slowly up Camden Street to the main road. Just to his right was the grandly named "University Cafe," known to the residents of the area as "Smokey Joe's." He entered. Seven or eight cheap aluminium and arborite table and chair sets were huddled in a small room, on one side of which was a long counter. On the counter a tired cold-drink machine rubbed shoulders with a tea urn and a glass-fronted cabinet in which languished an assortment of sandwiches, their stale edges curling, their lettuce leaves limp.

The walls were plaster, painted a hospital yellow, and adorned with fading posters of sunny Spain. A blackboard, nailed to the wall behind the counter, carried the menu, "Sausage and chips, egg and chips, sausage, egg and chips, bacon, egg and chips." The air was rank with the smell of frying fat and stale cigarette smoke.

Eamon walked over to the counter. A fat woman, in a once-white but now grease-stained apron, looked out from behind the tea urn.

"Yes, dear?"

"Egg and chips and a cup of tea, please."

She turned and shouted through a hatch in the wall behind her, "One egg and chips," and lifting a chipped mug from a convenient shelf, held it under the spout of the tea urn. The tea that filled the mug was stewed to a dark mahogany.

"Milk and sugar, dear?"

"Aye, both."

She slopped some milk from a white jug and ladled in a spoonful of sugar, finally handing Eamon the mug.

"Away on and sit down. I'll call you when it's ready."

Eamon, trying not to burn his fingers on the mug, sat at the nearest vacant table, studiously ignoring the other few diners, who in their turn ignored him. "Smokey's" was a good place to be alone and just now he wanted to be alone. He stared at the tabletop. A torn plastic, black-and-red checked tablecloth, eggstained at one corner, was set with four place settings, knife, fork, and spoon. A salt and pepper set, fake cut glass, sat in the middle of the table, along with a bottle of ketchup, the red desiccated smudges of ketchup at the bottle cap turning brown, and a half-full vinegar shaker.

He sat, sipping his tea with no great pleasure and wondering if he had time for a smoke before his food would be ready. Unable to decide, he let his eyes wander. Although the colours of the poster of Barcelona had faded, its blue, sunny skies contrasted sharply with the grey Belfast clouds that he could make out dimly through the streaked front window. The exhortation for holidaymakers to "get away from it all" struck him forcibly.

Get away? From the grime of Belfast, the sergeant, the grey-haired man? Eamon shuddered. Get away? He'd love to, but on what they paid him as a baker? Aye. Right. He'd go first class too. The fat woman called to him, "Your egg and chips is ready, dear."

He paid, collected his plate, and returned to his seat. First class. Jesus. The pile of chips was soggy, the egg white flecked brown with burnt cooking fat. The unappetizing whole was complemented with a single slice of thick white bread liberally coated with margarine. He tried to shake salt from the salt-cellar, but the grains had formed solid chunks in the damp air. He shrugged, sprinkled vinegar over the chips, and began to eat. He only managed three or four mouthfuls; the lard was already beginning to congeal on the roof of his mouth. There was a burning feeling just below his ribs.

He pushed his plate away, swallowed some more tea, and lit a cigarette. The burning in the pit of his stomach grew worse. It felt like a small animal with sharp incisors was chewing at his guts. He shifted in the hard seat, feeling his wallet dig into his hip. The note was in there, and as long as it stayed in there, the grey-haired man and his two friends would be safe, and, more important, Eamon would have nothing to fear from the IRA. But then, when would he get another chance to get the police off his back?

He coughed, sniffed, and looked furtively around, almost believing that the two women at the far table could hear his thoughts. What the police had done to him last night was bad enough. He massaged his finger gently. What the IRA would do, if they suspected, would make that outing look like a Sunday-school picnic.

He finished his, by now, lukewarm tea, left, and walked to the bus stop to wait for the red corporation bus that would take him to the dog stadium. He stood patiently in the queue, relentlessly considering his limited options, no closer to a decision.

He changed buses at the city hall. There were no seats. The bus was crammed with men in collarless shirts, woollen neck-scarves and raincoats. Most wore flat cloth caps, dunchers. He had joined the ranks of what, a century ago, would have been called "the fancy," the men who followed the sport of greyhound racing.

Eamon stood, hanging on to a leather strap, crushed between a short youth and a fat man with bad breath and appalling body odour. The two argued over the relative merits of two dogs. Eamon wished they would shut up. He had more important choices to make.

The bus lurched to a halt at the Dunmore Stadium stop. The fat man staggered and stepped on Eamon's injured instep. The pain made his eyes water, and for an instant he was back in the Land Rover. To hell with it. What the RUC knew had hurt him already. What the Provos did not know couldn't hurt him.

He left the bus, limping slightly as he joined the lines at the turnstiles. He pulled his duncher out of the pocket of his raincoat and put it on, pulling the peak down to shade his eyes. By the time he was paying for his admission, he was surprised to find that he felt calmer, now that he had made up his mind. He'd have to go and find the bookie called Rolston.

The floodlights were already on when he entered the stadium. He paused for a moment in the shadow of the entrance tunnel. Rows of concrete terraces encircled the red-surfaced track. He made his way towards a clear area, between the stands and the track railing. There the on-track bookmakers were calling the odds, taking bets from the punters and signals from the tic-tac men, changing the odds on the basis of the information received.

About twenty firms were working tonight, each at a raised lectern affair, above which stood the odds board where the bookie chalked the names of the dogs and their starting prices. He walked along the row of booths until he found the one he was looking for. A sign above the odds board read, "Honest John Rolston."

A small man wearing a bowler hat was hoarsely yelling, "Master Jim, five-to-four on, Carrickfergus Beauty, evens . . ." Eamon stood and watched. He could see the bookie's loudly checked jacket inside his unbuttoned raincoat. Eamon could feel his hands growing sweaty and his mouth was horribly dry. He started to tremble.

He watched as someone handed Rolston a banknote and received in return a ticket; a ticket to instant money if the dog won, dashed hopes if it lost. Eamon thought of the gamble he must take, shook his head—he couldn't go through with this—and retreated into the crowd. A thin drizzle started. He turned up his coat collar and hunched his narrow shoulders.

A tinny voice over the Tannoy announced the start. The electric hare appeared, rushing madly round the inside of the oval track, pursued by six lean, bounding dogs, each straining after its quarry. Christ, he thought, me and the fucking hare. Nowhere to go but in circles.

The results were announced and the lucky winners headed down to collect their winnings. All around Eamon, losers disgustedly tore up their tickets. He pulled his wallet from his pocket, slipped out the loaded fiver, took a deep breath, walked back to the bookie's stand, waited his turn, and handed the note to Rolston.

"The name's Eamon McCafferty." He saw the eyes widen in the man's florid face, but no other sign of recognition.

"What's your pick?"

"Michael's Rocket. On the nose." He waited for his ticket, noticing that Rolston had not put the banknote into his leather cash satchel but had stuffed it into a pocket of his trousers.

The ticket was handed over. "Good luck, young man. Come and see me again, soon." He was grinning, the shallow, empty grimace that bookies have for the chickens that they pluck every night. Eamon stepped away. That was it then. How Rolston passed on the message was none of Eamon's concern. He just wanted to get to hell out of there. He was halfway to the exit when the start was called. He hesitated, and turned. He did not recognize anyone in the immediate crowd, although that did not mean he was not being watched.

The drizzle had turned to steady rain. He stood waiting for the results, unable to leave until his bet on this race was run out, knowing full well that if it had not been for his passion for the dogs he would not have been in so deeply with another bookie, would not have had to steal the two hundred pounds, and would not be here now, wondering about what was going to happen next.

The dog lost. Eamon had had enough. He headed for the bus that would take him home.

The phone was ringing as he let himself into his flat. He hurried through the dark room, but the sound stopped just before he could lift the receiver. He stared at its familiar shape as if it was a malevolent thing.

He switched on the light, took off his sodden cap and raincoat, shook them and hung them on a peg. He sat down heavily, lit a cigarette, and waited. There were five half-smoked butts in the ashtray before the phone jangled again. He grabbed it before the first double ring was over.

"Hello."

"Eamon. How nice." The Antrim voice was gentle, coaxing. He didn't know what to say.

"Are you still there?"

"Aye." He scrabbled for another cigarette.

"Good. What would you like to tell me?"

To fuck off and leave me alone, Eamon thought, lighting his smoke. "There's a job tomorrow night. I've to drive."

"Oh?" The voice was even, noncommittal.

"Look. You've to look after me." Eamon surprised himself with the vehemence of his words.

"I will, son. I will." The voice hardened, slightly. "Tell me about the job."

Eamon inhaled smoke, closed his eyes, bit his lower lip, and let the smoke drift from his nostrils. "All right. I met a man yesterday . . ." Eamon opened his eyes. "He said, tomorrow night I've to drive a red car to—to Divis Flats and pick up himself and two other men."

"What time?" No mistaking the interest now.

"Eight-fifteen."

"Then what?"

"That's all I know."

"No it's not, son. What did the man you met look like?"

"I dunno."

"Eamon," the word cracked along the wires, "think."

Eamon thought, thought hard. He was sweating again, just like last night. After a moment he said, "He was about five-eight, five-nine, forty, forty-five, grey hair, moustache . . ."—just describing the man helped—". . . scar over his right eye."

"And he'll be with two other men, outside the Divis Flats at eight-fifteen tomorrow night?"

"Sure I already told you that." Eamon heard his own voice, shrill, petulant. What more did the man want? "What are you going to do?"

"Never you worry, son. You just listen to me, carefully."

Eamon sat straight, clenching his fingers round the phone.

"You get there, dead on time. You might see the police cars, you might even see an arrest." A dry laugh. "If I was you, I'd just keep on driving. No one on your side"—was there a hint of sarcasm?—"will blame you if you take off."

"Just like that?" It seemed too simple. "And that's an end to it?"

"Yes. Just like that. Oh, by the way, don't forget to have another flutter with Rolston." It still sounded like "Rowlston." Why couldn't the fucking sergeant say the bookie's name right? The line went dead.

Eamon held the receiver in front of his face. As he looked at it he thought about what he had done. Tears of shame, mixed with tears of relief, ran down his sallow cheeks. He replaced the receiver. By this time tomorrow night it would be all over, for good. The sergeant had said it would be an end to it, hadn't he?

Davy McCullough spent his day alone in his room attending to his work. He had learned his trade well in the Sappers. They had taught him about building bridges and blowing up bridges. He had learned that it was mining engineers who had first noticed that the manufacturer's name or trade-mark stamped into a batch of gun cotton, the precursor to plastique, was often deeply etched into the rock face after the blast.

The sergeant instructor had not been able to remember who had come up with the idea of seeing what would happen if, instead of sticking a flat lump of gun cotton on an obstacle, the explosive was hollowed into a concave shape first. He was happy to tell the class that the results had been spectacularly effective and by hollowing the charge, the force could be focused, delivering a vastly enhanced punch at a desired spot. He told them how the German paratroopers had used such devices on the great Belgian concrete fortress of Eban Emael in the early days of the Blitzkrieg.

Davy smiled, wondering if Sergeant Grant would be proud of his pupil today. Certainly a lot of pubs and several police stations would be in better repair but for Davy's expertise. He sat at the table, patiently carving a block of slate-blue plastique. That was something else he had learned. When Semtex explodes, the superheated gases expand at a rate of 26,400 feet per second. Short of a nuclear blast, there is no more destructive force than a shaped Semtex charge.

Davy hummed to himself gently as he worked, glancing from time to time at Maureen's picture. It was all very well for others to believe that they were fighting for the freedom of *Kathleen ni Houlihan*, Mother Ireland. That was their business. Davy had come into this because someone had to pay. He put one finished package of death aside and began working on the other.

There was no reason for Eamon to stay at home. He went to the bakery and attended to his work, hoping that the routine tasks might, in some small way, serve to keep his mind off what was to happen tonight.

The hours passed slowly. Finally it was time for home.

Eamon sat in his room smoking and watching the minutes, waiting until seven-thirty.

Seven o'clock. Only half an hour more to go.

"Come in." Davy ushered Bobby and Jimmy into the flat. He closed the door. "Sit down." He joined them at the table. The two charges, wired to their timers and detonators, lay with three automatic pistols on the tabletop. Jimmy hefted one of the guns.

Bobby smiled at him. "Put that down. You're too young to remember James Cagney."

Jimmy did as he was told.

Davy lifted an old suitcase from the floor and began to pack the tools of their trade. "You got the car?"

"Aye," said Jimmy, proudly, "a red four-door Ford. Bobby and me changed the licence plates."

Bobby tipped his chair back on two legs. "Your man here must've drove about a hundred miles round and round Camden Street before he could park where you told us. Near made me dizzy."

Davy was quick to bolster Jimmy's self-confidence. "You done good, Jim." He was gratified to watch the young man's slow smile.

Bobby asked, "You sure, Davy, that McCafferty'll be all right?"

Davy controlled his irritation. "Don't you start, Bobby. I met him yesterday. He's scared, but he's on our side. He'll do his job."

Jimmy looked at Bobby, a slightly superior smile on his lips.

Davy continued, "He'll be here at eight-fifteen. We'll have all we need in the suitcase here. No one will bother with us, among the other people on the street. We might look a bit suspicious later at night." He closed the lid. "We'll just take our time getting there."

"Where?" asked Jimmy, eagerly.

"Greyabbey." Davy's smile was peaceful, his words matter-of-fact. "We're going to take out a police barracks." He stood. "Anyone fancy a cup of tea?"

Eamon finished a last cigarette. Nearly seven-thirty. He put on his raincoat and his cap, let himself out. Sure enough, the keys were under the mat. He walked to the end of the street. A red Ford was parked where it was supposed to be. He tried the keys in the door lock, let himself in, sat, closed the door, and started the engine. He pulled away from the kerb, signalled for a right turn and moved out from Camden Street into the traffic of the Lisburn Road, heading for Shaftesbury Square and the centre of the city. He was going to be too early, but he knew that he could waste time in the city traffic. He intended to be just a minute or two late, just to be on the safe side. He tucked the car in behind a red double-decker bus and headed downtown, the long way round.

Davy took his time washing the teacups, keeping his back turned to Bobby and Jimmy, wishing the job over. He had not expected Bobby's reaction when, half an hour ago, the target had been announced.

"The barracks at Greyabbey? Jesus. That place is like a bloody fortress." Bobby had obviously been rattled.

Davy could not let his second-in-command infect Jimmy, who was looking at Bobby with his mouth open in an adenoidal stare. Davy laid a hand on Bobby's forearm. "The front is, Bobby. The front. But there's an alley round the back, the fence sits on a brick wall, and a wheen of the bricks are loose." He let go of Bobby's arm and directed his gaze to Jimmy. "I know the bricks are loose. I worked on them myself last week."

"Oh," said Bobby, seemingly satisfied.

"McCafferty will let us off on the Kirkubbin Road and we'll walk the last half-mile. Jimmy . . ."

Jimmy looked up expectantly.

"You're our lookout at the end of the alley."

"Right, Davy."

"Bobby, you help me get the bricks out, then cover my tail while I nip in the backyard. I'll be in and out like a ferret up a rat hole." He was pleased to see Bobby smile. He patted the suitcase. "These two charges on the back corners will bring the whole building down when they go off, but they're timed so that we'll be back in Newtownards before something a bit stronger than a spoon stirs the peelers' tea for them. Speaking of tea?"

"I'd go a cup," Jimmy said and Bobby nodded along.

Davy had put the kettle on to boil, paying no attention to the low conversation of his two companions. He didn't really want a cup himself, but he'd learnt long ago that going through the simple actions of everyday living calmed anxious men. Men like Jimmy. "Pass the sugar. Pass the milk." Pass the time.

Now that he'd finished washing the used cups Davy half-turned. "What time is it?"

"Eight," said Jimmy.

"Right. Getting to be about time." He crossed to the table, opened the case for one last check before snapping the catches shut. "I'm for a leak, anyone else need one?"

"Get on with it, Davy," Bobby said, rising.

Jimmy merely shook his head.

Davy went into the small bathroom. Knowing that excitement can slow the work of a man's kidneys, he was not surprised that he, the old hand, was the only one who had needed a piss. He opened the door. Bobby and Jimmy were waiting. Davy slipped into an old duffle jacket, picked up the suitcase, nodded at Maureen's picture, opened the door, and said, "Let's go."

Eamon had mistimed things. He could see the grey-haired man and his two companions standing on the corner two blocks away, staring in his direction. They'd just have to wait until this light changed. Where in hell were the police? Eamon's hands were clammy on the steering wheel. The light changed to green. Eamon let out the clutch and stalled the engine. It had not been deliberate. He had simply panicked. For a moment he failed to recognize what had happened and sat there, futilely depressing the accelerator. The driver of the car behind him was already impatiently blowing his horn. Eamon realized he had had a stroke of luck and fiddled with the starter, refusing to let the ignition catch until the light had once more turned red. He sat there watching.

Davy contained his impatience. Only a few more moments. He felt a tap on his shoulder and turned, expecting to have to pacify Jimmy or Bobby. A large man in a raincoat was standing there.

" 'Evening, sir. What's in the case?"

"Just some clothes . . ."

"Perhaps I could have a look. I'm a police officer. It's just a routine check. Nothing to be worried about."

Davy sized up his opponent, hoping to be able to belt him a quick one and make a run for it.

The big man opened his shoulders and nursed one hefty fist in his other palm. "I wouldn't try anything stupid, sir."

Davy shrugged and bent to set the case down on the pavement, placing his body between the officer and Jimmy and Bobby, trying to give them a chance to escape. He stood and realized as soon as he saw the four green-uniformed constables, two carrying Sten guns, that there would be no escape. From the tail of his eye, Davy caught a glimpse of Eamon's scared stare as the red Ford sped past. Go on, son. He wished Eamon well. No need for him to be taken too.

"Open it." The polite tone had gone.

Davy looked round once more, but there was no way out.

Eamon parked the stolen car on a side street off Donegal Road. His hands were trembling as he lit a cigarette. His initial terror had given way to startled relief. He'd got away with it, so far anyway. All he had to do was leave this car and walk the half-mile or so home. He got out, leaving the keys in the ignition, and slammed the door behind him.

It only took about fifteen minutes to walk back to Camden Street. He let himself in, pulled a half-bottle of Bushmills Irish Whiskey from a cupboard, and poured a generous measure into a glass. The spirits burned his throat as he took a large swallow. His hands were still shaking. Relief turned to despair once more. He pulled the curtains tightly shut, sure that he was being watched. He glanced nervously at the phone. It repaid his interest with stony silence. He sat at the table, whiskey glass clasped in both hands, and lowered his head.

After two weeks had gone by, two weeks of constant but diminishing worry, Eamon had a visitor. A short man, carrot-red hair, pasty-faced, hollow-cheeked, stood at the front door. He had a big innocent smile.

"Yes?"

"Eamon, I'm Rory. Brigade sent me."

Eamon's breath caught in his throat. Shit. They'd found out.

"Can I come in for a minute?"

Something about the way the man spoke seemed reassuring. Eamon stepped aside. "Sure." He closed the door and followed the stranger along the hall into the kitchen. "Have a seat?"

"No thanks. I'll only be a sec. Look," Rory smiled again. "I was meant to be driving the night Davy and the boys got lifted but I'd had my appendix out."

"Oh," said Eamon.

"Davy told me about you."

"Oh," said Eamon again, wondering what was coming next.

"I told Brigade, and they've finished the investigation."

Eamon's knees weakened. His eyes widened.

Rory laughed. "Don't look so worried. They reckon it was just bad luck. A routine check, but just in case someone spotted you, they won't be asking for your help for a brave while." Eamon could not believe his ears. He felt a smile start.

Rory turned to leave. "I'll see myself out. You keep your head down, just do your usual things." He held out his hand. Eamon shook it, thanking Rory as if he had just delivered a million pounds.

When Rory had left, Eamon let himself relax. He'd got away with it. He looked at the time. There would be racing at Dunmore tonight. He had been too scared even to think about the sergeant's promise about a payoff. He grabbed for his cap. He'd go and see Rolston tonight.

Later Eamon sat in his flat, nursing a very large Bushmills, savouring the peaty flavour, smoking a Gallagher's Green instead of his usual Woodbine. The two hundred pounds he had received from the bookie, even though Eamon's dog had lost, had rounded off what was turning into one of the best days of his life. He need not fear the Provos, Rory had said so, he was two hundred quid better off, and he was rid of the sergeant. He distinctly remembered the telephone conversation.

"Just like that, and that's an end to it?"

"Yes. Just like that."

He took a pull on his smoke, sipped his drink, and felt, smugly, that he had been one smart fellow.

He was still smiling when the phone rang.

"Hello, Eamon." The Antrim accent was unmistakable.

1990

On January 13, three men attempted to rob a bookmaker's in West Belfast. Undercover soldiers shot them dead.

On July 24, a 1,000-pound landmine, set by the Provisional IRA, exploded near the town of Armagh, killing three policemen. Sister Catherine Dunne, a nun, was driving past at the time. She died.

On July 30, Ian Gow, a Conservative Member of Parliament, was killed by a bomb in his car outside his home in Sussex. Shortly afterwards, two Provisional IRA death-lists were captured. Two hundred and fifty prominent British subjects had been targeted. Queen Elizabeth II's name did not appear on any such lists until 1996.

On September 30, Martin Peake and Karen Reilly stole a car and went joyriding. They were shot in the vehicle by soldiers.

On October 24, Patsy Gillespie was kidnapped by the Provisional IRA and his family held hostage. He was strapped into a van that was filled with explosives and forced to drive the bomb into a checkpoint on the Buncrana Road. The explosion killed him and five soldiers.

On November 10, four wildfowlers, two civilians, and two RUC officers were murdered in County Armagh.

1990 Dead 76   **Total Dead 2,949**

1991

On February 7, mortar bombs were fired from a van into the garden of 10 Downing Street by the Provisional IRA. Two bombs failed to detonate. One exploded fifteen feet from a room where the British War Cabinet was discussing the Gulf War.

On March 3, four Catholics were shot dead in Cappagh, County Tyrone, by members of the Ulster Volunteer Force.

On March 28, the UVF attacked a mobile shop in Craigavon, County Armagh. A man and two teenage girls died.

On June 3, soldiers ambushed and killed three Provisional IRA men in a stolen car at Coagh, County Tyrone.

On September 4, a lorry containing 8,000 pounds of explosives was found mired in a field near the Army checkpoint at Annaghmartin, County Fermanagh.

On November 2, two soldiers were killed and eighteen people injured when the Musgrave Park Hospital, Belfast, was bombed.

1991 Dead 94   **Total Dead 3,043**

ONLY
WOUNDED

"Ah, Jesus, not again." Bob Stevenson swore at the television set. "Would you look at that?"

Susan glanced up from her knitting. The news anchorman, his voice polished, impartial, read the headlines as the all-too-familiar pictures— torn buildings, rubble, weary firefighters, ambulances—flickered across the screen. "There was an explosion in Belfast today. Two people were killed and twenty-seven wounded," The Ulster Television *Nine O'Clock News* faded to the beginning of a commercial for women's tampons.

"It's disgusting." Bob rose, crossed the little room, and switched off the set.

She wasn't sure whether her husband was angry with the report or the commercial. Bob hated those Tampax ads. They embarrassed him.

She watched him standing there, shaking his head. "Come on and sit down." Susan patted the sofa cushion beside her. "You can do nothing about it."

"Aye. I know."

"You'd think we'd be used to it by now."

Bob sat beside her. She put her knitting away and snuggled against him. "Ach, Bobby, we don't know the ones that were killed. The others were only wounded."

He sighed. "Only wounded? Aye. I suppose you're right. It could've been worse."

She put a hand against his cheek, feeling the day's stubble. "Stop worrying about it. Give us a kiss." She saw him glance upward. "It's all right. John's asleep. Him and me's going shopping tomorrow."

John Stevenson was five. He was a happy child, curious in the way of all five-year-olds. His very best friend, Eileen, was going to have a birthday party and he was helping Mummy to find a present. He liked to go shopping. The people in the shops were nice and Mummy sometimes bought him peppermints.

He wriggled in the folding seat of the trolley and dropped his teddy bear onto the pile of groceries that Mummy had collected. He reached over to the nearest shelf and grabbed for a box of cereal. The little supermarket on Main Street was a delight to five-year-olds and the despair of their parents.

A casual observer among the other shoppers would have noticed John's mother. Susan Stevenson, née McNabb, had striking green eyes and long, glossy, auburn hair, but in truth, apart from her obvious good looks, there was nothing remarkable about Susan. She was twenty-six, and had worked as a shifter in the flax stink and ear-battering roar of the looms of a Belfast linen mill until six years ago when she had married her schooldays sweetheart, Bob Stevenson. The marriage had been her escape from the factory and from Belfast. The two had bought a little house in Bangor. Funny how the place was only twelve miles from Belfast and yet when she thought of what living in the city had been like, and how quiet Bangor was, the place could have been a hundred miles away.

John had been born within the year. Sometimes he could be a holy terror and on days like today she could wish herself single again, back at the mill with the other girls, no responsibilities, no house to run, no five-year-old to tie her down.

She sighed, took what seemed like the thousandth item from John's chubby paw, and replaced the garishly coloured box on the shelf. Her feet hurt, the minimarket was crowded, nothing seemed to be on the same shelves as last week, and John's unceasing interruptions were enough to test the patience of Job.

"Now, look." She pulled John's old teddy bear from the top of her purchases, handed it to her son, rattled the buggy, and looked sternly at the child. "I'm not telling you again. Leave-the-things-alone."

She had raised her voice as she spoke the last few words and was embarrassed to see a look of disapproval from a fat, middle-aged woman who was trying to wheel her own load of groceries past where Susan stood scolding her son. She forced a weak smile but the other woman pursed her lips and shook her head.

Old cow, Susan thought, noting the woman's pink plastic hair curlers, poorly hidden by a green headscarf. Mind your own business. She pushed the trolley, further irritated by her own embarrassment. She looked at John but saw Bob's fair hair and deep blue eyes. The grin on the little boy's face as he caught sight of the peppermints in the sweetie section was a smaller version of her husband's smile. He was a good man, her Bob. John's smile was widening, and the hopeful look in his eyes would have melted Pharaoh's hard heart.

"Oh, all right." She lifted a bag of round, white mints and put them in the trolley, well out of John's reach. "But you're not getting them 'til we get home, so you're not."

Willie Cauldwell paused from pushing his barrow. For the last forty-two years, rain and shine, he had walked this route as a council road-sweeper, shoving the refuse in the gutters before him with a stiff-bristled broom, down one side of the street, up the other, building little heaps of leaves, cigarette packet wrappers, fish-and-chip papers, dust. Lots of dust. He sneezed and pulled a grubby handkerchief from his trouser pocket, wrapping his bulbous red nose and honking to clear the irritation. He sniffed. His eyes watered.

He stuffed the handkerchief back into his pocket, leant the brush against the barrow—two dustbins mounted one behind the other between a pair of bicycle wheels—and pulled a shovel from its clips on the handle of the barrow. He used the broom to force the pile of rubbish onto the blade of the shovel and lifted the lid of one of the bins to deposit the load.

Shit. Those buggers at the depot were meant to empty the bins when he brought his barrow back in the evenings. They mustn't have bothered last night. Idle skitters. No wonder the bloody thing had seemed harder to push this morning. This bin was still half-full of dead leaves, yesterday's final sweepings from outside the Ward Park where great horse-chestnut trees drooped their boughs over the pavements of Upper Main Street. He emptied his shovel and closed the lid. He hoped there would be enough room to accommodate today's takings. He did not relish the thought of making an extra trip back to the depot. It was warm work, today. Willie looked down Main Street, squinting against the morning sun, past the McKee clock—sandstone, solid, two stories high—and on to the black, crooked finger of the North Pier. He could see Bangor Bay, lapis lazuli, veined with small flashes of white.

Willie wiped his forehead with the back of his hand, feeling the gritty dust mingle with his sweat. He pushed back his cloth cap to let the air at his forehead and looked out across the bay to Belfast Lough. An oil tanker, black sides rust-streaked, was anchored in the roads. Sailboats scudded towards the hills of Antrim on the far shore, all but hidden by the heat haze. He pushed his cap further back and thought, Boys a dear, yon's a pretty sight.

Willie wondered today, as he had often done in his sixty years, lived all in Bangor, if those far-off, shimmering hills were a foreign country. He had never quite managed to ask anyone. He shrugged. Sure what did it matter anyway? Wasn't he quite content living with his two cats, the three of them in the little cottage near the water, aye, and not too far from the pub? The pub. Jesus, but he'd go for a pint now.

He put the shovel back into its brackets, picked up his broom, and started sweeping, inwardly cursing the lazy buggers back at the depot, and the passersby who kept getting in his way. He thought, with relish, of the cool familiarity of the bar in the Marine Hotel where he'd pop in for a quick one on his way home tonight.

. . .

Molly Carmichael and Helen Grey left the butcher's shop on the bottom corner of the street. They always met on Tuesdays, made their purchases together, and stopped for lunch in one of the two Main Street cafés.

Molly was tall, hawk-nosed, and fiftyish, with the carriage and demeanour of a Victorian dowager. Helen was short, fair, slight, and shy, and walked in the shadow of her friend. They were in no great hurry. The sun was warm, their shopping bags full, and Bangor Main Street, which is on a hill, was crowded with shoppers and day trippers down from Belfast. Molly shifted her basket to her other hand. "I think we should go to the Singing Kettle today."

Helen heard the buttermilk of Molly's Ulster inflections surfacing through the cream of her affected Queen's English and observed, with just that tiny touch of malice a friend of many years can feel, how Molly's contralto voice had not quite responded to the attentions of the teachers, years ago, at a private girls' school. "All right, dear," Helen said, as always deferring to her friend's opinions. "Morning, Mrs. Wilson." She greeted a woman who was hurrying in the opposite direction and who acknowledged the salute with a smile and a wave. "Funny isn't it, how you get to know everybody?" Even as Helen spoke, she realized that Molly had not been paying attention.

"I beg your pardon?"

"I said, living in a place like this, you get to know everybody."

"Indeed, isn't that half the pleasure of living in Bangor? You simply— belong. I find it very comforting. You know everyone and everyone knows you."

"Yes, dear," said Helen, to her friend's back. Molly was busy exchanging a few pleasantries with a short, bald-headed man who was carrying his jacket over his arm, revealing a pair of bright red braces.

The two women took advantage of a gap in the flow of cars and crossed the road, Helen having to hurry to keep up with her companion's longer strides. As they walked on, up the Main Street, Molly began holding forth about some scandal at the Golf Club. "Why we let that bloody man in, I don't know. He's drunk as often as he's sober.

Last night he actually tried to pinch my bottom." Her shoulders stiffened, and Helen saw the flash in her friend's brown eyes.

"Oh dear," Helen said, helpfully.

"We'll just have to speak to the house committee and see about getting him out." Molly was in full cry.

Helen nodded vigorously. "Of course, dear." As far as she was concerned, it seemed to be a shame, getting excited about what was essentially so trivial a matter. She almost wished that someone would try to pinch her bottom.

They lapsed into a companionable silence, Helen still thinking, naughtily, about bottoms. It might be comforting to live in Bangor, but nothing much ever seemed to happen here. The Troubles, thank God, were in Belfast, or Londonderry or Crossmaglen. At least this episode at the Golf Club would give her something to tell Peter tonight when he came home from work. Perhaps she could entice him into pinching her bottom. That would be nice. She'd wear the short dress she'd bought last week. Peter said it made her look sexy.

Returning from her little fantasy, she noticed she was walking alone. She stopped and turned. Molly was a few paces behind, talking to Willie.

Willie touched his cap, politely. "Right enough, it's a grand day, so it is, Mrs. Carmichael."

"It is indeed, Willie. How are your cats?"

Helen bent and put her shopping bag on the pavement. She knew that when Molly got started on the subject of cats, she could be hard to stop. Helen smiled at her friend. For all her overbearing ways, Molly was a kind woman, the sort referred to in Ulster as having a heart of corn.

Susan collected her change from the cashier, and if only to gain a moment's respite from John's constant demands for a sweetie, handed him the bag of peppermints. She hefted two bulging brown paper bags and hustled her son out onto the crowded street.

"Come on, John." She motioned with a nod of her head, long auburn hair swinging thick below her shoulders. The little boy trotted after his mother, bag of peppermints in one hand, his teddy bear, constant companion on shopping expeditions, clutched by its nose in the other. Susan nodded at Helen Grey, who smiled back.

Susan started to elbow her way past the pedestrians who came and went along the pavement. She had to step aside to avoid a slim young man who was wearing trousers of a most unusual mustard colour. She did not recognize him as he bustled past to disappear in the crowd. She thought how funny the yellow pants looked—no Bangorian would wear anything like that—and almost collided with someone. She saw pink plastic curlers and a green headscarf, mouthed, "Sorry," and walked on.

Just as Susan was about to pass Mrs. Carmichael, who was talking to Willie Cauldwell about something, John decided to stop and see if Teddy would like a peppermint. Susan blew out her cheeks in exasperation, smiled wanly at Molly, turned, and yelled at her son.

"If you don't come here this minute, I'll have those sweeties off you."

The bright sunlight was dimmed by a brighter light and a thousand thunderclaps tore the gentle day apart as the ground-up ammonium nitrate, secreted the night before in one of Willie's bins, was ignited by its timed detonator.

The blast vapourized the bins, its violent heat melting the tarmac beneath the barrow, and blowing out the plate-glass windows for a radius of one hundred yards from the epicentre. Only the crystal tinkling of the falling glass broke the stunned, numbed silence.

Willie Cauldwell did not scream. Willie Cauldwell could not scream. The blast emptied his lungs of air milliseconds before turning half of his chest into a grisly pulp. Besides, he no longer had a head.

The hurtling blade of Willie's shovel cut the carotid artery in the neck of the unknown, slim young man in mustard yellow pants, a stranger, an American, come to Bangor to find his Irish roots. He bled to death.

Susan Stevenson didn't scream. Not at first. She simply stared through her scorched, tangled, auburn hair. She looked in stunned disbelief at the place where her left leg used to be, at the black streams of blood passively reflecting the sunlight as the gore trickled over the shattered remnants of Willie's broom. There was no pain. Not at first. Her only thought was for John.

She struggled to a half-sitting position, crying, "John. Joooohn. Johnnny."

She was still hoarsely calling his name when a man, face soot-blackened and blistered, but more alert than many of the others who stood or lay helplessly, wrapped a tourniquet around her stump, wrenched the strip of cloth tight and saved her life.

Helen Grey tried to scream but her howls, like herself, were small and subdued, unheard beneath a rising chorus of moans and prayers, curses and shouts and the "nee-naw, nee-naw" of the sirens of the emergency vehicles. She lay on her back, half in half out of a smashed shop window. A male mannequin lay on top of her in a grotesque parody of the copulatory act. She couldn't see. She couldn't see. She blinked again and again, rubbing her fists, grinding her knuckles into her blinded eyes, whimpering softly, terrified, alone, lost in her darkness.

Molly Carmichael was still standing. She made no sound. The blast that had destroyed Willie merely stripped her of her dress and one shoe. The force of the explosion also hurled a twelve-inch shard of window glass, sharp as a stiletto, vicious as the men who had set the explosives. The dagger had pierced her back, the point ripping deep into her body before coming to a halt buried in her left kidney. She just stood there, ashamed of her semi-nakedness, one hand trying to cover her breasts, her other hand clawing behind her for the thing that was tearing at her flesh.

Little Johnny Stevenson wept. He sat, rocking Teddy and telling him over and over, "I will be good. I will be good. . . ." He sat, surrounded by spilt groceries, blades of shattered glass, clutching his peppermints and Teddy. Mummy must be awful cross, and why could he not hear her? His tears flowed through his silence, making tiny soft splashes on Teddy's head. Trickles of blood from his ruptured eardrums stained his cheeks and mingled with his tears.

"There was an explosion in Bangor today. Two people were killed and fifteen wounded."

1992

On January 17, a landmine exploded at Teebane Crossroads, near Dungannon, County Tyrone. A vehicle carrying Protestant construction workers was passing. Eight men died.

On February 4, an off-duty Royal Ulster Constabulary officer entered the Sinn Fein offices in Belfast. He killed three people before committing suicide.

On February 5, two masked members of the Ulster Freedom Fighters shot and killed five Catholics in Sean Graham's bookmaker's shop on the Ormeau Road in Belfast. Fifteen-year-old James Hamilton said, just before he died, "Tell Mummy I love her." Seven other people were wounded.

On April 10, a van loaded with 100 pounds of Semtex exploded at the Baltic Exchange in London, killing three people including fifteen-year-old Danielle Carter.

1992 Dead 85   **Total Dead 3,128**

STRANGERS

The young barman took Alan's order, paused for a moment, smiled, and enquired, "The Wee North is it?" His brogue was soft.

"It is. County Down. Yourself?"

"Cavan." The barman left to fill the order.

Alan sighed. Was he losing his ear for accents? He would have taken his oath that he had just been talking with a Corkman.

The young man returned with a pint of Guinness, set it on the mahogany bar top, took Alan's payment, leant over, and asked, "You down here on business?"

"Aye." Alan sampled his pint. It was pleasantly bitter. He had no desire to talk about his work. Not tonight. "That's not a bad drop—for America."

The barman grinned, showing irregular teeth. "It's the way I pour them. Just like back home." He used a cloth to wipe imaginary beer spillings from the countertop. "Ah, you'll like the music later. The singer's grand, but he'll not be on for an hour or so."

Another customer came through the pub's swing doors. Alan watched as the man walked along the bare wooden planks of the floor, past the tiny stage at the far side of the room, past the half-dozen or so table and chair sets, and took a seat at the far end of the nearly deserted bar. The barman left to attend to the newcomer.

Alan turned away and hoisted his hip onto a tall stool. He sipped his drink and wondered how often he had drifted into so-called Irish pubs in cities all over America. When he had started working as a sales representative for a pharmaceutical company, the job had seemed glamorous. The personnel manager had promised Alan lots of travel. Now, after eighteen years of airport lineups, crowded flights, and medical convention centres full of snooty doctors who had no time for salesmen, the glamour had become tarnished. He was heartily sick of being alone in hotel rooms.

The advertisement in the Washington, D.C., *Yellow Pages* had said there would be live entertainment and a "convivial atmosphere" in the Dubliner pub. He wanted a bit of company. Left to himself his thoughts kept drifting back to Bangor, County Down, and he did not want to think about that. Not tonight.

He took another swallow and looked across to the stage. It was raised about four feet above the floor, and as far as Alan could see would give the singer enough room for his microphone, sound equipment, and precious little else. The flags of the four provinces of Ireland—Ulster and Munster to the left, Leinster and Connaught to the right—hung on dark wood-panelled walls, flanking the stage and framing a banner that hung above the little platform. Pseudo-Celtic script on the green material announced, "The Dubliner Proudly Presents." Beneath it a printed card said, "Tony Gallagher."

"He's a Kerryman."

Alan realized someone was speaking to him. He turned back towards the bar.

"Sorry?"

"Tony. He's from Kerry." The barman was back, polishing a straight glass with his dishcloth. "Nothing but the real MacCoy in here." He grinned. "I'm only off the boat a year myself. The name's Sean."

"Alan." He did not offer to shake hands. "I've been living in Canada for the last eighteen years. I'm just down here for a couple of days."

"Travel a lot, do you?"

"Too much." Alan coughed. "Sometimes I get fed up with my own company."

Sean set the glass back with its fellows. He inclined his head in the general direction of the tables. "It's pretty quiet now, but it'll start to

8STRANGERS 237

fill up. A lot of people who work for the American government like to drop in and take a taste of"—his accent changed to a Midwestern drawl—"li'l ol' Ireland."

Alan found himself laughing with the young man and was surprised when his new companion's smile faded and his tone became serious. "I don't mind them wearin' the green and shouting *Begorrah* but I wish some of them would mind their own business."

"What business?"

Sean propped one elbow on the counter, the other hand on his hip. "Well, it's hardly anything to do with me, being from the Republic, but I reckon smarter men than us have been at it for a brave while and they can't sort out Ulster."

"True enough."

Sean tilted his head and closed one eye, knowingly. "Then how the hell can Teddy Kennedy and Tip O'Neill and Bill Clinton have all the answers?"

Alan waited, surprised by the vehemence of the Southerner's opinion, one that for more personal reasons, he shared.

Sean opened his eye, nodded once, and continued, "They're after the Irish-American vote. You could meet some of that kind in here tonight." His seriousness went and he thickened his brogue. "Arragh, Lord Jasus, but there's nothing more Irish than a Yankee with a shamrock." He laughed and Alan joined in. "Still, there's a few decent lads come in. If you're after a bit of a blether I'll see what I can do." He looked along the bar. Alan's gaze followed. The bar's only other customer was beckoning to Sean, who grimaced and said, "Not him. He's a right gobshite. I'll be back."

Sean went to attend to the patron, leaving Alan to smile at the old Dublin expression of disapproval. It would be pleasant to find some company. This might be Washington, but Sean was like the publicans back home. Always ready to introduce a stranger to the locals. Alan lit a cigarette and looked at the row of bottles on a shelf behind the bar, and at a poor pencil sketch of James Joyce that hung, out of place, beside a well-executed watercolour of a sandy beach with green hills behind. The scene reminded him forcibly of the beach at Ballymacormick, near Bangor. There, little fields, gorse-green and turf-brown, bordered with dry-stone walls, met with the sand of the strand and the waters of Ballyholme Bay. Alan sighed.

"Nice picture," Sean said.

"Who's the artist?"

Sean peered at the signature. "Peter something-or-other." He un-hooked the painting from the wall and passed it over the bar. "What do you think?"

Alan admired the artist's technique. The man used firm economical brushstrokes and carefully shaded tints. "Can't see, but he's very good. Here."

Sean rehung the painting, turned, and leant with both forearms on the bar.

Alan's decision was spur-of-the-moment. "I don't suppose it would be for sale?"

"I've no idea. I'll ask when the manager comes in."

"Thanks." Alan stubbed out his cigarette. Dumb habit. Andy had disapproved of Alan's smoking. "It's very like a place back home. I used to go there with my brother when we were growing up."

"Brother still in Ireland?"

Alan set his empty glass on the counter, closed his eyes, and said quietly, "Oh, yes." He pointed at the painting. "I was back six months ago. I scattered his ashes on a beach like that."

Sean looked back to Alan. "Ah, Jesus. I'm sorry to hear that."

Alan shook his head. "Thanks, but it's all right."

"Still—"

Alan was surprised by the depth of concern in the Cavanman's eyes. "One of those things. Don't worry about it."

Sean nodded and walked along behind the counter. Alan watched him working the handle of a beer pump. Don't you worry about it, Sean, he thought, I can do all the worrying in the world. He lit another smoke and inhaled greedily, thinking about how much he missed Andy and his calm wisdom. Damn the Troubles. Damn them to hell. He looked at the painting once more. He and Andy had walked their beach—it must have been four or five years ago. The last time Alan had seen his older brother alive. Alan could imagine the pair of them, Andrew two years older, ruddy-cheeked from the wind, earnestly talking about the Troubles.

Sean set a fresh pint on the counter. "That's on me."

"Thanks."

The barman produced a small glass, looked furtively around, and poured himself a small Irish. "I'm not supposed to drink on duty." He raised his glass. "To your brother."

Alan hoisted his Guinness. "Andy." He drank and for a moment held Sean's eyes with his own. "Thanks again. But I told you, don't you worry about it."

Sean nodded once, slipped his now-empty glass among other used ones in a sink, and said, "Fair enough," before going into his stage Irish act. "Sure Lord Jasus, Mary, and all the little saints, don't us poor bog trotters have to stick together?" He grinned, showing his poorly cared-for teeth again. "I'll be back in a little minuit."

"*Sláinte*." Alan lifted his glass and toasted Sean's retreating back. Funny the young man from Cavan should say the Irish should stick together; that's what Andy had believed, with a passion. He'd worked so hard to try to bridge the gap between the two northern communities. Alan drank, wiping the foam from his upper lip with the back of his hand.

"Pint all right?" Sean was back at his post.

"It is."

"Good."

"And you're right. We should stick together."

"Us real Paddies," Sean said and then looked away. Alan followed the direction of Sean's gaze and saw a middle-aged man, business-suited, carrying a briefcase, come through the swing door and take a seat at a table. He heard Sean saying, quietly, "That fellow, just come in? Far as I know he's never been to Ireland in his life." Sean's lip curled. "Thinks he's a direct descendant of Brian Boru." He lifted a cardboard menu from under the countertop. "I'd better go and see what his majesty wants."

Alan was left alone again. He sat with his back to the bar. The place was beginning to fill up. Tables were being occupied by what seemed to him to be self-contained groups of friends, each table an island, entire unto itself, wishing no intercourse with its neighbour. Six smartly dressed young men had taken the stools to his right, four sitting, two standing, talking loudly about their office affairs, paying no attention to the man Sean had called a gobshite. Alan could see him sitting beside the newcomers, hunched over his drink.

At the other end of the bar, a woman wearing rhinestone-framed spectacles was treating her bottled-blonde friend to a cut-by-cut account of her recent hysterectomy. He could hear her sharp voice past the two men in work shirts who had taken the stools next-but-one to himself. Alan sipped his pint, looking at the empty stool beside him. Well, at least he'd had a bit of a blether with Sean, but he'd be too busy now, and it looked as though the other patrons had brought their own company, as if they were frightened of the possibility of having to talk to a stranger.

Sean must have forgotten his promise to introduce Alan to some of the regulars. Perhaps, once Sean had heard about Andy, he'd decided Alan might want to be left alone.

The volume of conversation all around rose. Cigarette smoke blued the air. A man carrying a guitar case pushed his way through the door. Alan surmised that this must be Gallagher, the singer. He was tall and heavily built, dressed in a pair of slacks and a green open-necked shirt, the front of which protruded over the waistband of his trousers. His face was round, fringed by a well-trimmed, chin-hugging ginger beard that turned sharply east and west at his ears to continue as a thin meridian of latitude around an otherwise bald and shining dome. His nose was large, his lips full. Close-set eyes twinkled beneath shaggy brows. His eyes, for all their laugh lines, spoke to Alan of innumerable nights in smoky bars, playing and singing tunes of Ireland that could scarcely be heard over the din of the mob.

Alan watched as the singer set up his equipment, wiring his guitar to a set of speakers. Loudspeakers. In Ireland, Alan thought, that would not have been necessary. There, he knew, the respect for the entertainer went right back to the old Celtic kingdoms where the *Filid*, the keepers of the oral traditions, were accorded places of great honour along with the King, and the givers of the law. Here in America—he looked round the crowded little room—the singer was like live elevator music. To compete with the background row of chatter, he had to become amplified. As he did, up went the level of raucous chattering of the patrons.

The entertainer stepped up to the microphone.

"Good evening, ladies and gentlemen. My name is Tony Gallagher, from County Kerry."

His brogue was as thick as a bowl of stirabout. "I am here to entertain you with songs of Ireland. If you like them," he indicated a small pile of tapes he had placed on a low stool, "you can pick up one of my cassettes."

Alan looked around. The man might as well have been talking to himself. He carried on.

"If you have any requests, write them on a piece of paper, and hand them up." He adjusted the guitar in its sling round his neck. "Now. Let's get your hands clapping. Do you know 'Whiskey in the Jar?' The chorus goes, 'Musha ringum a toorum anyah.' When I go, 'Anyah,' you go clap, clap, clap."

He demonstrated. One or two pairs of hands clapped feebly.

"Come on." He trotted out the old chestnut, "I know you're out there; I can hear you breathing."

Alan wondered how many bar singers he had heard use that one as Gallagher launched into his first number.

"As I was goin' over the far-famed Kerry Mountain,
I met with Captain Farrell and his money he was countin'. . . ."

Alan watched the other patrons. The bottled blonde was singing along off-key and clapping off the beat. One of the office workers was dancing something akin to a highland fling with both hands held high above his head. His friends seemed to think it was an Irish jig and were encouraging him with hoarse shouts. The general level of noise rose.

Gallagher was an accomplished guitar player, and even in his first number it was apparent that he had a soft, clear tenor voice that would be worth listening to. Alan took out his pen and reached for a napkin. He printed the title of a song and passed the napkin up to the stage. Gallagher looked at the paper, smiled, and nodded his agreement. He finished his first song.

"I have a request here for 'The Fields of Athenry.'" With no further ado, he struck the first chords and began to sing, softly and gently. Some of the customers actually stopped talking and turned to face the stage. Alan was surprised by the intensity of homesickness that welled within him. He ignored the other patrons. The cigarette smoke haze became a mist through which he could see Galway and the lonely prison wall, smell the hay drying, hear the young girl calling. Andy had loved that song. Alan felt his eyes fill. Surreptitiously he pushed an index finger between his spectacles and cheek, catching the errant tear before it could fall.

The singer continued to caress the notes of one of the saddest Irish songs of famine and criminal transportation to Australia. It made Alan think of his own transportion to Canada although that had been voluntary. Well, almost. Andy had tried to stand up to their father but the old man had been adamant. Alan had failed his medical school examinations once too often. A job had been arranged with a drug company in Calgary, and he was free to take it or leave it. There would, however, be no more paternal support. Calgary wasn't really such a bad old spot, he thought.

He listened to the last verse, cleared his throat, and bowed his head as a silent gesture of thanks to the singer. His nod was returned. Alan took a deep breath. Not moments ago he'd craved company but now he knew he would be quite happy to sit and listen to Gallagher. There was comfort in the old familiar songs.

Alan sensed movement to his left. A newcomer was pushing in to the bar. Alan slid his stool sideways and recognized the man Sean had earlier said claimed to be a descendant of Brian Boru.

The newcomer bent and set his briefcase between the brass rail and the foot of the bar, then straightened, clambered onto the empty stool beside Alan, and dusted a sleeve with the palm of one hand. "Thanks, buddy."

"You're welcome."

"You call for that last song?" His speech was slightly slurred.

"Yes."

"It's pretty." He smiled. "You Irish?"

The man had an open face. He was trying to be friendly, even if he was a pint or two ahead. Alan returned the smile. "Yes. From County Down but I live in Canada."

"I'm Irish too. Mayo County. I'm Bob." He held out his right hand.

Alan took the hand and said, "Alan," thinking as he did that there aren't too many folks from Mayo with a strong Boston accent. And a Mayo man would have said, "County Mayo," but no matter. He was someone to talk to.

Bob nodded at Alan's empty glass. "Would you like another, Alan?"

"Please."

Bob waved for Sean. "I was born there. My folks brought me to America when I was six months. Lived in Brookline, Mass., for years before I moved here. I'm going back to Mayo one day."

"It's a beautiful county," Alan said as he tried to listen to Tony Gallagher sing "The Travelling People," while Bob's "Two pints," and Sean's, "Right, Bob," intruded.

"He's good," said Bob, nodding at the singer.

Alan laid a finger against his lips. "Let's listen."

"Sure."

Alan hardly noticed the pints arrive and was grateful when Bob handed one over without speaking.

". . . *winds of change are blowing,*
old ways are going.
Your rambling days will soon be over."

Not if you're a salesman, Alan thought wryly as he lifted his glass to his new companion.

Gallagher unslung his guitar. "All right. This set's not over. I'll be back in a tick, but I have to go and shed a tear for the old country."

The entertainer's announcement of his need for a bathroom break provoked a chorus of laughter.

Alan did not join in. Too many tears had been shed, including his own. He did not want to think about them. He turned to Bob. "You like Irish music?"

"You bet." He took a deep drink. "I just wish Tony would sing some of the really good songs."

Alan frowned. "Good songs?"

"Yeah. You know. Like 'Four Green Fields,' or 'The Men Behind the Wire.'"

Alan's hand tightened round his glass. He felt a chill. Andy had detested the new folk songs that kept the flames alight or glorified the hard men of either persuasion. He spoke slowly, not wanting to start a discussion of the Troubles. "I don't think so."

"What?" Bob's eyes narrowed. "What's wrong with them?"

"I just don't think they help very much."

Bob blew out his cheeks. "I reckon anything that'll get the Brits out is great."

Alan heard Gallagher start the first verse of "The Galway Races." "As I roved out through Galway Town in search of recreation . . ." which, Alan thought, is what he was doing tonight. Still, this conversation, which had started so inconsequentially, was taking a turn that he desperately wanted to avoid.

Bob bent, opened his briefcase, and produced a newspaper.

"Take a look at this." He thrust the broadsheet under Alan's nose.

Alan saw immediately that it was the NORAID newspaper, the *Irish People.* He pushed it away like an unclean thing, unable to control a swallow of total revulsion. He would read nothing in the organ of NO-RAID, the Northern Irish Aid Committee. "No thanks."

"Shit," said Bob, "call yourself Irish. I suppose you don't want a united Ireland. One nation, strong and free?"

Alan looked around and was grateful to see Sean moving along to their end of the bar, eyes raised, head shaking. Alan shrugged and inclined his head towards his companion. He felt Bob's hand on his shoulder and heard him say, "I want the tyrants gone." The man was mouthing slogans that were hangovers from the Anglo-Irish War of the twenties.

Alan tried to ignore him, but the grip on his shoulder tightened. He turned to Bob. "Please take your hand away."

Bob's nostrils flared. "I suppose you're a bloody Prod."

Alan stood. "No. I'm a Catholic."

"All right." Bob let his hand fall on the bar. "Here." He pulled an envelope from his jacket pocket. "Show me. Make a donation to NO-RAID."

Alan clenched his teeth and closed his eyes. "No."

He heard Sean try to intervene. "Leave it be, Bob."

As Alan opened his eyes, Bob swung on the barman, snarled, "Fuck off," and turned back to stare at Alan. Alan saw how the man's pupils had dilated even though he softened his voice as he said, "Come on. You don't live there anymore, but you can help. You're a Catholic and an Irishman. The least you can do is put your hand in your pocket. Every dollar for NORAID goes to support the cause." He held out the envelope in his well-manicured hand as if collecting for the Cancer Society.

And he was, Alan thought. Money for the cause. The cancer of Ireland. He barely heard Bob's voice, hectoring now. "Have you any idea what one automatic rifle costs? Do you know where the money for the guns comes from?"

Andy had had his cause, too. His cause had been peace. He'd given his life for it when he had stepped between a Provo gunman and a young Protestant and his daughter. It hadn't mattered. They'd all been killed, cut down with an Armalite bought with NORAID money.

"I know," he whispered, as his eyes pricked. "I know." And in the background he heard Tony Gallagher finish his song.

"There were half a million people there of all denominations.
The Catholic, the Protestant, the Jew, the Presbyterian,
And yet no animosity, no matter what persuasion,
But fáilte—*hospitality inducing fresh acquaintance."*

1993

On January 3, in a grocery shop in Pomeroy, County Tyrone, a Catholic father and son were murdered by members of the UVF.

On March 7, the second bomb attack in five months was made on Bangor, County Down. Five police officers were injured.

On May 20, a 1,000-pound bomb exploded outside the Grand Opera House in Belfast.

On October 23, the IRA bomber himself and nine other people died in an explosion in a fish shop on the Shankill Road.

On October 30, seven patrons of the Rising Sun pub in Greysteel were murdered by members of the UFF.

On December 12, the IRA shot two RUC officers to death in Fivemiletown, County Tyrone.

1993 Dead 84   **Total Dead 3,212**

BIRDSONG
IN THE
MORNING

"Another cup of tea?" She held the pot in her big, reddened left hand and reached for his cup with the other. He hardly seemed to hear her. She tried again, more loudly this time. "More tea?"

"What?"

She watched his eyes, blue-green eyes, focus on the teapot, as if not recognizing it for what it was. She thought he looked so young, vulnerable, just a boy really, not much older than her Brian had been. "Tea. I asked if you wanted more tea."

He shook his head, lips pursed.

She tried not to look at his hands, which he kept beneath the table to hide the chain between his wrists and the handcuffs encircling them. His forearms rested on the rough serge of his trousers. His fingers, held loosely between his legs, tapped, one tip against the others, as if practising scales on a penny whistle. She looked away, busying herself with the teapot and milk jug. Blue delft. Why she had seen fit to use her Sunday best she couldn't say. It wasn't as if the boy, sitting silently in the chair that he had occupied since his arrival, was a special guest.

She took the teapot to the sink, removed the lid, and tipped the contents of the pot into the plug hole. The warm, mahogany fluid, like the blood that spilled when she butchered a pig, flowed away leaving only a few tea leaves to mark its passage. She turned the tap on, rinsing the teapot and the last remaining leaves before inverting the pot on the draining board, to keep company with the plate and knife and fork that had been washed moments before. What a waste. The congealed bacon and eggs now lay in the slop bucket beneath the sink. He'd hardly touched any of it. She turned off the tap, giving silent thanks, as she did every time she used it, that her husband, Michael, had installed the water supply and that she no longer needed to fill pails from the well at the other side of the farmyard. Brian used to do that for her. The water had come to the farmhouse at the same time the county council had brought telephone service to the townland.

She heard the boy moving behind her and turned, drying her hands on her calico pinafore. He had risen and was standing, head drooping, cuffed hands held in front of his crotch.

"'Scuse me, missus."

He was polite enough.

"I . . ." He began again, "I need to," he hesitated, "pee."

She finished drying her hands, smiling at his embarrassment. "Do you now?"

"Aye. Please."

She heard the flat vowels, the Belfast intonation, and knew that his speech would sound foreign, here in the depths of County Tyrone. "Come on then." She held out one hand.

He stepped toward her, arms outstretched, palms together, like a supplicant priest. She took his right upper arm in her hand, feeling the tense muscles beneath his striped, collarless shirt. He resisted her gentle urging, saying, apologetically, "They took away my boots." He nodded towards the floor and she looked down at his wool socks, noting the hole where his left great toe stuck through.

She shook her head. Men. So useless when it came to women's work. "I should darn that for you." Usually she could no more ignore mending that needed to be done than a baby that needed to be changed. God alone knew—she brushed a stray lock of hair away with the back of her hand—how many pairs of socks she had darned for Michael, aye, and Brian.

She left him, crossed the scrubbed sandstone floor to where a pair of black rubber Wellington boots stood, the insteps flecked with blotches of dried cow clap, picked up the boots, and brought them to him. "Here. Put those on you."

He winced as he used his manacled hands to force his feet into the boots. "They're a bit tight. I thought your man would've had bigger feet."

"Them's not Michael's. Brian used to wear them."

"Brian?"

She folded her arms, right hand massaging her left shoulder. "Our young lad."

They had told her, when they brought the boy to the farmhouse, in the dark just before the dawn, that she was not to try to get to know the prisoner, nor to let him get to know her. No names. No unnecessary chatter. She remembered that now and shook her head. "Come on, now." She took his arm again, guiding him through the kitchen, out of the door with its black-painted iron snib, and out into the farmyard, past the rooster and few chickens that pecked round the kennel where an old border collie lay, head between his forepaws, watching. The dog raised his head, porcelain-pale eyes fixed on the stranger. A dull, insistent rumbling started in his throat.

"Away to hell out of that, Shep." She waved one hand imperiously at the animal, who retreated, muttering, into his kennel. "Pay no heed to him."

He walked at her side, awkward in his ill-fitting boots, breathing in the air redolent with the aroma of cattle and the mown hay that lay in the fields beyond a blackthorn hedge. He stopped for a moment, staring at the fields—yellow gorse and brown bracken, dry-stone walls and bright green grass—rolling in gentle hills to the windbreak of heavy-leaved poplars in the distance. Away, far to the right, a curl of blue smoke from the chimney of a whitewashed, thatched cottage ascended softly to join a few wisps of white clouds.

A look of despair had taken the smile from the young man's face just as a wavelet washes a child's sandcastle into the infinite ocean. She waited for him to speak, but he just stood there, rocking gently, one hand massaging the other wrist where the cuff chafed. He looked at her, his blue eyes pleading. He whispered, "I'm scared, missus." His eyes blurred and silent tears spilled. "They're going to kill me." His voice was flat, matter of fact. "They think I've informed."

She could find no words to comfort him. "They," the men who had brought the boy here, were strangers to her, but Michael had known them. Two, big, brusque, hard men, balaclava-covered heads like khaki woollen skulls, camouflage jackets, rasping voices. Little had been said but instructions to feed and house the prisoner until Army Council decided what was to be done with him. The men had left as suddenly as they had come, refusing her offer of breakfast, but taking Michael with them. Her soul ached and she wondered if Brian had been scared, had had time enough to be scared.

She went to the boy and clasped him to her, holding his head on her breast, stroking his ginger hair. His hot tears wet the front of her pinafore. She made inchoate, murmuring noises, soothing, shushing.

He pulled away from her, straightening his shoulders and wiping the run from his nose with the back of one hand, the other following its partner in silent, manacled protest. "I'm all right. All right." He sniffed and made a noise in the back of his throat. "Right," he said, "I'm bustin', so I am."

She smiled at him, sadly, giving him back his man's pride. "Come on, then." She took his arm again and guided him to the privy, holding the door open for him and closing it behind him, standing waiting, hearing the sudden plashing in the good earth.

He reopened the door with his shoulder, standing there, embarrassed. He held his hands out, helplessly. "I can't do up my pants."

She looked down, seeing the tail of his shirt caught in the zipper, hanging limply like a tiny grey penis. She pulled the material from between the teeth of the fastener, tucked the cloth back inside, and zipped him up. "There."

"Thanks."

Together they walked back, side by side, through the warmth of the late-summer day towards the cool of the kitchen, and overhead the larks sang and in the hedgerow the linnet and thrush, blackbird and wren trilled, and gave their bright music to the morning.

. . .

She could not sleep that night, thinking of the boy and thinking of Brian. She could hear her prisoner, next door. She had followed her instructions, unlocking one cuff and snapping it closed around one of the pillars of the big brass bed. He had made no protest. The walls were thin and now his snores reverberated. Still, snores were better than the muted sobs that had preceded them.

She turned onto her side, pummelling the pillow, feeling the emptiness on Michael's side of the bed. Surely to God, he'd be back soon. She needed him now, the strong sweaty smell of him after a day's haying, the hardness of his muscles that even now, after nearly twenty-five years of marriage, excited her as much as they had done when he had been a young man courting her, late of a night, snuggled in a hayrick, exploring the places and the deeds that the priest had said would lead to damnation.

She felt herself growing damp at the thought of those days and Michael. She slid a hand between her legs, feeling the frisson as her fingers found the tiny bud, pausing, listening to the snores from next door, knowing that the boy would not hear her little whimperings as she moved her fingers, rhythmically, faster, until like a great sneeze, climax came, washing over her, taking her to another place.

She rolled onto her back, her long dark hair spilling down the pillow to the sheet beside her, the black of it glowing, the silver streaks shining in the moonbeams that lit the wall beside her and the picture of the bleeding heart of Jesus.

Why? she sighed. Dear Mother of Christ, why? Life had been so good. Michael, the farm here in Tyrone only a few miles from the Donegal border, the animals and the crops, the cycle of the seasons, the rightness of it. She sat up, hugging her knees, her night-dress rumpled under her. She had never needed towns or cities or the world and its troubles. She loved it here where—a line of Yeats came unbidden—"Peace comes dropping slow." When had it all changed?

A single tear crept into her right eye, hesitated, stumbled at the edge and fell, sliding like a first raindrop down the windowpane of her cheek. She held her legs more tightly, rocking slightly, alone in the big bed. Brian had been born here, seventeen years ago. He had been their miracle.

After seven years they had stopped trying. The doctors in Belfast, with all their tests and indignities, had not been able to discover why she could not conceive. But she had, one year later, unexpectedly, wondrously. The insides of her arms touched her breasts. He had been delivered in this bed by the old midwife and—she tightened her arms—these breasts had given him suck.

She threw back the bedclothes and padded barefoot to the window, opened the curtains to stand looking over the moonwashed farmyard, seeing the ghost of her son, her only child, fair and lightfooted, running after Michael who sat on the tractor, begging to ride beside his daddy.

Next door the boy moved. She could hear the rustling of the sheets, the groaning of the bedsprings. He muttered something, perhaps awake, perhaps talking in his sleep. How many nights had she listened to the sounds from that room, Brian's room? Her own mother had told her that mothers could hear their children's dreams, and, as he had grown, Brian had had dreams, but she hadn't heard them.

She stepped back to the bed and sat on its edge, bare feet cold on the linoleum floor. Damn the Gaelic Athletic Association, damn them and their talk of Maeve, Princess Macha, Deirdre and Cu Chulainn and the Knights of the Red Branch. Stuff and nonsense of Celtic Twilight to fill the head of a sixteen-year-old who had only joined to play hurling, sweeping the field with his ball and hurley, running in the heat of youth, laughing on the green fields of Tyrone. The stories were as old as those fields, the hurling matches the only battles that Brian needed to fight.

If only the men of the club had kept to the ancient tales, the magic of faeries and the little people, the Firbolg and Milesians, but no, curse them. They had to tell of the heroes of '16, Padràic Pearse and James Connolly, executed by the British, Bobby Sands of modern days, starving himself to death. Why should she and Michael and Brian care, here in their rural isolation? But Brian had cared, snared by the men who sought cannon fodder for their "struggle."

She knew that she would not sleep now, so she walked to the dresser, lifting a jug from the basin where it stood. The splash of the cold water on her face stung and she rapidly dried the rivulets from her cheeks and the hollow of her neck, laying the damp, rough towel, neatly folded, back in its place beside the wash jug. Her slippers waited beside the dresser. The felt was warm against her chilled feet. She walked quietly across the floor, took her dressing gown from its peg and opened the door, slowly, lest the creaking of the hinges disturb the boy. She stood for a moment on the landing, head cocked, listening. But only the sound of his deep breathing came from his room. She inhaled deeply, sorrowful for him, fearful of what his awakening might bring.

She slipped along the landing, avoiding the places where from long experience she knew the floorboards would complain, down the stairs and into the kitchen. The range, black and bulking in the darkness, radiated a comforting heat. The smell of turf burning mingled with a faint whisper of peeled onions. Kitchen smells. Homely. Familiar.

She lifted the kettle, filled since last night, and set it on the range to wait until she had thrust some peat bricks into the still-warm embers below. Once satisfied that the turf had caught, she set the kettle in the glowing aperture.

When the water had boiled, she warmed the teapot and spooned in the leaves from a metal tea caddy decorated with a picture of the Pope blessing the crowd on his last visit to Ireland. She was confident in the timeless acts of starting another day. She poured herself a cup of tea, holding it between her hands for the warmth, and carried her drink to the table where she sat, looking up, hearing the boy moving in his sleep.

How many times had she risen before dawn, the good farmer's wife, to make tea and stirabout for her menfolk? She sighed. Brian had refused to eat his porridge on that last morning. He had been too excited to eat, waiting, eager, impatient for the men to come in the car that would take him on his first operation for the cause.

Grey fingers of the dawn's light began to play on the stone of the kitchen floor, motes of dust catching the rays, shadows appearing, cast by the milk jug and sugar bowl on the table. It had been much darker when, almost a year ago now, they had brought her son home, bleeding, dying.

She held herself, hugging her pain, looking up again as she heard the boy call out in his sleep. She could not hate as Michael had started to hate, could take no solace from the revenge her man had taken, joining the Provos in his son's place, growing hard, growing bitter. She had grieved for her lost boy, silently, with dignity, privately. No more deaths would bring Brian back. She could remember, as a girl, hearing Pandit Nehru on the wireless giving the eulogy for the assassinated Gandhi. His words came back, poignant, and so true. "The light has gone out of our life."

Yet she could not but be loyal to Michael and had raised no protest when he had told her that she must be gaoler to the boy upstairs. Her tea was finished. She set the cup in its saucer and stretched her arms across the smooth pine wood of the tabletop, laying her cheek on her arms, suddenly tired. She dozed, barely hearing the crow of the rooster as he sounded his call to the new day.

From somewhere between sleep and waking she heard Shep's bark, insistent, fierce—not his welcome when Michael returned but a warning that strangers were in the farmyard. She roused herself and went to the door, opening it to a grey day, mist heavy on the far hills, veiling their crests, hiding the sun.

A black car was parked in the farmyard. Three men strode purposefully towards her—Michael, a stranger, and a priest, black in his cassock, a crow of ill omen. Her hand went to her throat when she saw the grim look on Michael's unshaven face and noticed the way the priest would not meet her eyes.

No words were spoken as the three men went past her into her kitchen. She closed the door and stood with her back to it, feeling the roughness of the planks. Michael turned to her, brushing his lips lightly on her cheek.

"We've come for him." The words were staccato, bereft of hope.

She would make no complaint, no protest. It was man's work and though her soul wept for the young man, for all the young men, she would not try to interfere. "He's upstairs."

She saw that the stranger had seated himself at the kitchen table. The priest came to her and put an arm round her shoulder. He smelt vaguely of cologne, and his pink, scrubbed cheeks shone. "Will you bring him down, daughter?" By the lilt of his voice she recognized him for a Southerner.

She nodded once, disengaged herself from the man's encircling arm, gathered the hem of her dressing gown and night-dress in one hand, and went to climb the stairs.

He was sitting up in the bed, his right hand behind him, cuffed to the bedpost. She thought he looked as if he had the jaundice, the way the whites of his eyes reflected the yellow of the bruises. His pupils were wide, staring. "I heard a car." His lower lip trembled. "Is it them?"

She could not bring herself to speak but simply nodded, seeing his fear and wanting to smooth his hair, tousled from his night's sleep.

"Oh, God." His eyes darted like a cornered animal seeking any avenue of escape. The chain rattled against the brass as he jerked his wrist. "Don't let them take me, missus." The hand behind him clenched into a fist, the other was outstretched, pleading.

She fumbled in the pocket of her dressing gown, removed the key, and unlocked the cuff from the bedpost. "You'll want to get washed." She remembered his embarrassment of yesterday when he could not fasten his trousers. "There's a pot under the bed and soap and water on the washstand." She turned to go. "I'll wait outside." He threw back the bedclothes, and as she left, she caught a glimpse of his toe, still poking through his sock.

She waited on the landing, hearing the deep voices of the men below, the splashing of the water from the room behind her. The splashing stopped and the door opened. He stood there, hair combed, holding his hands meekly for her to refasten the cuffs, but she shook her head. She turned and he followed her downstairs, sharply drawing in his breath when he saw the three men sitting at the kitchen table.

The stranger rose and gestured to an empty chair. "Sit."

She stepped aside.

As the boy made his way to the hard-backed chair, Michael spoke. "Wait upstairs, Mary. It's no place for a woman."

To love, honour, and obey. She looked at her man, saw the acid eating him, yet knew she still loved him, ached for his bitterness. She obeyed, climbing the stairs, hearing the scrape of the legs of the chair as the boy was seated, hearing the big man speak. She hesitated on the landing, the words drifting upwards.

"Cahal O'Rourke, you know I'm here from Brigade, to inform you of the sentence, duly passed by a properly constituted court-martial of the *Oglàigh na hEirann*?" The accent of the Falls, nasal flat, a working man's voice, made to sound important by hiding behind formal phrases, dignified by using the Erse for "Army of Ireland." There was no reply. The disembodied voice continued. "You were properly instructed in the Green Book by the officer that recruited you?"

"Aye."

"Are you sure?"

Could she detect a hopeful note in the man's voice?

"You know that if you have not been, you have grounds for appeal?"

"For fuck's sake, Brendan," she heard the scrape of the chair legs. Was the boy standing? "Wasn't it you that recruited me?"

"Sit down, Cahal." The voice was tired. "I have to do this right."

"Right?" she heard a catch now, the momentary defiance gone. "Would an appeal do me any fucking good?"

"No."

A silence hung, ominous, lengthening. Brendan coughed, then said, "It was the verdict of the court-martial that you, Cahal O'Rourke, are guilty, as charged, of treason by reason of passing army information to the forces of the occupying power."

"I never did." She heard his voice rise in pitch. "Honest to God, Brendan."

"The findings have been upheld by Army Council."

"I never grassed." He was sobbing quietly. "I never."

The voice continued, raised to cover the boy's whimpering. "The sentence is death."

The boy wailed, a long keening moan, rending her like the scream of a hare half-shot. Her head drooped on her chest. Death. Holy Mary, no more killing. Cahal was little more than a child.

She could hear movement below, footsteps, the boy's ill-formed cries and the Latin droning of the priest. She heard the door open. Enough. She ran down the stairs, only to be caught and held firmly by Michael, who alone remained in the kitchen.

She held her face up to him as he stood looking down at her. "Sweet Jesus, Michael, can you not stop them?"

He shook his head, sadly, she thought.

"Michael. He's only a baby, just like Brian. He's only a baby."

"Brian died for Ireland. That wee rat betrayed her. He has to pay."

She tore herself free. "God. God." She loved him for his strength, hated him for his hardness. "Michael, Michael. Killing that boy won't give us Brian back. Killing him won't—"

The telephone rang.

Michael picked it up. "Hello."

She watched his lined face—dark where the stubble grew, darker yet beneath his eyes, which widened as he said, "What?"

What was being said?

Michael's shoulders sagged. "I don't believe it. Are you sure? Tell me again." He waited, shook his head and slowly replaced the handset into its cradle.

"What is it, Michael?"

"Mary, that was Brigade. I don't believe it. Gerry Adams has called for a truce. Sinn Fein wants to talk to John Major."

"I don't understand."

"Nor me." He took a deep breath and stared through the open door. "The lad's sentence is to be held off."

"He's not to be shot?"

"Aye. He's going to get away with it."

"Oh, Michael. Can you not forgive him? These last years, have you liked what you've done?"

He shook his head. "I was doing it for Brian."

She took his hard hand in hers. "I know, love." Mary lifted her face to him. "Then save Cahal. Now. For me."

He stared at her and nodded slowly.

She pushed him. "Run, man. Away you after them. Go on with you." God, she thought, but he can be stubborn. "Michael, will you go?"

He walked to the door.

"Move, Michael."

He began to run, long strides across the farmyard.

She ran to the doorway, willing her man to fly, watching his boots pound through the grass as he raced along the tracks left in the dew by three earlier pairs of feet, seeing him disappear over the rise and down into a hollow, willing him to be in time.

"Call out to them, Michael," she cried, but no sounds came back.

She stood watching as the morning sun began to melt the misty tendrils which, like the gauze pubic coverings so favoured by Renaissance painters of saints, still clung modestly to the hills and treetops. She held her breath, praying that Mrs. O'Rourke, wherever she was, would be spared the anguish that she, Mary, had known since the lunacy had taken their Brian.

As if to bring her comfort, overhead a lark sang and in the hedgerow linnet and thrush, blackbird and wren trilled and gave their bright music.

Then two shots—flat, deadly in their finality—clamoured from the hollow and echoed back from the mist and the hills, and at their sound the birds fell silent.

1994

On February 10, Dominic McGlinchy, former leader of the Irish National Liberation Army, was shot to death.

On April 24, the IRA killed two Protestants in Garvagh, County Londonderry.

On May 8, Roseanne Mallon, aged 76, was murdered by the UVF near Dungannon, County Tyrone.

On June 18, UVF gunmen killed six customers in the pub shooting at Loughisland, County Down.

On July 17, a Catholic woman was abducted from Belfast by the IRA, who subsequently killed her.

On August 7, Kathleen O'Hagan, mother of five and pregnant again, was shot to death by members of the UVF.

1994 Dead 56   **Total Dead 3,268**

BURRARD INLET
1994

"They're a damn sight bigger than the Mournes." Neill sat up on the port side staring past the curve of the boat's headsail to the North Shore Mountains.

Pat nodded. "You get used to them after five years."

"It's that long since you left Toronto?"

"Aye." Pat pointed to two peaks higher than the rest. "That's Lion Mountain. Phyllis calls the bits sticking up, 'the lion's ears.'" He hoped Neill would laugh.

Neill didn't laugh but instead took an appraising look all around then aft to where Pat sat holding the tiller. "This is Burrard Inlet? It's a bit like Belfast Lough."

"Aye," said Pat. "Same size, more or less, but look at all the anchored bulk carriers and container ships. Lot more traffic." He refrained from remarking, "Quieter too. No one's going, 'Bang.'" The last thing Neill needed was to be reminded that this was the twenty-fifth year of the civil war in Ulster. It had taken a great deal of coercion over the trans-Atlantic telephone before Pat could persuade Neill to come out for a visit. Pat watched Neill. He'd always been slim, but now he looked gaunt. His black hair, unruly as ever, was streaked with grey. Not silver but dirty grey, like an old smoker's moustache. The planes of his face were more angular, and those dark circles under his eyes had never been there before. We're both getting on, Pat thought, but Neill is aging faster. No wonder.

Pat heard the leech of the genoa start to flap. "Could you trim the jib? It's a bit loose."

Neill took a turn of the sheet round a winch and pulled, tightening the genoa. The boat heeled under the pressure of the wind in the well-filled sail. "Lap of luxury, this, after *Gannet*."

Pat looked up at the pleasing symmetry of the white triangles of the main- and headsails, clean wings against an azure sky. Fifteen knots of wind, filling the taut fabric, drove the boat's sharp bows through the low swell, cleaving the water and sending spray aft to sparkle down the lee scuppers. "*Gannet*? She'd be making heavy weather in this wind. I wonder who has her now?" Pat immediately regretted his remark. It didn't seem to bother Neill.

"No idea." He stood up and stretched, balancing himself against the heel. "You didn't call this one *Gannet 2*?"

"*Tarka*. Tarka the otter. You remember we saw one at Ballysallagh?"

"I do. Pretty little animals. Do you have them out here?"

Pat gently moved the helm towards himself, correcting *Tarka's* urge to sail closer to the wind. "Over in the Gulf Islands. I've seen them at Prevost." He looked over his shoulder out across Georgia Strait to where the peaks of Vancouver Island seemed to be painted against the sky, a stage backdrop to the low humps of the Valdes and Gabriola, shimmering in the heat haze. "Would you like to go over there?"

"How far is it?"

"About twenty miles."

"We'd not be able to do it today."

"No. I meant in the next week or two."

Neill did smile now. "I'd like that. A lot."

"Done. We'll head over next Tuesday. The anchorages are always full at the weekends. Might even find some orcas."

"Killer whales? I've always wanted to see a whale."

"Right. We'll go next week, but I can't promise whales."

"Never worry." Neill yawned. "Sorry. It was a long flight."

"I know. Tell you what. Why don't you go below and get your head down? I'll give you a yell when we get to Caulfeild Cove."

"You don't mind?" Neill yawned again. "It's the jet lag."

"Not at all. Go on."

"Right." Neill headed for the companionway. "Get me up when it's time to anchor."

Pat watched his friend go below and hoped that he would sleep. Perhaps the gentle pitching of *Tarka* would help.

Pat lay back against the transom, tiller held loosely in one hand. Sleep well, Neill. Pat felt the good wind on his cheek, the roll of the boat, the tiny tugs of the tiller. He held a course for the cove on the North Shore. They would be there in about an hour. All he could hear was the singing of the shrouds, the slaps as *Tarka*'s prow cut through the waves, and a gentle snoring coming from below. He smiled.

He looked around again from Point Grey to the Lion's Gate Bridge, just visible under the foot of the mainsail. The high-rises of Vancouver were disappearing behind the trees of Stanley Park as *Tarka* slipped effortlessly along. The late August sun warmed him and twinkled from the sea. A good day to be alive. A great day to be on the water with Neill, even if he wasn't the Neill of old.

Bring her head up just a bit. He put the helm down and stooped to tighten the sheets. Should fetch Caulfeild on this tack. Pat watched the shore come closer, settled himself more comfortably, and watched a pair of Canada geese fly lazily overhead. They took his thoughts to the Long Island. Neill and Grouse and himself, waiting for the dawn. Waiting for the ducks. There were lots of ducks out here but Pat hadn't lifted a gun for years. He'd decided that waterfowl were more beautiful alive than dead. Pity some of the hard men back home didn't think about people that way. How did Neill stick it in Ulster, year after year? Particularly now, since Helen had left him.

Pat could imagine her so clearly, laughing with them the night they had brought the trout home from Ballysallagh, pleased to meet Neill's friend Pat. She was tall, as blonde as Neill was dark, with eyes like pansies, blue and shining. She had the walk of a Celtic princess and a softness to her Galway accent. An Irish girl. Pat looked to the waves. Not as blue as Helen's eyes. If he hadn't been married he could have fallen for her himself, but she obviously had doted on Neill. Then. Neill had been besotted. It was just like him not even to mention her until he sprang the surprise, after the fishing at Ballysallagh. Seemed her first husband had been with the Bank of Ireland and had been posted to Bangor. When they'd split up, she'd kept the house and stayed on in the North.

It had been no trouble, none at all, to go and stand best man for Neill ten years ago. Pat had gone back again three years ago and he had found that Helen had become even more lovely. He hadn't noticed anything wrong and if he had, could he have done anything from 5,000 miles away? Not likely.

Pat looked at the open hatch. He didn't go in much for the North American obsession with intensive counselling, and the need for catharsis, for incessant talking, on and on, about one's "problems." But all Neill had said was, "Helen's gone back to The Republic," coldly, matter-of-factly, about eighteen months ago. He had refused to say any more on the phone. Nor would he say much last year when Pat had travelled back, ostensibly to a legal convention in London but in truth to go over to Ulster to see Neill. He had found his friend changed, a man turned into himself, quiet, dry-eyed, and withdrawn. Maybe he might be ready to open up a bit now. In his own time. Perhaps next week when the pair of them would be alone in the Gulf Islands.

Certainly since he'd arrived, a couple of days ago, he'd seemed a bit more like his old self, but there was still a wariness and lapses into silence.

Pat worried at the thought like a terrier at a bone, turning it over and over, careless of the need to steer a straight course.

The slatting of the sails brought his attention back to the job of helming. He'd let *Tarka*'s head come too close to the wind. He let her bows fall off and saw that they were nearly at their destination. Time to call Neill. Keep the mood light. "All hands on deck." Nothing. He cupped a hand to his mouth. "All hands on deck."

"Coming."

Pat heard the thump of Neill's feet on the sole. His head appeared at the hatchway. "All hands on deck? It's a twenty-six-foot sloop, not a bloody windjammer." He was smiling and Pat chuckled.

"Sleep well?"

"Lovely." Neill warbled a snatch from an old hymn. "Rocked in the cradle of the deep."

"Good." Pat was pleased for his friend and could see that Neill was making the effort to remain cheerful. "Up forrard, Mr. Mate. Break out the anchor."

"Right, me hearties," said Neill, making his way along the lee scuppers. Pat lost sight of him behind the mainsail. He slackened the jib sheet, hauled in on the self-furling line, and wrapped the headsail round the forestay to give Neill more room to work.

Neill jumped back into the cockpit. "Mainsail?"

"Uh-huh." Pat bent and switched on the diesel, as always disliking its noisy clatter. "Hang on, I'll bring her head to wind. Here." He handed Neill the sail ties. "I'll work the halyard. You get the sail down."

"Aye aye, sir."

Almost like old times. Pat put the helm over and listened to the mainsail flapping as the wind spilled. "Coming down." He paid out the halyard and watched Neill flake the fabric on the boom. He hadn't lost his touch.

Neill came aft. "Nice little anchorage."

Pat steered into the small cove, tucked in between low cliffs. "Good holding in about five fathoms. Go on forrard again. I'll tell you when to drop."

"OK."

Pat busied himself with the routine of mooring, satisfied himself that the anchor had set firmly, and turned off the engine. "That's better." Quieter now but not as quiet as Strangford. He could just hear the noises of the traffic on the Upper Levels Highway not far inland.

Neill was back in the cockpit. "Jesus," he said, "it's hot." He stripped off his shirt.

Not a pick of extra flesh, Pat thought, guiltily patting his own waistline. "Would you like a swim?"

"That's a thought." Neill kicked off his shoes and clambered down the stern ladder to dip an exploratory toe into the water. He pulled it out again. Quickly. "It's bloody freezing."

"Not as cold as Strangford the day I went after the goose."

Neill came back inboard. "That's a brave while ago."

"Aye. It is. I'd not do it now."

"Nor me." Neill sat on the rail staring back over Burrard Inlet towards the towers of the University of British Columbia, tiny on the far shore. "Would you look at that? It's gorgeous." He slipped back into the well of the boat. "I thought you were mad to leave Ulster. You weren't."

"I know. But once in a while, not as often now, I still get a notion to go back."

Neill shrugged. "Who said, 'You can never go home'?"

"I don't know, but my life's here now. Colin and Anne are Canadians. Phyllis is back at work." Pat hooked his thumbs in the armholes of his T-shirt and said sonorously, "I'm a pillar of the legal community."

Neill laughed. "Some pillar." His face clouded. "I could no more leave the North. Too many memories and," he hesitated, "I'm nearer to Helen's boys. I got close to them over the years. They're two good lads. She lets them come and see me once in a while."

Pat waited. Neill hadn't mentioned Helen since he'd arrived in Canada. Was he going to say more?

"I'm famished. Is there any grub aboard?"

Pat exhaled. He'd hoped for a moment—ah well. "Below. I'll nip down and get it."

He left Neill with legs stretched out, eyes shut, basking like a beached seal, an underweight seal, and went below to the galley.

"Here." He handed up a small styrofoam cooler and scrambled up the companionway. "Beer?"

"No, thanks. Have you a lemonade?"

Lemonade, Pat thought. Now there's a thing from back home. Lemonade, a fizzy soft drink that was simply not obtainable in Canada. "No, but there's Coke."

"That'll do."

Pat opened a can, handed it to Neill, took a beer for himself, and passed Neill a kaiser roll stuffed with cheese, lettuce, and tomato. "Here."

"Great."

Pat sat on deck, eating, sipping his cold beer, and luxuriating in the warmth of the day. He didn't speak for some time. Neither did Neill. Pat finished his drink and rummaged in the cooler for another. "More Coke?"

"No, thanks."

"Not like you to turn down a jar." He looked up and saw a look of sadness on Neill's face. "You all right?"

"Not really." Neill looked at the shiny red and silver Coke can. "I hate this stuff."

Pat sat up straight. "There's some Canada Dry below."

"No. I mean I'm sick of Coca-Cola, but," Neill dropped his eyes, "I got too much of a taste for the other—after she left."

Pat waited. He hadn't known that Neill had been hitting the bottle.

Neill took a deep breath. "I miss her. A lot."

Was he going to talk about her? "I know." It sounded trite. Pat sought for better words of comfort, but none would come. He laid his hand on Neill's arm and saw the pleading in his friend's dark eyes.

"It was so bloody stupid." Neill pursed his lips and shook his head. "We lived through years of bombs and bloodshed. It never touched us. Not really. And then, out of the blue she just says, 'I've had enough. I'm going home.'" The look on Neill's face made Pat think of a small child in a fairground who'd turned round and found his parents gone. "I didn't know what the hell she was talking about. 'They're not all mad in Galway,' she said. I couldn't stop her, and I couldn't go with her. No work down there. I tried, but Galway's a small city."

Neill leant forward and held his head in his big hands, rubbing the fingers up and down his forehead. He swallowed. "I loved her, Pat." He looked up. Pat wasn't sure if the misty look in Neill's eyes was an effect of the salt spray on his own spectacles or whether Neill was close to tears. "I still do."

"Ach, Neill." Pat did not turn away. If Neill wanted to cry, who else better to weep with? "Can you do nothing?"

"I don't know." Neill sat back against the side of the boat. It wasn't salt. His eyes were clear now. "I've phoned her a couple of times."

That was news. "And?"

"She says she misses me. The boys miss me."

"Is there no chance she might come back?"

Neill shook his head. "I asked her. She says she won't live in a country where you can't go into a shop without being searched, when you don't know when your world's going to blow up in your face." He crushed the Coke can. "I think it was the bomb right in Bangor that did it. Pushed her over the edge. I never saw it coming. The second one, last year, didn't help. Here." He handed the mangled aluminium back to Pat. "Have you a place for this?"

"Aye." Pat took the piece of battered metal. "What would she do if there was peace?"

"Peace?" Neill's laugh was a dry bark. "Peace? There'll never be peace in the North of Ireland. Too many scars. Too many wounds."

Pat could only nod. "Stupid question. I'm away too long."

Neill stood. "Best thing you ever did. You couldn't find a better place to live than this. It's got everything." He managed a small smile. "And it's quiet. No bangs."

Pat blinked. He'd been thinking the very same thing himself not a couple of hours ago.

"I should have got out too. Brought Helen here. She'd have loved it."

"Is there no chance for that now?"

"Who's going to hire a fellow damn near fifty?"

Pat sighed. Neill was right. He felt a hand on his shoulder and looked up. Neill had a smile on his face. Why?

"You know, Pat, I've mostly sorted it out for myself. We'd a lot of good years together, her and me. I'd have her back tomorrow if she'd come. But no peace. No Helen. I've my friends back home, the trout's still in Ballysallagh, I've a bit of roughshooting at Saintfield—and a new dog. Dirk. He's not old Grouse, but he's a good pup."

Pat returned the smile, wondering if Neill was fooling himself, wondering how wounded his old friend really was. "I'm glad to hear that."

"Aye," said Neill, "and I always know where to find you, you old bugger."

Pat stood, took Neill's hand in his own, and clasped his friend's arm with the other hand. "Aye. You do."

Pat held on silently, knowing nothing needed to be said.

"Now," Neill said, "unless I'm mistaken, the wind's getting up and," he pointed to the far shore, "if that's where I think your dock is, we could have a good run home. I want to see if this big tub can go down wind like old *Gannet*."

Pat released his hold. "You sure?"

Neill winked. "I needed to get that off my chest, but I'm not for spending the next three weeks like a ghost at a wedding feast. Come on, fire up the diesel. I'll get the hook up."

Pat looked at his watch. "It's time to go. Phyllis is going to meet us at the yacht club."

Neill laughed. "We'd better not be late then. I mind the night she called me a 'scutter.'"

Pat did too. Too many jars in the Mermaid. "Right. If you really want to see how *Tarka* goes, let's get the main up first and I'll get the gennaker ready."

"Aye aye, skipper. I'll look after the main."

Pat went below and shoved a bulky sailbag through the forehatch. He hauled himself on deck, stripped the bag from the gennaker that was hidden inside its long, dun outer-cover, shoved the now empty bag back down the hatch, and dogged it shut. He busied himself with shackles and sheets, finishing the foredeck work by attaching the halyard to the fitting on the sail. He walked back to the cockpit.

Neill had the main fully hoisted. It shivered as the anchor held the boat head to wind. Pat hauled on the gennaker halyard, sending the packed sail to the head of the mast, forgetting in his haste exactly what the brown material hid.

"What the hell's that?" Neill was looking forrard.

"We didn't have one of these on *Gannet*. It's like a spinnaker only easier to handle. The sail's in the bag. Once we're underway, you helm. I'll set the gennaker. Go and get the anchor up and stowed."

"Right."

Neill hurried to the bows.

Pat waited until Neill had returned to the cockpit. "Get your shirt on. It'll be cold out there. The wind's picked up." He let *Tarka*'s head fall off, paying out the main sheet until the sail stood out at right angles from the boat and she was running free. "Here." He gave the tiller to Neill. "Hold her on that course and here," he handed Neill the gennaker sheet, "as soon as I've it set, sheet in."

"Right."

Pat scrambled forward, grabbed the downhaul, and stripped the outer covering upwards, freeing the great, thin nylon sail. He craned his head back to watch the light fabric burgeon and fill, ballooning out its vast, multihued curve ahead of the bow. Oh, Jesus, Pat thought as he ran aft, but Neill gave a yell that sounded like pure animal delight. He thumped Pat on the shoulder. "Trust you, you Orange bastard!" He pointed at the gennaker. "Only a Protestant would have a sail made from a bloody great Union Jack." The nylon fibres snapped and crackled like pistol shots as Neill hardened the sheet.

Pat realized he need not have worried about upsetting his friend. "Sorry about that. It came with the boat."

"Sorry, be buggered," said Neill. "It's perfect. Main to port, gennaker to starboard, wing-on-wing, *Tarka*'s flying."

Pat sat beside Neill, taking the gennaker sheet and adjusting it until he was satisfied with the set of the sail as *Tarka* sped down the sea. She pitched as the crests hurried under her keel and surfed over the waves while the red-white-and-blue fabric of the headsail swelled with pride.

"Look at that," said Neill, grinning hugely and pointing at the knot-meter. "Six knots."

Pat saw Neill's face open, content, at peace, at least for now. Pat hoped, that as *Tarka* ran down Burrard Inlet carrying two friends of forty years, the wind driving her would blow some of Neill's pain with it. He looked across to Kitsilano. At this speed they should be home in another half-hour. He lost himself in the business of sail trimming, the rhythm of the ocean, and the pleasure of the day.

"Jesus," said Neill, as they walked up to the yacht club, "that was great."

"Glad you enjoyed it. And Neill?" Pat stopped for a moment. "I'm glad we talked."

Neill pursed his lips. "Me too." He looked to the door of the clubhouse. "Is that Phyllis?"

"Aye. What's up with her? She's jumping up and down like a monkey on a stick." Pat hurried his pace.

"Pat," she called. "Pat."

He could hear the excitement in her voice. "What's up?"

"It's great." She hugged him.

He laughed. "What's great?"

"It's been on the news all day. Since just after you two left this morning."

"What has?"

"Sinn Fein."

Pat stopped dead. He felt a sudden chill. "Sinn Fein? What have they done now?" He stole a glance at Neill and saw how crestfallen he looked. "Tell me."

"There's a ceasefire. They've called for a truce. They want peace talks with the British government."

"What? I don't believe it." But he knew from the shine in her hazel eyes that it was the truth. "A truce. My God. What do you think of that, Neill?"

Neill did not answer for a moment, then said, slowly. "I'll believe it when I see it. I don't trust Sinn Fein." Then he smiled. "But we can hope. We can always hope." He looked at his watch. "Four o'clock. What time's that back home?"

"Midnight. Why?"

"Too late today."

"For what?"

Pat watched as Neill took a very deep breath. "I'd like to call Galway, but it'll keep till the morning."

IN LATE AUGUST 1994, SINN FEIN ANNOUNCED A CEASEFIRE AND CALLED FOR PEACE TALKS WITH THE BRITISH GOVERNMENT.

GLOSSARY

Some nuances of Northern Irish speech, some Irish historical figures, and all aspects of Ulster politics can be confusing. This short glossary is offered to provide the reader with a few explanations. It is arranged in sections: Paramilitary and Political Organizations, Security Forces, and General Information.

PARAMILITARY AND POLITICAL ORGANIZATIONS
(R) denotes Republican, (L) Loyalist.

Irish National Liberation Army (INLA) (R): Never thought to have had more than fifty active members, this extreme Marxist group broke away from the Provisional Irish Republican Army (PIRA) and was responsible for the murder of British MP Airey Neave and the Droppin' Well bombing. The PIRA has taken action against the INLA, assassinating some of its more prominent members. In 1987, the INLA splintered further with the formation of the Irish People's Liberation Organization.

Irish Republican Army (IRA) (R): Formed in 1919 from the Irish Volunteers, the IRA refused to give up the struggle with Great Britain after partition of Ireland into Northern Ireland and the Irish Free State. It bombed targets in Britain and Northern Ireland in 1939, and began "operation harvest" on December 11, 1956, against targets in Northern Ireland. Lack of results and losses in the ranks led the IRA to call its men off active service on February 26, 1962. Largely a spent force by the end of the sixties, it proved unwilling or unable to protect the Catholic ghettoes during the 1969 riots. A split occurred in the ranks leading to the formation of the Provisional IRA. The term "IRA" is frequently used to identify the Republican paramilitary organization. As the official IRA is inactive, reference should properly be made to the PIRA.

Orange Order (L): Founded in 1795 as a defensive association of fraternal lodges, the Orange Order swore to "Defend the King and his heirs so long as he or they support the Protestant Ascendancy" and has consistently opposed any suggestion of home rule for Ireland or union with the Republic of Ireland. Its massive parades, to commemorate the victories of King William of Orange (Protestant) over King James Stuart (Catholic), particularly on July 12, are well known. Many of the banners carried in these parades bear the slogan "Civil and Religious Liberty for All." The Order is, however, anti-Catholic. It is not active militarily, although many of its members belong to Loyalist paramilitary groups.

Provisional IRA (PIRA) (R): In December 1969 a Marxist group, led by Sean MacStiofàin (an Englishman) and Rauiri O'Bradaigh, split from the official IRA. A military organization was established. Later, the brigade and battalion structure was largely replaced by Active Service Units of five-man cells. Specialists or special cells became responsible for such functions as bomb making, arms procurement, intelligence, or assassinations. By 1978, it was estimated that the organization had 1,700 active members and possessed 4,000 handguns and rifles. In 1987, ordnance destined for the PIRA and captured aboard the motor vessel *Eksund*, included AK-47s, 12.7mm heavy machine guns, two tons of Semtex, and SAM-70 ground-to-air missiles. The PIRA is responsible for most of the Republican-backed atrocities. The political arm of the PIRA is known as Sinn Fein, an Erse expression meaning "ourselves." Originally formed as a separatist, non-violent organization in 1907, Sinn Fein became active militarily under the command of Eamon DeValera in 1919. It was declared illegal in September of that year.

After partition, Sinn Fein reverted to being a political party in Northern Ireland. At the same time as the PIRA split from the official IRA, Provisional Sinn Fein was established. Throughout the book, only the term "Sinn Fein" has been used, as this is common usage to this day in Northern Ireland.

Ulster Defence Association (UDA) (L): The Troubles have spawned a large number of Loyalist paramilitary groups. The UDA was founded in 1971 to protect Protestant districts in Belfast and Derry. Originally it was a legal political organization. During the seventies and eighties the UDA ran protection rackets. In August 1992, the UDA was legally proscribed by the British Parliament, which because of the organization's known criminal activities was no longer prepared to recognize the UDA's legitimacy. Protestant terrorists were believed to have been responsible for 29 percent of all murders and 10 percent of all explosions between 1969 and 1990. Much of the weaponry used by the Loyalists was supplied by South Africa in return for military secrets stolen from the Short Brothers aircraft and missile factory.

Ulster Freedom Fighters (UFF) (L): A cover name for the terrorist activities of the UDA, the UFF was not as well organized as the PIRA until 1991 when it adopted the cell structure of the Provisionals. It was actively involved in reprisal killings of Sinn Fein and PIRA targets. From January to April 1992, the UFF murdered thirteen people and the PIRA twelve.

Ulster Volunteer Force (UVF) (L): Attempts to give Ireland home rule in the early years of this century were bitterly opposed by the Protestants of Northern Ireland. The Ulster Unionists were prepared to resist, with force if necessary. To this end, a body of 90,000 men, the Ulster Volunteer Force, was raised and trained in 1913. With the outbreak of the First World War, 35,000 of these men enlisted in the British Army and were kept together as the Ulster Division. In the first two days of the Battle of the Somme, 1916, 5,500 men were killed and four Victoria Crosses won. In 1966, on the fiftieth anniversary of the Somme battle, Loyalist militants meeting in the Standard Bar on the Shankill Road formed a paramilitary group and named it the Ulster Volunteer Force. On May 21, the UVF released the following statement: "From this day we declare war against the IRA and its splinter groups. Known IRA men will be executed mercilessly and without hesitation." The UVF was active until the late seventies when the Shankill Butchers, all members of the UVF, were jailed. A splinter group formed, the Protestant Action Force (PAF), which was active in the late eighties and early nineties.

Other Protestant paramilitary organizations are known to exist, including the Orange Volunteers (OV); Loyalist Defence Volunteers (LDV); Red Hand Commando (RHC); and the "Third Force," which held a parade of 15,000 men in Newtownards in 1981.

SECURITY FORCES

British Army: Units of the British Army, originally inserted to keep the sectarian factions apart, are now expected to achieve three goals: reassure the general public through the presence of visible patrols, interdict terrorist attacks by the use of patrols and checkpoints, and directly attack terrorist activities by arresting terrorists and seizing weapons and explosives. By 1992, there had been more than 400 fatalities and 4,700 injuries among service personnel stationed in Northern Ireland.

Garda (plural Gardai) Siochana: The "State Guards," the uniformed police force of the Republic of Ireland is 11,000 strong, and unarmed except for the elite Special Branch. There are direct links between the Garda and the Royal Ulster Constabulary. The Garda are often supported in anti-terrorist actions within the Republic of Ireland by the Irish Defence Forces.

Irish Defence Forces: The Armed Forces of the Republic of Ireland have an establishment of 13,000 regulars and 15,000 reservists. Three infantry battalions and an armoured car squadron are deployed along The Border. These troops can only operate, within the Republic, at the specific request of a Garda officer of the rank of inspector or higher. Irish Naval Service maintains antigunrunning patrols with a fleet of one helicopter-equipped patrol vessel, three mine-sweepers, a second patrol vessel, and two smaller coastal patrol ships.

Royal Ulster Constabulary (RUC): Formed April 5, 1922, the police force of Northern Ireland in its familiar dark green uniforms, was, even prior to the 1969–94 Troubles, the only armed police force in the United Kingdom. Its establishment is 8,250 full-time and 4,500 part-time members. By the end of 1991, 284 police officers had been killed and 6,800 wounded.

Ulster Defence Regiment (UDR): In 1970, the B Specials (Ulster Special Constabulary), were disbanded. These part-time police officers were believed to have been too partisan (Loyalist). The Specials were replaced by a regiment of the British Army drawn from both Catholic and Protestant recruits. In the first two years, 18 percent of the troops were Catholic. In 1972, 95 percent of the unit's strength was made up of part-time soldiers. These part-timers lived in their communities. By 1992, when the regiment was merged with the Royal Irish Rangers, 244 fatal casualties had been suffered, 155 when the soldiers were off duty and 47 after the victims had left the regiment.

GENERAL INFORMATION

Black and Tans: First World War ex-servicemen were recruited to act as additional security forces during the Troubles of the 1920s and were so-called because of their uniform, black jackets and khaki trousers.

Bonnaught: Irish mercenaries, hired by Norman overlords in the fourteenth century.

Boyne: The river around which Catholic and Protestant forces clashed on July 1, 1690. The result was a Protestant victory. At the time, the Protestant King William of Orange was allied with the Pope. Today, some Orange supporters celebrate the Battle of the Boyne on July 12 (New Calendar), which is also the date of the final battle of the campaign, Aughrim, fought in 1691.

Brian Boru (or Boruma): Last Àrd Ri (High King) of Ireland. Killed at the battle of Clontarf, 1014.

Caltach: The Book of Battles or Battler. One of the earliest seventh-century illuminated manuscripts. Its authorship is attributed to Saint Columba. Its possession was believed to confer invincible powers to any Irish army.

Celtic Twilight: Term used in conjunction with the revival of interest in Irish literature, art, and language in the late nineteenth century, spearheaded by Lady Gregory, William Butler Yeats, and John Millington Synge. Today, it is often used in a derogatory fashion to denote unrealistic dreams of Irish greatness.

Connolly & Pearse: James Connolly and Padràic Pearse. Two of the leaders of the 1916 rebellion. Executed by British Army firing squad.

Crack: Vernacular expression used to denote convivial conversation, not cocaine.

Cu Chulainn, Deirdre, Maeve, Princess Macha, Knights of the Red Branch: Celtic heroes, mostly described in the oral saga *Tàin Bo Cuàilnge*, The Cattle Raid of Cooley, which was first put into written form at Bangor Abbey.

Erse: The Irish language, often referred to as Gaelic.

Fenian: Derogatory term for Catholic.

Fenian Brotherhood: A militantly nationalistic political movement that arose during the Great Famine of the 1840s.

Finn McCool: Legendary Irish giant. Credited with many superhuman deeds including creating the Giant's Causeway, a remarkable geological formation on the County Antrim coast.

Firbolg: Pre-Celtic invaders of Ireland. Probably from Greece. Described in the *Lebor Gabala*, The Book of Invasions.

Gallowglass: Scottish fighting men, clad in chain mail, helmeted and armed with tall battle-axes. Originally imported in the eleventh century to check the Norman advance. Gallowglasses remained in the forefront of Irish armies until the sixteenth century.

General Assembly: Annual meeting of the Presbyterian Church in Ireland.

Green Book: The constitution, aims, objectives, and disciplinary procedures of the Irish Republican Army. The possibility of a reprieve for the character in "Birdsong in the Morning" on the grounds that he had not been instructed in The Green Book is found in General Order No. 15.

Kathleen ni Houlihan: Poetic name for Ireland.

Milesians: Pre-Celtic invaders. Also described in The Book of Invasions.

Nationalist: Generic term for anyone who subscribes to the belief that the Republic of Ireland and Northern Ireland should be united.

No Mission: Belfast vernacular meaning absolutely no chance that the desired outcome will occur.

NORAID: The Irish Northern Aid Committee was founded in 1969 in America ostensibly to raise money for the dependents of IRA prisoners and victims of the Troubles. In 1969 it raised $600,000, most or all of which went directly to Provisional IRA war funds. NORAID also bought and supplied arms.

Northern Ireland: The part of Ireland that remains within the United Kingdom of Great Britain and Northern Ireland. It is comprised of six of the old nine counties of the Irish Province of Ulster (see map 2).

Palace Barracks: Major British Army camp on the outskirts of Holywood, County Down.

People's Democracy: This protest movement of students and some faculty of the Queen's University of Belfast was largely Protestant and was formed on October 6, 1968. Its basic platform was to demand equal rights for Catholics.

Republic of Ireland: A sovereign state of twenty-six counties. It has variously been known as "The Irish Free State" and "Eire" (see map 1).

Snib: Vernacular term for a door latch.

Stormont: The East Belfast seat of the Northern Parliament was opened in 1932 and prorogued in 1972 when the British Parliament took over direct rule of Northern Ireland.

Taioseach: (Erse). The prime minister of the Irish Republic.

Townland: A small rural community, the boundaries of which often had been established centuries ago.

Ulster: The old Irish province included the six counties and Cavan, Donegal, and Monaghan. The term "Ulster" is used by many simply to denote the present six counties, but is geographically incorrect (see map 2). The name is derived from the people who originally dwelt there, the *Ulàidh*, and *Tir*, Erse for "land of," hence, "*Ulàidh Tir*." This was corrupted by the Vikings to "Uladztir" and by transliteration became Ulster. The provincial flag is a red hand on a white background.

Unionist: In 1886, the Liberal and Conservative parties of the United Kingdom joined to oppose home rule for Ireland. They adopted the name "Unionist." The Unionist Party is still a major political force in Northern Ireland and indeed in British political life. It sends members to the Westminister Parliament. Technically, to be a Unionist an individual must be a dues-paying member of the party. The term is often used in the same way as "Loyalist" to denote someone with a clear desire to avoid union with the Republic of Ireland and to remain a citizen of the United Kingdom. It is used as an antonym to "Nationalist."

Wolf Tone: Theobald Wolf Tone was a Dublin lawyer and leader of the United Irishmen, a group of dissenting Protestants and Catholics who wished to sever ties with Great Britain. The abortive United Irishmen rising, aided by the landing of French troops in County Mayo in 1798, was crushed. Tone was captured and condemned to death. He slit his own throat and died seven days later.

SUGGESTED READING

"25 Years of Terror." *Belfast Telegraph*, Monday, August 15, 1994, p. 11 (The numbers of those killed in each year were taken from this article).

Bardon, J. *A History of Ulster*. Belfast: The Blackstaff Press, 1992.

Bell, J. B. *The Irish Troubles: A Generation of Violence, 1967–1992*. Dublin: Gill & MacMillan, 1993.

Bishop, P., and Mallie, E. *The Provisional IRA*. London: Hamish Hamilton, 1987.

Buckland, P. *A History of Northern Ireland*. Dublin: Gill & MacMillan, 1981.

Chadwick, N. *The Celts*. London: Pelican Books, 1971.

Dillon, M. *The Dirty War*. London: Hutchinson, 1990.

Dillon, M. *The Shankill Butchers*. London: Hutchinson, 1989.

Johnson, P. *Ireland*. Chicago: Academy Chicago Publishers, 1980.

Ripley, T., and Chappell, M. *Security Forces in Northern Ireland, 1969–92*. London: Osprey Publishing Ltd, 1993.

ABOUT THE AUTHOR

Patrick Taylor, M.D., was born and raised in Bangor, County Down, in Northern Ireland. He is the *New York Times* bestselling author of the nine-volume Irish Country series that began with *An Irish Country Doctor.* Dr. Taylor is a distinguished medical researcher, off-shore sailor, model-boat builder, and father of two grown children. He now lives on Saltspring Island, British Columbia.

www.patricktaylor.ca